Petals and Plot Twists

Petals and Plot Twists

JENNY PROCTOR

To anyone who has ever wished on a birthday candle or tried to blow away dandelion fluff all in one breath or whispered dreams into a night sky streaked with shooting stars. Believing in a little bit of magic is fun. But don't forget—the real magic has always been you.

Chapter One
Sophie

IF MY LIFE were a romantic comedy, I'm not sure I'd be the main character.

I have more of a quirky sidekick vibe. Bubbly, supportive personality. Big hair. A treasure trove of funny anecdotes—mostly dating mishaps—to make the main character feel good about her own life and prospects.

I *do* want to fall in love. More than anything. I just haven't figured out the secret. I haven't figured out how to capture that main character energy.

Or maybe the problem is that I haven't found my hero. If he's even out there at all.

These are my thoughts as I slide my trowel through a planter of beautiful black dirt, scooping out a row of holes just the right size for the bright pink petunias I picked up at the nursery this morning.

Petunias don't really have main character energy either. They're incredible flowers. Easy to grow and a great complement to other plants since they come in so many colors. But they're never going to be the showstopper. The main feature.

They're a sidekick.

Just like me.

I add the petunias to the planter, covering their roots with soil, then slip off my gardening gloves. I've been working in the rooftop garden at The Serendipity all afternoon, and my back aches from the effort. But I wouldn't trade the feeling.

There's a lot to love about the quirky apartment building in Serendipity Springs that I call home. The grand winding staircase. The crown molding and original wood floors. The beautiful courtyard with a pool and a gorgeous fountain. But the rooftop garden is my favorite.

As a landscape architect, I spend a lot more time behind a desk than people usually think, particularly working for Leonard Trowbridge and Associates. Junior designers in the firm rarely have the privilege of being on site when plants are going into the ground. Or being outside at all. I mostly work from home, aside from a once-a-week in-person meeting at the office, and I spend ninety-nine percent of my working hours on the computer, creating designs, doing research, and outlining plans.

But my undergrad degree is in botany, so tending the rooftop garden has become a magical kind of therapy for me. When I'm close to losing my mind and I need a dose of sunshine, I leave my first-floor apartment and come upstairs to garden. I get my hands dirty. I cultivate. I create. And the perk is that I get to do it on The Serendipity's dime. The garden is a community space, and lots of residents come up to enjoy it on a regular basis. Especially now that winter has surrendered to a gloriously warm and beautiful spring.

Everyone knows it's my job to make the space beautiful. And it *is* beautiful.

Narrow concrete planters full of colorful annuals line the perimeter of the garden, bracketed by larger planters full of hardier trees and perennials that can withstand Mass-achusetts winters. A rose trellis supports heirloom roses, and a second trellis arches overhead, draped in wispy purple wisteria. Fairy lights adorn the entire space, giving the garden a cozy, magical feel, especially at night.

I pull out my phone and take a photo of the newly filled planters, then text it to my best friend, Peter.

His response comes through almost immediately.

PETER

Incredible. As always. The petunias look especially good.

SOPHIE

My petunias say thank you. Are you hungry? Are you home?

PETER

Yes to both. Just got home.

SOPHIE

Perfect. Can I come over? Maybe we can figure out dinner together?

PETER

So what I'm hearing you say is: Peter, can you feed me please?

SOPHIE

You know me so well.

Peter lives one floor above me in The Serendipity, which honestly feels too good to be true. How lucky is it that my two best friends both live in my apartment building? To be fair, I suppose Willa became a best friend *because* we live in the same building. We met not long after I moved in and bonded over books, which we both love to read, and sugar cookies, which Willa loves to bake...and I love to eat.

Peter, on the other hand, snatched up an empty apartment because I begged him to the minute he finished grad school and came home.

The summer before I started tenth grade, my mom moved us one town over to Serendipity Springs so she could marry Charles Crooksley. Charles's name should have been a warning, but I loved him at first. Mostly because my mother had been serial dating for years, one man after another, after another. I was just thrilled to see her settle down. Charles was stable, he had a steady job as a financial planner, and he adored my mother.

Until he didn't anymore. Two years after their wedding, he cleaned out her bank accounts and disappeared. All my mom's savings, including everything she'd set aside for me to go to college. It was all gone. He took every last penny.

Twice burned, my mom said in the days after their divorce. First my dad, then my stepdad. I doubt she'll ever get married again.

Still, I can't regret moving to Serendipity Springs. Moving here brought me to Peter. And there's nothing to regret about him.

And not just because he's so good at feeding me.

SOPHIE

Yes, please. I'll be down in a sec.

I gather up my tools and carry them to the storage shed by the stairs, but I pause on my way when Mr. and Mrs. Hathaway walk into the garden. Mr. Hathaway is using a cane, but he is no less attentive to his wife, keeping his free hand on the small of her back as they slowly make their way into the garden.

I dart forward, setting my tools on the ground so I can coil up the garden hose currently snaking across the path. I've never seen the elderly couple on the roof before, and I'm looking at the space with new eyes, searching for any obstacle that might hinder their progress.

I haven't done an official survey, but the Hathaways have

to be the oldest residents at The Serendipity. Though they have family members close by who are constantly checking on them, they're spry enough to live independently, and it seems like they still get around pretty easily. But that doesn't mean I want them tripping over a garden hose.

I refuse to be responsible for one of the Hathaways finally breaking a hip.

I scoop up the offending hose and coil it up, shifting it out of the way just in time.

"Sorry about that," I say. "I did some planting today, so I needed to water everything, but I shouldn't have left the hose out."

They finally reach the nearest bench, the one just in front of the rose trellis. Mr. Hathaway holds his wife's hand while she lowers herself to the bench, then he sits down beside her.

"It looks wonderful," Mrs. Hathaway says. "You've been busy."

"I have been. Do you guys come up to the garden often?" I see the Hathaways frequently—they live on the first floor just a few doors down from me—but I've never run into them up here, which doesn't necessarily mean anything. I'm usually only up here evenings and weekends.

"We come up every day after lunch," Mr. Hathaway says. "The doctor says a little bit of sunshine is good for us."

"Even in the winter," his wife adds. "Nothing is more fortifying than a little cold Massachusetts air."

"It seems to be working for you," I say. "You look like you're aging backwards."

"Oh, you," Mrs. Hathaway says. "That's just silly."

Mr. Hathaway squeezes her hand. "She's right, dear. You've never looked more beautiful."

Um, hello. Could these two *be* any cuter?

"We're only coming up late today because we spent the day with our granddaughter. We thought about skipping it, but the weather is so nice, we figured a later visit would still be good for us, even if we missed the sunshine."

Dusk has definitely settled in Serendipity Springs, the sun dropping below the horizon.

"I like it up here in the evenings," I say. "It's romantic."

Mr. Hathaway slips his arm around his wife's shoulders. "I agree."

"Well, enjoy yourselves," I say, smiling at the couple. I turn away to retrieve the tools I abandoned earlier, but then I pause, my gaze snagging on a flower I'm not expecting to see. I let out a little gasp as I step closer to inspect the plant.

The plant's wide, flat leaves wind their way up the trunk of the Japanese maple just past the rose trellis. And a single white bloom, about the size of my palm, shimmers under the fairy lights that decorate the tree.

I know everything there is to know about plants. I have a bachelor's degree that *taught* me everything there is to know. But *this* plant is a mystery that's been stumping me for weeks.

I didn't plant it. I can't identify it. And so far, I've only seen it in bloom once.

Until right now.

The white petals are full and open, revealing a deep pink center. It's beautiful, but it also doesn't look like anything I've seen before. It looks like some sort of cross between an orchid and a lily, but it grows more like a hibiscus. I see a few smaller buds among the leaves, but none of them look anywhere close to blooming. The last time it bloomed, there was only one flower, and now, again, there's just one.

Since this is a community garden, any number of residents could have brought the plant up and added it to the planter. Or it could be a volunteer, a seed carried on the wind or by a bird. It could even be a bulb that lay dormant and finally decided to grow this spring.

Then again, knowing The Serendipity, the flower could have just poofed into existence.

It wouldn't be the strangest thing that's happened around here lately.

Still. My very scientific, very educated brain *really* wants to know where it came from. Bare minimum, it'd be nice to have a *name* for the mystery plant.

I pull out my phone from the back pocket of my overalls and take a picture of the flower. The lighting isn't great, but it's still clear enough that I can run an image search on Google and see if it pulls up any hits.

"It's beautiful, isn't it?" Mrs. Hathaway says. "The love flower?"

I turn to face her, still crouched in front of the plant. "What did you just call it?"

"The love flower, dear. Isn't that what it's called?"

"I don't know," I say. "I've been trying to identify it for weeks, but I haven't been able to find anything official. You wouldn't happen to know its scientific name, would you?"

"Oh, I don't know anything about scientific names," Mrs. Hathaway says. "I just remember my friend Beatrice had a painting of a love flower in her apartment." She looks over at her husband. "Do you remember her? She passed last summer. She was an artist, and the painting she did of the love flower was her favorite one. I could be wrong, but it looks just like that bloom."

"Is she the one who made that coffee cake that I liked so much?" Mr. Hathaway asks, and his wife nods.

"And you're sure it's the same flower?" I ask. I don't want to pester the elderly couple, but I've been searching in vain for weeks. I'm more than a little excited to have any kind of hint about the plant's identity. "I know this one doesn't bloom very often, so if you need to take a closer look..."

Mrs. Hathaway furrows her brow. "I've seen it every day

since the weather warmed up. I know well enough what the bloom looks like."

I stand and pocket my phone. "You've seen *this* flower bloom?" I point at the plant just to make sure. "The white one with the pink center?"

The Hathaways stare at me like I've lost every single one of my marbles.

"Yes," Mrs. Hathaway says slowly. "The love flower. As I said."

I look back at the flower, my brain trying and failing to puzzle it out. Maybe it only blooms at certain times of the day?

But I've been up here all afternoon, and there were zero blooms until just now. Maybe it only blooms in the evening? Like a moon flower? But that doesn't make any sense, because the Hathaways just told me it's in bloom whenever they come up at lunch time.

"I remember thinking it was a little early for flowers to be blooming the first time we saw it," her husband adds. "A flower like that looks more like a summer bloom."

It does look like a summer bloom. Like something tropical that would love a warmer, more humid climate. But the leaves are more like a rhododendron leaf—like the plant is built for a harsher climate. I've never seen anything like it.

"Huh," I finally say as I sink back on my heels.

"What's the matter, dear?" Mrs. Hathaway asks.

"It's just unusual for me to come across a flower I've never heard of," I say. "But it's good to know it's called a love flower. That gives me another thing to search."

Mr. Hathaway chuckles. "Better be careful, Miss Sophie," he says, echoing my earlier thoughts. "A mystery flower even a botanist such as yourself can't identify? Strange things might be afoot at The Serendipity."

Chapter Two
Sophie

WILLA LIVES a few doors down from Peter's second-floor apartment, so I stop on my way to his place and knock on her door. She knows a thing or two about "strange things at The Serendipity," and she'll probably have an opinion on Mr. Hathaway's twinkle-eyed suggestion.

Last month, Willa had a series of mysterious experiences when she went into her own closet and somehow wound up two floors away in a *different* closet.

That closet belonged to Archer Gaines, our very grumpy building owner, who is now Willa's not-as-grumpy boyfriend.

We still have no idea how she was basically transported from one closet to the other, but the why is completely obvious.

Willa and Archer were meant to fall in love.

Considering Willa's experience, a mystery flower in the rooftop garden is mere child's play. Not that my flower *is* magic, or even anything extraordinary. I'm just saying, considering The Serendipity's history, I'm not willing to rule out the possibility.

I wait outside Willa's door for almost a minute before

remembering that she and Archer are going out tonight, something I know because she swung by my apartment to borrow a dress. Apparently, Archer wanted to take her somewhere special. I had the perfect thing to loan her—because of course I did. It is my moral imperative as the trusty sidekick to always have the perfect dress hanging in my closet, even if I'm never the one who gets to wear it.

Not that I fault Willa for her happiness.

Nothing made me happier than watching her main character romance play out. And she and Archer really are perfect for each other.

But thinking about their love story does make me a little wistful. Willa wasn't even looking. Her happily-ever-after fell right into her lap. Or right into Archer's closet?

Either way, it looks like Willa's already gone, so I abandon her door and walk the short distance to Peter's place.

Luckily, he opens on the first knock.

"What took you so long?" he says, stepping aside to make room for me to enter. "I'm hungry enough to eat my arm."

"The Hathaways came up to the garden, so I talked to them for a bit," I say. "Then I stopped at Willa's on my way."

"I love it so much when you remind me that I'm your second choice." He grabs my hand, picking it up to study my fingernails. "Please wash these before you touch anything in here."

I roll my eyes but move into his kitchen to scrub the dirt off my hands. "You're not my second choice. You're just not... *Willa*."

"Hmm," Peter says as he sits down at his kitchen table, his laptop open in front of him. "Does not make me feel better."

I reach for the hand towel sitting beside Peter's sink and dry my hands. "Shut up. You know I love you the most."

He raises an eyebrow, but he doesn't glance away from his

laptop as he says, "Just because you've loved me the longest doesn't mean you love me the most."

Peter *definitely* has main character energy.

On my first day of high school in Serendipity Springs, he was randomly assigned to be my lab partner in AP Chemistry. It only took a couple of weeks to realize he wasn't just the smartest person in our class, he was the smartest in our entire grade—by a longshot.

Still, as smart as he is, he is not your stereotypical nerd. While he isn't very social, it's not because he's incapable of interacting with people. He's well-spoken and thoughtful and kind, but he doesn't need people's approval to feel good about himself. He has this quiet, peaceful confidence that comes entirely from within. I've always admired that about him—I still do.

High school Peter didn't care about being popular or being liked. About going to football games or even the prom. He did his schoolwork. He swam on the swim team. And he ran the math club. That was pretty much it, and that was enough for him.

My tenth-grade self craved that level of confidence, that easy self-assurance, so I made it my mission to make Peter Stone my best friend. I think I thought he might rub off on me, but I also felt safer around Peter than I did anyone else.

It took a few months, but I was persistent. When I invited him over to study for probably the eighteenth time, he finally said yes.

We've been best friends ever since, no matter what he says about me liking Willa more.

I drop into the chair across from him. "Not true. And it's not personal. Sometimes I just need a girl to talk to."

Orrrr someone who won't scoff at my speculation that my mystery flower might have an origin that isn't entirely logical.

But I choose not to volunteer that particular piece of information to Peter just yet.

He was understandably skeptical when I told him what happened with Willa and her closet. He's a data scientist. He believes in numbers. In logic. In hard, evidentiary facts. I can't fault him for his struggle to fully embrace a situation that has no logical explanation.

He no longer protests when I talk about Willa's experience, mostly because he's heard Willa *and* Archer share their own retellings of what happened. He can't dispute it. But if he can't explain it, I think he'd rather not talk about it.

I give the table a nudge to get Peter's attention—a totally juvenile move but one I know will work without annoying him because we've both been doing it since high school.

Peter breathes out a patient sigh and lifts his gaze to mine, peering at me over the top of his computer.

I grin. "Hi."

"Hi," he repeats...definitely *not* returning my grin, though I see humor behind his brown eyes.

"What's up? It's after six o'clock on a Saturday. Are you working?"

He closes his laptop. "Just answering a few emails."

"How did things go at your parents' house?"

Sadness flickers behind his eyes, but he quickly masks it. He hasn't said much about his parents' planned move but knowing Peter and how close he is to his family, it has to be hitting him pretty hard.

"I brought home most of my LEGO sets," he finally says.

I let out a little gasp, sitting up a little taller in my seat. "All of them?"

"As much as I could fit in my car without taking them apart."

I look around his kitchen. "You brought them here? Where are they?"

Peter slips his fingers under his glasses and presses them into his eyes. Then he runs his hands through his light brown hair. "In my office. That's why my laptop is out here. I don't have enough room in there anymore."

I stand and dart through the kitchen, ignoring Peter's calls to be careful as I fling open his office door.

On every surface. On top of his desk, on every bookshelf, on every available inch of floor space. Peter's office is filled with LEGO models. Cars, trains, airplanes. Even the super expensive Starship Enterprise that he got for his sixteenth birthday and spent an entire summer putting together.

I feel Peter approach behind me, the heat of his six-foot frame warming my back.

"It looks like so much more in this smaller space," I say, looking over my shoulder.

"Yeah," he says, the word sounding heavy.

I turn to face him. "How are you feeling?"

He shrugs. "It's finally starting to seem real, I guess."

I study Peter's expression, sensing how much he *isn't* saying. His parents are selling the house where he grew up, the house *they've* lived in since before Peter was born. They're selling, and they're *moving.* All the way to South Carolina, where they're planning to live it up as retirees in a state where it only snows once every ten years.

"I can't believe they're taking Allison, too," I say. I step into the room and adjust the wheels on a bright red racecar.

"Allison is an adult," Peter says. "They aren't *taking* her; she's moving because she wants to. She's excited about the warm weather, and she needs a new start."

Allison broke up with her fiancé of two years over Christmas, so sure, I can see her wanting a new start, especially since she and her ex currently work at the same accounting firm. But does her new start really have to be five states away?

I turn to face Peter, pushing my hands into my back pockets and feeling indignant on his behalf.

His parents only told him three weeks ago that they were putting their house on the market. I know he's feeling things, but I can't get him to talk to me about it.

I know Peter.

He keeps his social circle small, but once you're in that circle, he is fiercely loyal, and his family is right at the center of it. His parents are kind and supportive, likable and easy to be around, and his sister is just as amazing. The four of them talk frequently and have family dinners at least a few times a month.

He must hate everything about them leaving, and I'm worried that by not saying it, admitting it out loud, he's setting himself up for some kind of crash.

But then, what do I know? I speak all my feelings out loud the minute they pop into my brain.

"Peter, you know you can talk to me, right? You don't have to pretend like their move doesn't bother you."

His jaw tightens the slightest bit. "It doesn't bother me. It's right for them."

"Maybe. But it can be right for them and still suck for you. Both things can be true at once."

He takes a deep breath. "I know. And I appreciate your concern, Soph. But I promise I'm okay."

I swallow any further protests—they won't do me any good, at this point—and turn my attention back to the LEGO sets. "So, you got them all."

"It was either that or the donation pile. This isn't even all of them. I still have to go back to get the bins of loose pieces."

"Where will you put those?"

"I was hoping the basement? I don't keep much in my storage space down there."

"That should work," I say. "Or you could keep some at my place. The closet in my office is basically empty." I leave the racecar and move toward a replica of Notre-Dame Cathedral. "Why not display some around the apartment?" I ask. "Put a few in the living room, a few more in here. Maybe some in your bedroom?"

Peter gives me a wry look. "My LEGO collection is not a flex, Soph. That won't help my already dismal dating life."

I roll my eyes. "Exactly how many dates have you invited over in the past year?" I push a hand into his chest, nudging him out of the way so I can move back into the kitchen. I open his pantry and pull out a box of Cheez-Its, dumping a handful of the crackers into my palm. "If you never invite anyone over, it doesn't matter. A woman can't be bothered by a LEGO collection she's never seen."

"I've invited women over," he says, following behind me. He takes the box of crackers and reaches in for his own handful. "At least two in the past six months. Which I'm pretty sure is two more than *you*."

"I have definitely been out with more than two guys," I say, yanking the box of crackers out of his hands.

"Yeah? Name them."

I shove at least twenty crackers into my mouth at once, and Peter smirks like he knows exactly what I'm doing.

"Bon, and Babid, and Beb," I say, crumbs spilling out of my mouth and onto the floor.

"Bon and Babid," Peter repeats. "I'm so sorry I didn't get to meet them."

"Don't judge me," I say. "You know I'm terrible at dating. But you aren't. I could list half a dozen women who would love to go out with you, right here on the spot."

I really could list off six women. Maybe twice that many. Peter doesn't have the same sidekick curse that I do. He might not be in-your-face-hot like the typical romcom hero, but he's mastered the sexy professor vibe. The glasses, the dry sense of humor. The enormous brain. The only reason he's still on the market is because he just doesn't date enough.

I, on the other hand, have had no shortage of dates. I just can't seem to make any of them go anywhere.

In my lowest moments, I'm convinced there's something wrong with me. That it's a Stewart family curse, and I'm destined to live out my days like my mother, ever the date, never the wife. But I don't want to be like my mother. And sidekick energy or not, I have a lot going for me. I'm gainfully employed, even if I *do* have a billion dollars in student loan debt—thank you, Charles Crooksley—I'm funny, I'm a very loyal friend, and I have zero food intolerances or allergies.

I should be the easiest date ever.

But nothing ever sticks.

Willa thinks the problem is that I always seem to pick the wrong guy. As she once so aptly described, my *ick* detector is broken. The red flags most women sense on the first date don't even register for me. Not until I'm at least four or five dates in.

If I *have* been dating less, it's only because I'm tired of striking out. Of getting excited then having everything come crashing down when I discover the really cute high school gym teacher I thought might be my soulmate has a list of non-negotiables, including a Star Trek-themed wedding, costumes *not* optional.

I have a strong appreciation of nerd culture. I love Peter's LEGO collection. And I respect the dedication of the people who dress up in cosplay for midnight movie releases of their favorite franchise films. But I draw the line at walking down the aisle in Spock ears.

"Come on," I say, finally setting down the Cheez-Its. "You know why I don't date. You don't have the same excuse."

Something flickers behind Peter's gaze, an emotion I can't

quite read, but then he rubs a hand down his face, and whatever I saw is hidden behind a mask of indifference. "I *don't* know why you don't date," he says. "I know why you *say* you don't date, but I think that's an excuse."

"My broken ick detector is not an excuse."

"Yes, it is," he argues. He brushes the Cheez-It crumbs from his fingers and moves over to the table to grab his phone. "Do you want Chinese?"

"Yes, please."

He nods and focuses on his screen long enough to order our favorites, then sets the phone face-down on the counter. His t-shirt stretches across his shoulders, and I find myself wondering if he's been working out lately. Peter has always had a lanky swimmer's body, but it definitely seems like there's a little more bulk to him than I've ever noticed before.

"What if you're just looking in the wrong places?" he asks, snapping my attention back to his face.

"What do you mean?"

He shrugs. "Maybe the guy you're supposed to be with isn't on a dating app. Maybe he's someone you already know." He lifts a hand and hooks it around the back of his neck. "Someone you work with, maybe. Or...I don't know. Someone you met in school."

I frown. "Wouldn't I have realized it if I had? Felt something? Noticed some kind of chemistry?"

"People change, Sophie," Peter says easily. "Just open your eyes a little. Maybe you'll see someone in a new light."

For a split second, I wonder if Peter is talking about *him*. Does he want me to see *him* in a different light? But I quickly dismiss the thought.

It's not that I haven't considered it. For a brief stretch during our senior year, I nursed a pretty intense crush on Peter. But after several weeks of dropping what I thought were obvious hints, he didn't take the bait, so I filed away my crush and leaned hard into the friendzone. And I don't have any regrets about that. Peter is an amazing best friend, and I don't want to do anything to mess that up. With how easily I seem to crash and burn with men, I probably *would* mess things up. Which is all the more reason to steer clear.

"Okay, I'll try looking at people in a new light if *you* agree to go out with Miranda."

"Who's Miranda?"

"The woman who runs Spring View Nursery. She sells me all my plants."

Peter grunts. "I'll go out with Miranda if *you* spend as much time on dates as you do with your plants."

I scowl. "That's not fair, and you know it."

"No deal, then," Peter says. "I'm not caving if you won't."

I sigh and push away from the counter. "What do you know about my plants anyway? It's not like you ever come up to my garden." I move back into Peter's office and retrieve the model of Notre-Dame. It's one of those architectural ones that looks less like a toy. He can absolutely put this one in his living room.

"Only because spring is basically here, and I don't have a death wish," Peter says when I reappear in the kitchen. "I'll go once all the pollen has settled."

"You should," I say as I move into the living room. "It looks amazing." I set Notre-Dame on the top of the low-profile bookshelf behind his couch. "You should leave this one out here. It's cool enough it won't scare any women away."

I turn to see Peter looking at me, hands pushed into his pockets. "Will you go with me? When I pick up the rest?"

It feels big that he's asking. Peter doesn't usually *ask* for anything. Especially not company. If we hang out, it's because I show up. If we go places, it's because I drag him there. I know he enjoys my company. He's told me as much multiple times. But I'm pretty sure he prefers his *own* company just as much.

Which is why I have to say yes. He wouldn't be asking if he didn't really need me.

"Of course I will," I say.

"Good. Thanks," Peter says, the sincerity in his expression giving me pause. "I appreciate it."

"You're welcome," I manage to say. But for the rest of the night, I can't quite shake the feeling that there's something else behind Peter's invitation.

I just can't put my finger on what it is.

Chapter Three

Peter

As a data scientist, I have a graduate degree that taught me how to analyze information, look for trends, interpret patterns in data, and make projections about what's likely to happen next.

Which is why, when all evidence indicates my emotions will not be returned, it makes no logical sense for me to be in love with my best friend.

And yet, here I am. Soaking up every minute of her company. Saying yes every time she wants to see me because I am incapable of telling her no. Throwing logs onto the embers of my affection, hoping that maybe, just maybe, she'll feel an ounce of the heat and something will spark for her, too.

"Hey," Sophie says, holding up her iPad. "What do you think of this one?" She's nestled on the opposite end of my couch, working on sketches while we binge episodes of *Ted Lasso.*

Sophie has landscape design software she uses for everything she gives to her clients, but when she's brainstorming, she sketches on her iPad. This particular sketch is of a series of tiered planters moving down a hillside.

If I asked, Sophie could tell me the name of every plant she's included in the design.

"Looks great," I say. "I like the taller bushes over on the left side."

"Yeah? They're blueberry bushes." She tucks a springy brown curl behind her ear. "They didn't explicitly ask for them, but I'm hoping they'll like the suggestion."

Her eyes drop back to her iPad, and I take advantage of the opportunity to study her profile. The line of her neck, the mass of curly hair piled on top of her head.

A wave of yearning pushes through me, but I tamp it down just like I always do. I've had a lot of practice—though to be fair, it hasn't always been this bad.

In the almost decade we've been friends, I've gone long stretches of time when friendship has been enough. I even had a fairly serious girlfriend through most of grad school, though I'm sure that was only possible because I was in Boston, at MIT, and Sophie was across the state at UMass.

Still, she was always in the back of my mind, the standard by which I measured every woman I met. When my girlfriend, Penelope, hinted she was ready for a proposal, I realized with startling clarity that I couldn't marry her when Sophie still occupied so many of my thoughts.

I'm beginning to think I'll never meet anyone who measures up, which is admittedly concerning. I'm not an idiot. I know I can't live like this forever. That at some point, I'm going to have to tell her the truth. Lately, I've been feeling the pressure to do it sooner than later.

I just can't figure out how.

"Oh! I forgot to tell you," Sophie says. "The author you love—what's her name? The woman who writes the books bigger than my head?"

"Silvie Wainwright?" I ask.

"Yes! That's her," Sophie says. "So I guess she's coming to Serendipity Springs for a book signing next month. I happened to be walking by the bookstore when they were putting a poster in the front window about ticket sales, and I recognized the book cover..." She pauses and points at the most recent Silvie Wainwright book sitting on my coffee table. "That one! I'm not sure I would have remembered her name otherwise, but that cover is gorgeous, so I knew she was the one you love."

"They sell the tickets online," I say. "I tried to get one, but they sold out in seconds."

"That's exactly what the bookstore lady told me," she says. "But then I spent ten minutes explaining how she could revive her fiddle-leaf fig from the brink of death, and she was so grateful for the advice, she gave me her comp tickets to the signing."

"You're kidding," I say.

"Why would I kid about that? They're VIP tickets and everything, so you get to go to this question-and-answer thing, and you won't have to wait in a holy long line to get your books signed."

"Sophie, that's incredible. And she just gave them to you for free? How did you manage it?"

"It's not a big deal," she says easily. "Her plant really needed help. And I guess it wasn't entirely free, because I promised I'd stop by next week and drop off some of my favorite homemade plant food. Fiddle-leaf figs love it, so I really think it will help her."

While I am genuinely excited about the opportunity to meet Silvie Wainwright, right now, I'm more preoccupied with the ease of Sophie's interactions in the world. The fact that she just waltzed into the bookstore and became best friends with the employees—it's so far outside of anything I would ever do.

I don't mind talking to people. But I'm generally comfortable with my own company, so I don't often think about putting myself out there.

Sophie is good for me in that way. She pushes me to be more social, to let people in when it's generally against my nature to do so.

"It is a big deal," I say. "Thank you. You'll come with me, right?"

She looks over and smiles. "Of course I will."

As I take in her smile, it occurs to me that my sudden pressing need to be honest about my feelings might have something to do with my parents' move.

The two people who have always been my safety net, my safe place, announced they are leaving Massachusetts and driving a thousand miles south for warmer temperatures and year-round tee times.

And they're taking my sister with them.

My parents are good people. And my sister Allison, even though she's my polar opposite, is the only person I like to be around as much as Sophie.

I hate to see them go, but I also want them to be happy, and this move is exactly what they all want. Which means I have to figure out how to live my life without my family nearby.

Maybe I'm realizing I can't lose Sophie, too. And if she falls in love with someone else, which she's bound to do eventually, I will.

Not unless she falls in love with me first.

"So...do you want to play another episode?" Sophie asks. "Or are we just going to sit here in the quiet?"

My eyes dart up to meet hers, heat flushing my face. I've been staring. Did she realize I was staring? Can she see, just by looking at me, what thoughts were coursing through my mind?

"Let's do another," I say, reaching for the remote. "Definitely another. You want popcorn? I want popcorn." I quickly stand and move into the kitchen.

While I wait for the popcorn, I try to regroup and come up with some sort of plan.

Do I just...tell her? Make a move somehow?

Or do I need to be more methodical about it? Drop hints, make suggestions.

None of this comes naturally to me. The only reason Sophie and I are friends is because she made it happen, not giving me much choice in the matter.

I don't have moves.

I don't even know what it means to have moves.

Allison reads a lot of romance novels, and so does Sophie. Maybe I could borrow a few and read them as a means of collecting data—see if I can come up with some clear methodology. If I'm going to risk our friendship by asking for more, I have to do it right.

Sophie jokes about her unlucky dating life, but she doesn't have a whole lot of reason to trust men. Her parents split when she was six, and her dad has been pretty much absent her entire life. They talk on the phone a few times a year, but he lives a few counties over with a new wife and four kids Sophie has only met a handful of times.

Sophie's stepdad wasn't much better. He was only around for a couple of years while we were in high school, and while he was nice on the surface, he was a master manipulator, practically a con artist. I'll never forget the afternoon Sophie told me all the money her mom had set aside for college was gone.

That's twice she's been betrayed, and there's no way it hasn't had an impact.

I sometimes wonder if Sophie's lack of serious relationships has to do with her pushing men away before they get close enough to hurt her. If it does, she doesn't realize it. But I could see the same fear keeping her from wanting a relationship with me. I'm safe when we're just friends. I don't think relationships feel safe to her. Which means I have to tread carefully.

When the popcorn is finally ready, I carry it back to the living room, pausing before sitting down on the couch. Should I try to sit closer to her—create an opportunity for a little more physical contact? Not side by side. That might seem too suspicious. But I could sit just close enough that if I stretch my arm across the back of the couch, I could possibly touch her shoulder.

Not that I would. I don't want to be creepy. Just more intentional than I have been in the past.

I'm waffling, deciding how or even if I should make a move, when Sophie takes the popcorn bowl out of my hands.

"Here. Sit closer," she says, tapping the cushion beside her. "It'll be easier to share."

I almost laugh as I sit down directly beside her. As per the usual, she makes everything easier for me.

I sit, and Sophie closes the cover on her iPad and puts it on the side table next to the couch. She leans into me, her shoulder pressing into my arm as she tucks her legs up under her and spreads a blanket across her lap. "Want to share?" she asks as she holds up the blanket.

"Yeah. Great." I take the blanket and pull it across my lap. I look over at her iPad. "What were you working on? Was that the same design as before?"

"Nah," Sophie says. "I was just messing around."

"It looked really good."

Sophie doesn't like to call herself an artist, claiming her drawings are more utilitarian than true art, but I don't think she gives herself enough credit. Her sketches are beautiful.

"You think?" she asks.

"I always do."

She seems to consider her words for a moment before finally saying, "I was drawing this new flower I found in the garden. I can't figure out what it is, and it's bugging me."

"Have you googled it?"

She shoots me a dry look. "Only about a million times," she says. "I can't find anything like it. I've seen it bloom twice now, and it really doesn't seem like a Massachusetts flower. It looks rare and exotic and tropical. The Hathaways called it a love flower, but I've never heard of such a thing."

"A love flower? And that doesn't show up in any searches either?"

"That only happened tonight, so I haven't really tried yet. But I don't remember learning about it in school, and I basically memorized the common and scientific names of every plant species that grows in the state. There is no love flower on that list."

"So what *do* you know?" I say. "Tell me about it."

She shifts and turns her body to more fully face me, tucking her knees up to her chest and slipping her toes under the side of my thigh.

It's not lost on me that she does this easily, initiating contact like it's no big deal, while I deliberated for a ridiculous number of seconds about where to even sit on the couch.

"The first time it bloomed," she says, "it was at night, and I haven't seen it bloom again until today. Also at night, but the Hathaways say it's always in bloom when they're on the roof at lunchtime. Which means it *can* bloom during the day. But I've yet to see any discarded petals or blooms. There are several smaller buds that aren't close to blooming, but it looks like the same flower just keeps opening up, then closing again, which doesn't make any sense. It's not behaving like a regular flower—at least, not one that grows here."

"I doubt Venus flytraps made sense when they were first discovered," I say. "Maybe you've discovered something new. That could be a big deal, right? Would you get to name it?"

"Probably. But the process is long and really hard to prove. And I'm not convinced—" Her words cut off and she gives her head a little shake. "No, never mind."

Emboldened by her proximity—and by how easily she seems to be touching me—I reach down and grab Sophie's foot, wrapping my palm around her foot and giving it a little squeeze. "Just say what you're thinking." When she doesn't pull away, I shift over my other hand and start massaging the sole of her foot.

She leans back and closes her eyes and lets out a moan that makes my blood heat. "Oh man, that feels good." She's quiet for several long moments before she says, "Maybe it's because of everything that happened with Willa, but I just keep wondering if the flower is different because The Serendipity is different."

It goes against everything in me to accept the *differences* Sophie is referencing. But she isn't a liar, and neither is Willa. And last month, Willa really did experience something extraordinary. I can't explain it, but I also can't deny that it happened. Or that *something* happened, at least.

Whether it occurred exactly how Willa described is another question.

Sophie is fully convinced, but it's hard to wrap my head around something that doesn't fit within the bounds of science and logic.

When I explained as much to Sophie, she only laughed. "So much of the world doesn't fit within those bounds," she argued. "If you look for miracles, for magic, you can always find it."

I give Sophie's foot what I hope is an encouraging

squeeze. "Maybe it is different. Either way, I'm sure you'll figure it out."

She raises an eyebrow. "You aren't going to lecture me on science and practicality and realism?"

It's tempting. But if I'm going to convince Sophie to give me a chance, I'm not about to scoff at the idea of magic. Because honestly, I could use a little magic of my own. Even if I don't fully believe it's real.

"Is there any point when we're talking about The Serendipity?" I ask.

"Honestly, even that feels like a concession for a data scientist," she says as she reaches for the popcorn.

"Trust me," I say. "It's not an easy one to make."

Sophie spins back around and drops her feet onto the ottoman next to mine. "Come on. Let's watch one more episode before I fall asleep."

She settles against my side, her shoulder pressed against mine, her leg touching my leg. All the contact makes it impossible for me to relax, which is ridiculous. It's not like we've never touched before. But I'm so practiced at suppressing my feelings, at keeping Sophie solidly in the friendzone, that I don't frequently let myself think about it. Now, I'm hyperaware of every move her body makes, every place the heat of her registers against my skin.

Finally, halfway through the next episode, I lift my arm and extend it in Sophie's direction across the back of the couch. With my shoulder gone, she shifts, leaning into me even more.

I hold my breath, waiting for her to move away, but she doesn't even look up. She does the opposite, snuggling in closer, leaning her head against my chest.

"Mmm. You smell good," she says.

"Do I?" I ask.

"Yeah. Is it a new deodorant?" She turns her face and buries it in my shirt, taking a deep breath. "I really like it."

With any other woman, I might feel a twinge of victory. But Sophie is acting like this physical contact, like intentionally smelling me, is no big deal.

Which can only mean for her, it *isn't* a big deal.

"Yeah, I picked a new scent," I say, trying not to feel discouraged.

She lets out a yawn. "It's a shame you're wasting it on me instead of a date."

Okay, this definitely feels like a setback. But I don't know what else to do but persist.

The more I think about my future, the more I'm coming to accept the uncomfortable reality that if I am ever going to fall in love with someone else, Sophie's going to have to break my heart first.

And that won't ever happen if I don't try.

Chapter Four
Sophie

"If I bring you a latte, will you feed me cookies for breakfast?"

Willa yawns into the phone. "That's an offer I can't refuse. Come on over. I'm up."

I pocket my phone as I shuffle forward in the line at Serendipi-Tea. It's early on a Tuesday morning, and I have final design plans I'm supposed to submit by noon, but I'm nearly finished. Finished enough that I can absolutely spend a few hours with Willa before I add the final touches to the design.

The senior designers are probably going to overhaul the whole thing anyway. Well. Maybe overhaul isn't the right word. More like they'll keep all the infrastructure but gut the project of anything that gives it character. I've been told my designs are a little too whimsical for my firm and I'd increase my chances of advancement if I could "dial it back" a little.

I'd like to tell *them* what they can dial. My designs *are* whimsical. That's what makes them so amazing. Everything else that comes out of Trowbridge and Associates is as boring as Leonard Trowbridge himself.

Still. It's a decent job. A steady paycheck. And the convenience of working from home is amazing. If I can stick to my three-year plan, saving and paying down my loans, once everything is paid off, I'll have the freedom to find something else, maybe even branch out on my own. Until then, I just have to deal with senior architects sucking the heart and soul right out of my terraced gardens in favor of right angles, retaining walls, and orderly boxwoods.

It's finally my turn, and I step up to place my order. I add a couple of breakfast sandwiches, hoping at least a little protein will offset the many, *many* grams of sugar I plan to consume as soon as I reach Willa's. Probably too little too late, but I still have plenty of time to make healthy dietary choices.

And I will.

When I'm thirty.

With breakfast in hand, I return to my car and drive the short distance back to The Serendipity where I park, then take the grand staircase up to the second floor.

Willa opens her door after just one knock and motions me inside. The scent of sugar and vanilla fills my nose. She doesn't even bake up here, but somehow, her apartment still smells like a giant sugar cookie. Or maybe *she* smells like a cookie? Either way, I love it almost as much as I love her.

I hold up the bag. "I brought us protein."

"Look at you being healthy."

"I'm not sure sausage, eggs, and cheese layered inside a croissant qualifies as healthy, but Peter is always telling me I should have protein before I have my carbs, so…I guess I'm trying?"

"Peter is too logical for his own good," Willa says as she moves into the kitchen. She holds out a tin of unfrosted sugar cookie pieces—all the discarded broken bits left over from her bakery business. A dish of frosting already sits on the counter—because Willa knows I won't eat her cookies without it.

"True," I say using a boot-shaped cookie piece to scoop up a dollop of frosting. "Peter *is* too logical for his own good."

"How is he, by the way?" Willa asks. "I feel like I haven't seen him in forever."

At her question, my mind shifts back to Saturday night when Peter and I watched a few episodes of *Ted Lasso*. When we *snuggled* and watched *Ted Lasso*. Usually, whenever we hang out, Peter is pretty reserved when it comes to touching. He doesn't get weird about it, but he doesn't really initiate it either. I've always just assumed he's not as touchy-feely as I am. But that night, he leaned in like he's never leaned in before.

And I—weirdly—really liked it.

I don't admit this to Willa, though, because she will absolutely turn it into something it is not.

"He's good," I say instead. I settle onto a barstool and pull the sandwiches out of the Serendipi-Tea bag and hand one over to Willa. "He's been focused on a big project at work that's sucked up all his time. That, and moving all his stuff out of his parents' house."

"That's right. They're moving soon, aren't they?"

I nod. "It's happening so fast. And Peter won't really talk to me about it. I know he's bummed."

"They're close?"

"So close. They genuinely like to hang out together. I think he feels like he's supposed to be happy for them, so he's not letting himself be *sad,* and that's making him all weird and stuff."

Willa lifts an eyebrow. "Why did you just blush when you said *weird and stuff?*"

I lift my hands to my cheeks. "I did not blush."

"Yes, you did," she says back. "And now it's getting worse, so there's definitely something you aren't telling me."

I roll my eyes. "No, there isn't."

"Sophie. Spill it," Willa says, her tone leaving zero room for argument.

I huff out a breath. "It really is nothing. It's just—we hung out on Saturday night, and Peter was—I don't know. He was super clingy. Sitting closer than he usually sits. Touching me more." I reach for another cookie. "Not that I minded. You know me. I'm happy hugging total strangers. But Peter isn't like that, so it just felt...odd."

"You and Peter never touch?" she asks.

I shake my head. "No, it's not like that. We do. But it felt more intentional somehow? I'm usually the one who initiates, but he totally was. Giving me foot rubs, putting his arm around me. Plus, he asked me to go with him to pick up the rest of his LEGO collection. That's a thing he would usually want to do by himself."

"Why do you say that?"

"Because he prefers to do most things by himself."

Willa laughs. "You guys really are polar opposites."

"That's why he's so good for me," I say. "He makes me slow down and be still. And I remind him he doesn't actually hate people and socializing can be fun."

Willa opens her breakfast sandwich and takes a big bite. "Oh, gosh, this is amazing," she says through a mouthful of food. "Tell Peter thank you for making you order protein." She swallows, then takes a sip of her latte before saying, "So, I'm guessing by your earlier blush that you know what I'm going to ask you, right?"

I dig into my own breakfast sandwich, because she's right, and I'll happily delay her question as long as possible. The sandwich really is delicious, and I let out a little moan, surrendering to the momentary distraction, then chase the bite with a sip of my latte.

"You can ask," I finally say, "but that doesn't mean I'm going to give you a different answer."

"Come on," Willa says. "You guys seriously have so much chemistry. I just don't buy that you've *never* thought about dating him."

I breathe out a sigh. Willa and I have this conversation every few months, usually when I've had a bad date and feel like complaining about the sad selection of men in Serendipity Springs. Her argument every single time is that I could save myself a lot of trouble by dating the guy who already loves me.

Which...Peter and I *do* say I love you to each other. But only in a friend way. It would be colossally weird for him to actually catch feelings.

Wouldn't it?

"It just doesn't work that way," I say, pushing my uncertainty away and reaching for my tried-and-true argument yet again. "He's my best friend. We've always been best friends. It would be stupid to mess that up."

"It just doesn't work that way?" she repeats as she rolls her eyes. "Says who? Maybe he's acting a little differently because he's into you, and you're just being stubborn."

My heart rate increases the slightest bit as I think about how good Peter smelled on Saturday night. About the weight of his arm around my shoulders, the gentle press of his thumbs into my tired feet.

Ten years of friendship, and Peter has never given me a foot rub before.

"That is absolutely not what's happening," I say, but even I can hear the uncertainty in my voice.

"What makes you so sure?" she asks.

"The fact that I am absolutely not Peter's type."

"Does Peter even have a type?" Willa asks. "I've literally never seen him dating anyone."

"He dated this woman in college," I say. "Penelope. She was bookish and quiet and very put together."

Willa laughs. "Okay, yeah. Except for the bookish part, that is nothing like you."

I feel weirdly offended by her laugh, which makes zero sense, because I'm the one who made the comparison first.

"The thing is," Willa continues, "Peter didn't wind up with Penelope, right? So maybe you shouldn't assume she's his type." She reaches into the tin and takes a piece of cookie. "I could be wrong. You definitely know him better than I do. But just think about it. Let it simmer in the back of your mind whenever you guys are together and see if you notice anything else. You have to at least admit, Soph, Peter *is* pretty cute."

On that point, at least, she doesn't have to convince me. Peter has a great smile and great hair. Light brown eyes that I really love. And a great jawline. I reach for another cookie and swirl it through the icing. "Of course he is. I never said he wasn't."

She grins like I've made some monumental concession.

"But I still don't think that's what's going on," I say. "He's just sad because his family is moving, and since I'm the next best thing, he's holding me a little tighter than normal."

"Okay," she concedes. "You would know better than me."

"He could also just feel sorry for me because my other best friend is spending all her time with her new boyfriend."

It's a deflection, and I'm sure Willa recognizes it as one. But I can't wrap my head around the possibility of Peter having real, actual feelings for me. I can't, because I can't lose Peter. And if my track record is any indication, dating him would definitely mean losing him.

Willa scoffs. "I'm here, aren't I? Having breakfast with you?"

"Sure. But you're probably still thinking about him," I say. "Counting down the minutes until you get to see him again."

A goofy smile stretches across Willa's face before she nudges the cookies toward me. "Shut up and eat another cookie," she says playfully. "Sugar makes you happier than protein."

I do as she asks, then finish the last of my latte before remembering why I wanted to come see Willa in the first place.

I spend the next few minutes filling her in on everything I've learned about the love flower in my garden—which is, admittedly, not very much.

Since she and Archer were on the roof the first time the flower bloomed, she's been invested in my progress, so she's excited to hear about the Hathaways' name for it. But there's little to tell beyond that. Adding "love flower" to my searches didn't pull up any new hits, and my reverse image search of the bloom pulled up a lot of similar flowers but none that were an exact match.

"I just think I need to narrow my search to Serendipity Springs history," I say. "Has a flower like this ever shown up before? Could it be connected to the spring? I've even wondered if there's something else going on. Like, I know it sounds crazy, but what if the flower actually bloomed *for* the Hathaways? Like, it bloomed because they were on the roof?"

"Maybe because they're in love?" Willa says. "You did say they called it a love flower."

"That tracks," I say, "because the first time it bloomed, you and Archer were present. But that still feels like a pretty big stretch."

"Really?" she says. "And a portal in my closet *isn't* a stretch?

Mr. Hathaway said strange things might be afoot. I'm just trying to think outside the box a little."

I sigh, suddenly weary. "I have no idea. Maybe I'm overthinking and it's a weed I should have pulled the minute it popped up."

"It's way too pretty to be a weed," Willa says. "Just keep researching. Have you searched the library downstairs?"

I nod. "Yeah, but I didn't find anything."

"Then you should go to the one downtown. They have a ton of local history books. Maybe you'll find something there?" Willa gathers up our trash and turns, dumping it all in the bin beside her fridge.

"That's actually a good idea," I say.

"Don't act so surprised," she says. "I'm full of good ideas. Which is why you should also consider what I said about Peter. You never know, Soph."

"I will do no such thing, because it's a ridiculous suggestion, and Peter does not like me like that."

He doesn't.

He can't.

But as I say goodbye to Willa and head back downstairs to get to work, I can't help but wonder.

What would it be like if he did?

And why does the thought make my stomach flip?

Chapter Five
Sophie

THE DOWNTOWN BRANCH of the library in Serendipity Springs is just as charming as the rest of downtown. It's in an old stone building at the edge of Oldford Park, and whenever I venture inside, I always feel a pang of sadness that with modern technology, we all have fewer reasons to spend time in libraries.

I have a reason to be here today, though. Because the library really does have a killer collection on Serendipity Springs. I've never specifically looked for botany-themed history, but I'm banking on there being something in the vein of what I'm looking for. There has to be. The room that houses the collection is huge.

I wave at Sissy, the elderly head librarian sitting behind the main circulation desk, and make a beeline for the glass-walled room that fills the back left corner of the first floor. Last time I ran into Sissy, she nearly convinced me to spend twenty-seven dollars on a contour stick I definitely didn't need. When she isn't doing the librarian thing, Sissy sells makeup, and she is *very* persuasive. But I definitely don't have time to talk about accenting my cheekbones—at least not today. I have another work deadline at five, so I probably shouldn't be taking the morning to research a flower that has absolutely nothing to do with my paycheck.

Then again, I had to work until almost nine twice last week to finish up a different deadline that was entirely unreasonable given the scope of the project. So maybe I don't feel guilty about a little time off.

I push open the door of the Serendipity Springs collection room and slip inside. I'm the only one here, and it's ten times quieter than the rest of the library. Quiet enough that I almost feel like I should tiptoe.

A computer station sits in the corner, providing access to a digital catalog for the collection, but there are also plaques affixed to the wooden shelves lining the walls, and I trail my hand over them as I read each one.

Political History. Culture. The Revolutionary War. Founding Fathers. And so many others.

The last time I was in this room, I was a senior in high school, and Peter and I were working on our final research papers for our history class.

Maybe it's the smell of the room or the peaceful solemnity of all the history lining the shelves, but the memory of that afternoon pops into my brain with startling clarity.

Peter was naturally focused on his work, while I was focused, for reasons I can't remember, on counting the number of times I could make Peter smile. I jostled the table, making his pencil roll. There was one. I whispered a knock-knock joke. There was two. I pretended to read out loud from the history text I was reading, but I changed the words, creating an outlandish narrative about a mercenary who stole George Washington's horse.

I think I even made him full-on laugh with that one.

But then I'd gotten bolder, and I'd shifted from the seat across from Peter to the one right beside him. Heat climbs up my cheeks as I remember the way I boldly reached over and tried to tickle his waist, my fingers dipping under the hem of his t-shirt. It was totally innocent, and I barely touched his ribs, but Peter reached down and grabbed my wrist, tugging my hand away.

"Sophie, you can't touch me like that," he said, eyes wide and serious.

"Sorry," I quickly said. "I didn't know it would make you mad."

"I'm not mad," he explained. "It's fine. I just...wish you wouldn't."

It wasn't like we never touched. Our relationship wasn't super physical, but we'd hugged multiple times and teased and joked around a lot, so his reaction completely took me by surprise.

I'm not sure I ever really understood it, and since we only had a few more weeks before we graduated, we never talked about it again.

After my conversation with Willa, I have to wonder if Peter acted so weird that day because he really *did* have feelings for me.

But even if he did, that doesn't mean he does *now*. That was such a long time ago, and he seemed perfectly fine with all the touching we did on Saturday. Either way, he's been way too top-of-mind the last few days, and I only have an hour to research before I need to get back to work.

I finally reach a plaque that reads *Natural History*, and I force my brain back to the task at hand.

After sifting through several titles, I finally find a three-volume set of books by a Massachusetts naturalist who wrote extensively about the flora and fauna he encountered in his travels around the state. I carry it over to the table and read for close to an hour, but I don't find anything notable.

When I'm returning the books to the shelf, Sissy lets

herself into the room. "Just wanted to check in and see if I could help you find anything."

I almost wave her away, but Sissy Mayhew has to be close to eighty, if not older. I don't think she's native to Massachusetts—she sounds like she's from the South, Texas, maybe?—but she's lived here at least as long as I have, and aren't old people supposed to be full of knowledge? Especially old people who are also librarians?

"I'm not sure if you can, but it's worth a shot. I'm looking for information about a flower that just popped up in my garden. I've never seen it before, and I haven't been able to find anything about it on the internet. So I'm trying to figure out if it's native to Massachusetts or if anyone else in Serendipity Springs has ever seen it. I think locals might call it a love flower?"

She reaches up and pats her very poufy hair. "A love flower, you say? Over at The Serendipity? I wonder..." She moves to a shelf labeled *Oral Histories* and runs her hand along the spines. "Ah," she finally says. "Here it is."

She carries the book over in wobbly hands. "Maybe look through this one? I think I remember a story in here about a love flower."

I take the book. "Really? You've read it?"

"I've read a lot of things. I don't *just* know about makeup. Though I really do think you should consider the new blush palette I have at the circulation desk. It'll brighten your face right up."

Sissy doesn't leave me to the book until I promise to stop by and let her try the blush on me before I go. Pretty sure I'm getting the short end of the stick with this deal until I find the story she was referencing.

Because there's a drawing above the chapter heading, and it looks exactly like my flower.

I quickly read the story, heart pounding as I reach the concluding paragraph:

After weeks of gathering data, I am forced to conclude the unusual bloom is a respecter not just of persons, but of emotions. It does not bloom according to time or temperature or season. It blooms according to love. But there are qualifiers. The love must be romantic in nature. Friendship or familial love does not trigger a bloom. However, it is not required that the love be fully developed or even yet acknowledged. I have witnessed many blooms for couples in the early stages of their courtship. In that sense, the flower is somewhat of a fortune teller, forecasting the possibility of love. The only thing still inconclusive is the timing of what makes the flower appear and disappear. In my four years of observation, the flower appeared three different times. Each time, it remained anywhere from two to six months. I was not able to detect a pattern. Certainly seasons had no influence, as I saw it bloom in the snow as frequently as the sun. Though I cannot prove as much, my personal feeling is the flower appears when it's needed. When lonely hearts need a helping hand or lovers need a nudge in the right direction.

I read the paragraph a second, then a third time, then flip back to the beginning of the book to note the copyright date: 1954.

The truth is, Serendipity Springs is full of stories just like this one. Tales of magic and mysterious happenings and spring waters that bring good luck. The stories give the town flavor and are fun for tourists, but I've never had reason to truly believe them until Willa was whisked into Archer's closet.

Now, every single thing that has happened with the love flower fits the story on the pages in front of me. It's a story that feels like a folk tale or a legend, even a fairy tale. Except it's real life. *My real life.*

I close the book, mind reeling. The description of the flower matches perfectly. A vine growing up the base of a tree. Wide, flat leaves. Deep green color. White bloom with a deep pink center that opens and closes without wilting. And the author of the story lived in The Serendipity just like I do. Apparently, the building used to be a college dormitory, something I vaguely remember hearing but have never really taken note of until now.

Same building. Same flower. And the circumstances of when I've seen it bloom match what the story describes.

The flower bloomed when Archer and Willa were present, and I know how much they love each other. And it bloomed for the Hathaways—only the cutest couple on the planet—who have been married at least a million years.

It fits.

It *all* fits.

I pull out my phone, opening the book one more time so I can snap a quick photo of the sketch of the flower at the beginning of the story, then another of the concluding paragraph.

I stand and return the book to the shelf, anxious to get back to The Serendipity.

I try my best to sneak out the door without Sissy noticing, but she's quick for an old lady, and she corners me by the door, blush brush in hand. If I wasn't in such a hurry, I might try to protest, but letting her do my makeup will probably get me out of the library faster, so I stand patiently while she loads what feels like an inordinate amount of blush, then bronzer onto my cheeks.

This has to be against library policy, but for all I know, Sissy is the one who *sets* library policy, so it feels fruitless to register a complaint.

"There. You look beautiful," Sissy says, her Southern drawl a little thicker than usual. "I wish I had a mirror so you can see. Oh! I do have my phone. A teenager in here the other day told me you can use the camera as a mirror."

"Thank you so much, Sissy," I say. "But I've really got to run. I'll look in the mirror at home and let you know what I think the next time I'm here."

I dart out the door before she can apply the lipstick she's pulling out of her pocket and hoof it back to The Serendipity.

Despite the very convincing history I just read, I still want to gather my own evidence. Which means I need to be on the roof with other couples. Couples who are *in love* and not just together. If my mother's recent dating history is any indication, one doesn't always indicate the other.

But who? People who already live in the building would be the easiest place to start.

Maybe I could convince Archer to give me a list of all the apartments that are double occupancy? But then what? Would I just randomly knock on doors and ask people to venture up to the rooftop? I like people, and I have no problem talking to strangers, but that feels like a lot even for me.

Honestly, enough people frequent the garden that if I hang out long enough, a few couples probably will just come up. Since I'm usually up there in the evenings, I often see people on dates, especially in the spring and summer when the wisteria and the twinkle lights make it so incredibly romantic.

I finally reach The Serendipity and head inside, mind still puzzling out the fastest way to test the aptly named love flower, when I run directly into a broad, well-muscled chest.

Peter's broad, well-muscled chest.

He catches me as I bounce off his body, his arms wrapping around my waist as I find my balance.

I lean back and take him in. He's wearing a suit, which is entirely unlike him, and his hair is styled, glasses in place. He looks good—*really good*—and he smells amazing, just like he did the other night when we were watching *Ted Lasso*.

A weird, fluttery sensation stirs just behind my breastbone, something I blame entirely on Willa. If she hadn't mentioned the possibility of Peter liking me, I would not be reacting to his presence like this. But *man*, he really does smell good.

His eyebrows lift as I look up at him, and a smile slowly stretches across his face. I get the sense that he's trying not to laugh, which makes me frown.

"What? What's so funny?"

"Nothing," he says a little too quickly. "Nothing. It's just..." His arms drop from my waist, and he pulls out his phone. He pulls up his camera, then turns it around so I can see my reflection on his screen.

Annnd that's when I see Sissy's handiwork for the first time.

My hands lift to my cheeks. "Oh my gosh. For real?"

"It's a good color on you," Peter says through a laugh, and I reach out and push against his chest.

"Stop laughing at me. It's not funny!"

"It really *is*," he says. "What happened to you?"

"Sissy freaking Mayhew happened to me."

"Who?"

"The librarian at the...you know what? Never mind." I scrub at my cheeks. "She's too hard to explain."

"You're just making it worse," Peter says. "Here." He reaches into the bag hooked over his shoulder and pulls out a wet wipe from a little resealable travel pouch.

I'm not even a little surprised Peter has wet wipes in his work bag. He's always been fastidious about keeping his hands clean—just one of the many quirky things that make Peter *Peter*.

He lifts it to my face, knocking my hands out of the way so he can hold my chin and wipe off my cheeks. His touch is gentle, his focus entirely on me in a way that makes my skin prickle with awareness.

"Where are you going?" I ask. "Work?"

He nods. "Yeah. Got a meeting they won't let me do over teleconference."

"The horror," I say in a mocking tone, and he grins.

"Right? It's been so long since I've worn my suit, I had to dust off the shoulders."

"You look nice," I say as he shifts from my left cheek to my right one. I lift a hand and slide it down the front of his tie. "I like your tie. It's been forever since I've seen you in a suit."

"Want to know a secret?" he asks.

"Always."

"It was kind of nice to have a reason to put one on."

"I'm immediately calling your boss to tell him," I say.

He smirks. "That might actually help," he says. "The meeting is a performance review, and if it goes well, I could be offered a promotion."

"Are you serious? That's amazing! And that would mean you'll have to wear a suit more?"

He nods. "I'll spend a lot more time at the office if I get the job."

He brushes the wipe over my cheeks one last time, his fingers lingering before he reaches forward and tucks a stray curl behind my ear. The gesture sends a delicious shiver down my spine, and I suck in a tiny gasp.

Peter's gaze jumps to mine, and I know, instinctively, that he heard the gasp and knows it was his touch that pulled it out of me. "Done," he says, his voice low. "Back to normal."

His hands fall from my face, and he takes a few steps to the side to toss the wipe into the trashcan near the door.

"Thanks," I say, my throat suddenly dry.

"No problem." He glances at his watch and frowns. "I really have to go. Will I see you later?" he asks, his tone hopeful.

More hopeful than usual?

Or maybe I'm just reading into things.

"Definitely," I say. "Good luck at your meeting."

I watch as Peter disappears out the front door, thoughts spinning, but then my new friend Iris and her boyfriend, Matteo, appear at the bottom of the stairs, and I remember my purpose.

I dart over to them. I don't know Iris super well, but we bonded last month when she randomly brought several bags of potting soil I desperately needed up to the garden. I'd say we're definitely on friendly enough terms that my request is only going to sound *slightly* strange and not entirely deranged.

"Iris! Hi." I look over at Matteo. "Hi, Matteo. Listen. Are you guys busy? Can you come up to the roof with me? I need a quick..." Oh, geez. What do I need? Maybe I can just be vague? "A favor!" I say a little too loudly. "A tiny one. A very tiny favor."

Matteo gives me a wide-eyed look, and Iris bites her lip, like she can't quite figure out how to respond.

"I promise it'll only take a second," I say, still struggling to read their expressions.

Finally, Iris looks up at Matteo with a sweet expression on her face. "What do you think? Do we have time to go up to the roof?"

Matteo shrugs his shoulders. "I'm game if you are." He looks at me. "I heard you've put some new flowers in. I'd like to see them anyway."

"Yes. Perfect. Thank you!" I lead the way as we head

upstairs, Iris and Matteo holding hands the entire time. If the flower doesn't bloom for these two, I'm declaring the story at the library completely bogus because there is no way they aren't in love.

Sure enough, as soon as we step up to the plant, the largest bud slowly unfurls, revealing its deep pink center.

I lift my hands over my head and let out a cheer. I've never seen it happen in real time, and the sight completely takes my breath away.

"What?" Iris asks. "What is it?"

"Nothing," I say. "Just that my favorite flower has finally bloomed. That's what I wanted to show you." I point at the white and pink bloom. "See? There it is!"

Matteo wrinkles his brow. "I thought you needed a favor."

I could just explain. But I'm not sure I know Iris and Matteo well enough to fill them in when I'm still trying to wrap my head around an actual fortune-telling, matchmaking, magical flower.

"Right," I say. "A favor. You know what? I forgot. I already did it. There were some bags of compost I needed to put away, but ha! Silly me. I did it last night."

Iris looks at me funny. As she should because I sound like an utter and complete moron.

"Okay," Iris says. "Well, the flower is really pretty. Thanks for showing it to us."

"The garden looks great, Sophie," Matteo adds.

I linger on the roof while Matteo and Iris head back downstairs, watching and holding my breath as the flower slowly folds in on itself, the bud closing up tight.

I shake my head, still in awe that this is even happening. It blooms for Archer and Willa. It blooms for the Hathaways. It blooms for Iris and Matteo. All couples who are in love, or at least very close to it.

But if the story in the library is true, it should also bloom for people who only have the *potential* for true love. New couples who are on their way there. Even strangers who are destined to fall in love but don't know it yet.

I drop onto the bench beside the flower and pull out my phone so I can look at the images I took at the library, but I'm momentarily distracted by a text from my mom.

MOM

Just saying hi! We're in port in Honduras so I'll only have service for a minute. But look at this view!

Mom is currently on an eighty-day cruise with her boyfriend, Pierre, so an update like this makes sense. But the picture in Mom's second message doesn't make any sense. Because it's a selfie of her and a man who is *not* Pierre. I zoom in on the photo and look a little closer. The two of them are standing on a balcony, bright blue ocean glittering on one half of the background, and what I'm guessing is Honduras filling up the other half, tree-covered hills gently rolling into each other before turning into sandy beaches, then foamy waves. The view *is* beautiful, and my mom looks great. As gorgeous as ever. But I have never seen the man standing beside her.

I sigh and key out a response.

SOPHIE

Amazing view. But who is the guy?

Mom must still be within cell range, because her reply comes through pretty quickly.

MOM

His name is Jean-Luc. Isn't he dreamy?

SOPHIE

Mom. Where is Pierre?

Only my mother could start an eighty-day cruise with one man and end it with another. Without even getting off the boat.

I heart Mom's last message, doing my best to ignore the tightness in my chest that comes whenever I think about my mother's ridiculous dating history. I get that she's been hurt. I'm just not sure this is the healthiest way to cope.

I sigh and close out our text thread, then navigate back to the images from the library.

I zoom in on the paragraph I photographed and read it one more time.

Willa's closet didn't toss her into Archer's apartment until she was ready to find love. At least, that's my theory. And the love flower didn't appear in my garden until now, even though I've been tending the garden since I moved in.

If this story is correct, the timing is significant.

Maybe I'm supposed to use the flower to help others find love?

Or maybe...it appeared because it's *my turn* to find love?

A breeze picks up and ruffles the leaves on the maple tree behind me. I don't know why, but it feels like confirmation, and I'm filled with a trembly sense of anticipation.

If I bring my dates up here, it won't matter if my *ick* detector is broken.

Because the flower will tell me once and for all if a guy has potential—if he's truly meant for me.

It's the ultimate dating hack.

But do I want to start dating again? It's been kind of nice lately, not worrying about it. I've been spending more time with Peter. And I've had a much easier time staying on budget without all the drinks and dining out.

But if the flower could help—if I could do it without all the pointless searching and bad dates—the process would be so much easier.

I think of Willa's suggestion about Peter one more time. Her words *have* made me look at him differently the last few days. At least in small ways. But I doubt very seriously I would need a magic flower if Peter were the one who's meant for me. Besides, a decade is a very long time to never make a move. If Peter had feelings for me, wouldn't he have said something by now?

No matter how I shake it, the most important thing is that I have the opportunity *right now* to use the flower to find my match.

Willa's closet eventually stopped acting as a portal, which means my flower could disappear at any point. It would be irresponsible not to take advantage.

What if this is it?

What if it's finally my turn?

My main character moment.

The love flower in my garden is going to help me find my soulmate.

I just have to figure out how to use it.

Chapter Six
Peter

I'M in my bedroom adding clothes to a duffel bag when a series of frantic knocks sound at my door. The knocking is insistent enough that I half wonder if the building is on fire, and this is my warning to evacuate. But when I leave the now-full duffel bag in the kitchen and swing open my front door, I only find Sophie, cheeks flushed, eyes bright, looking more alive and beautiful than ever.

"You okay?" I say as she barrels into the apartment. "Who's chasing you?"

Sophie's smile stretches wide as she puts her hands on my shoulders and gives me a little shake. "No chasing. Just very exciting news."

My eyebrows lift, even as my heart pounds a little faster for how close she's standing. I haven't seen Sophie since I ran into her on my way to the office. That was only two days ago, which isn't that long. When we're both busy, we'll often go twice that or longer without seeing each other in person. But with how much I've been thinking about her lately, two days felt like ten, so it feels good to see her, to have her here. "Let me hear it, then," I say.

Sophie grins. "Okay, I need you to brace yourself, because what I'm about to tell you isn't going to make any sense."

"Are we talking Willa teleporting into Archer's closet kind of stuff? Or more like...you ran into your high school boyfriend, and he pretended like he didn't know you kind of stuff?"

She scrunches her brow. "Maybe somewhere in the middle?"

"Okay. Shoot."

She grins. "I figured it out."

A pulse of trepidation pushes through me.

She figured out what, exactly? That I like her? That through all these years of friendship, I've always been low-key obsessed with her?

It's a stupid thought. Putting my arm around her was a bold move *for me,* but Sophie hugs people she meets in line at the grocery store. She wouldn't read into something like that without any other evidence.

Sophie gives my shoulders a squeeze, forcing me to focus on the here and now instead of my own spiraling worries. "Do you remember the mystery flower I found in my garden?" she asks.

Relief washes over me, but I feel a tinge of disappointment mixed in, too. It would definitely make things easier on me if Sophie really *had* figured out how I feel. "The love flower?" I ask. "The one you were sketching on your iPad? Did you figure out what it is?"

"Sort of?" she says, eyes sparkling. "I still have no idea what it's called, but I *did* figure out what makes it bloom." Her hands fall away, and I immediately miss the warmth of her standing so close, but Sophie is clearly too full of energy to stand still. I watch as Sophie moves into my living room and rearranges my throw pillows, moving one from the chair to the couch, then swapping the ones on the sofa so the colors alternate.

Even just that subtle shift makes the living room look better. She *always* makes everything better.

"I'm on pins and needles, Soph," I say.

She props her hands on her hips, biting her lip as she takes a deep breath. "The flower really *is* a love flower," she says. "It blooms in the presence of love."

I let out a scoff. Because...*what?* "It does what?"

"I know it sounds crazy, but it's true. When two people who are in love stand in its presence, the flower blooms." She sits, so I move into the living room and join her, sitting down in the armchair perpendicular to the couch.

"Do you remember the Serendipity Springs history room at the downtown library?" she asks. "Where we went to work on our final research papers senior year?"

I nod. "Yeah. Of course I do." We spent hours in that room—usually alone—talking as much as we were studying. That was the room where Sophie discovered a chart on the inside of my history notebook filled with numbers. She asked me what it was, and I made up something about the number of times I wanted to play through a certain video game before I left for college.

Really, it was a chart counting down the number of days we had before we both left for college—the number of days we had left together.

"I went to the library searching, hoping I might find something on local flora and fauna. That idea didn't pan out at all, but then the librarian helped me find a book of oral histories," Sophie says, "published in 1954, and it includes a story from a college student who lived *here,* in The Serendipity, while it was still a women's dorm. She wrote about a flower just like mine. She even included a sketch, and it's absolutely the same flower. Same leaves, same bloom. It was her theory that the flower blooms in the presence of love."

"So, are you only going off what you read? Or..."

"No," Sophie says. "Everything I read totally tracks with what I've observed on my own. The flower bloomed once when Willa and Archer were nearby, then again for the Hathaways. After I read the story, I came back to The Serendipity and took Iris and Matteo up on the roof, and sure enough, it bloomed right then and there. I watched it open with my own two eyeballs. And the flower closed up again when they left."

I resist the urge to reject what Sophie is telling me as fantastical, even ridiculous. But flowers that sense feelings? It's not quite as outlandish as a teleporting closet, but it's close.

"Matteo and Iris?" I ask. The names sound familiar, but I don't think I know them.

She nods. "They live on the third floor. Just started dating."

"Huh. I hadn't heard they got together. That's cool." It's an inane thing to say, but it's innocuous, and that's what I need right now. To say meaningless words while my brain tries to wrap itself around Sophie's claims.

"Anyway, even though three couples felt like pretty good evidence," she continues, "I still wanted *more* proof, so I basically spent the last two days entirely in the garden, waiting for couples to show up."

"You just sat up there and waited?"

My tone is more judgmental than I mean for it to be, and Sophie bristles.

"What else was I supposed to do?" she asks. "I wasn't going to just knock on random people's doors. And a lot of people come up to the garden"—she shoots me a look— "unlike *some* people I know, so it didn't take that long."

"I get it," I say. "I'm sorry. I was mostly just thinking about your work schedule."

She winces. "Okay, that's fair. I tried to take my laptop with me, but without my desk setup, I was pretty much useless, so I basically did nothing for two solid days. I'll have to play catch-up to meet my next deadline, but this was important, and I honestly thought it would take longer. Two days feels pretty reasonable, all things considered."

There is nothing reasonable about this conversation, though I can't quite tell if I feel that way because we're talking about love and Sophie and that's making me nervous, or if it's just because of the whole magical flower thing.

I want to believe her, for her sake, if nothing else. But the mental gymnastics required to do so still feel just out of reach.

"So you think you finally proved it, then?" I ask. "You saw enough couples come into the garden?"

"Six couples in total," she says. "It was amazing."

"That many?"

"Wild, right?" She lets out a little laugh. "But that's not even the best part." She moves into the kitchen, still buzzing with energy, and helps herself to a huge glass of water. She stands beside the counter and chugs it down while I do my best not to stare at the shape of her. She's wearing bright orange overalls over a white tank top, an outfit that does excellent things for her curves.

When she finally turns to face me again, I force my gaze to her face, not wanting her to catch me checking her out. If she does notice, she doesn't care enough to say anything.

"So, the story I read speculated that the flower also blooms when there is the *potential* for love," Sophie says as she moves back into the living room. "I wasn't sure how I was going to test that part, but then, this guy, Jason, the dentist who lives on the fourth floor, brought a date onto the roof, and it was their *first date*. They barely know each other, so they definitely aren't in love yet, but the flower bloomed anyway. Do you know what that means?"

"That Jason's probably going to have a good time tonight?"

"Exactly! Because they're going to fall in love! The flower is a freaking fortune teller. A mystical, magical, love-finding fortune teller." Sophie looks around, like she's finally come down off her high enough to notice where she is. Her eyes catch on the duffel bag in the kitchen. "Are you going somewhere?"

It takes me a second to register her question. I'm still hung up on the last part of Sophie's discovery because I can't stop wondering: if she and I were on the roof together, would the flower bloom for *us*?

Not that I believe in Sophie's magic love flower. I don't.

But if I did believe, and I went onto the roof with Sophie and the flower *didn't* bloom, would that mean love would never be possible?

The more important question might be: Would *Sophie* take it to mean love would never be possible?

I clear my throat and force myself to focus on Sophie's immediate question.

"Uh, yeah, actually," I say. "I'm going to go stay with my parents for a few days."

"What? Why?" she asks.

As if to answer her question, the lights in my living room start flashing, repeated flickers as they brighten, then dim, then turn off completely before repeating the cycle over and over again. Sophie shields her eyes to the strobe-like effect. After twenty or so seconds, the flickering stops.

"That's why," I say, pointing to the ceiling. "They've been doing that for two days, but it's gotten worse this afternoon. I can't get them to stop, and I can't work as long as they're blinking. It's driving me crazy."

"Can't you just leave them off? Use the natural light from the windows?" she asks.

"It doesn't matter if they're off. They still flicker. It's happening in the bedroom too. I've barely slept the past two nights."

She crosses into my living room and stares up at the light fixture. "Why not just take out all your lightbulbs?"

"And then what? Use candlelight after seven p.m.?"

The lights flicker one more time.

"It has to be better than *that*," Sophie says, pointing toward the ceiling. "Did you call Steve? Or Archer?"

I've talked to The Serendipity's building manager at least ten times today, but so far, our conversations haven't been very productive.

"Yeah, Steve brought an electrician by today, but they couldn't find anything wrong. That's the main reason I'm leaving. They're going to have to remove some sections of wall to get to all the old wiring, and I really don't want to live in a construction zone."

Sophie frowns. "Is your parent's place going to be any better? With all the packing they're doing?"

It's a valid question. I'm not particularly excited about witnessing the dismantling of my childhood home, but Mom assured me my bedroom is still functional, if completely devoid of LEGO sets, so it has to be better than here.

"It's free and it's close," I say. "Plus, I'm supposed to pick up the rest of my LEGO bricks anyway."

"But we're doing that together," she says. "Why not just come crash at my place? My couch is super comfortable, and then you'll still be close to all your stuff."

I prop my hands on my hips, considering. It *would* be easier to stay with Sophie. That way, if I need anything from home, I'm only a floor away. It would also give us more time together—and maybe give *me* more opportunity to talk to her about how I feel.

Then again, if I tell her, ask her out, and she says no, would I have to keep living at her place like everything is normal?

In that circumstance, I probably could just bail and go stay with Mom and Dad.

"Come on," Sophie says. "It'll be fun. Besides, if you're staying with me, it'll only be easier for you to help me with my new plan."

"Your new plan?"

"Yep," she says brightly. "I'm going to use my magic flower to find love."

Chapter Seven
Sophie

"Okay," I call to Willa, who is waiting just inside the stairwell with Archer. "Come on out!"

I focus my phone camera right on the love flower and wait for what I know is going to happen. Sure enough, as soon as Willa and Archer are within sight, the closed bud on the flower slowly unfurls, revealing the creamy white petals and dark pink center. It's the first time I've gotten the entire process on film, and I just barely keep myself from squealing.

I'm still getting to know Archer, but I know enough to guess he's not the kind of man who appreciates a good squeal.

"Did you get it?" Willa asks.

"I totally did," I say. I open my gallery to watch the video. The actual process of blooming doesn't look all that different from that of a moon flower, though a moon flower doesn't bloom quite so quickly.

"Look," I say as I pull up the video, turning so Willa and Archer can watch too.

Except, there's nothing to watch.

The video plays, but the image on the screen is completely blurry. "What on earth? I swear, it was totally clear while I was filming. I was staring at the screen the whole time."

"Maybe you moved a little?" Archer suggests.

"Or maybe the flower just doesn't want to be filmed," Willa says.

I give her a dubious look, and she rolls her eyes.

"So you think it blooms in the presence of true love, but you're too much of a skeptic to think it doesn't want to be caught on camera?"

"Okay, fair point," I say. "But this totally sucks. I really wanted to show Peter, and he's still refusing to come up and see it for himself."

"Why?" Willa asks. "He loves your garden."

"Not in the spring. He has terrible seasonal allergies. Once the pollen dies down, he'll come."

"Honestly," Archer says, "maybe it's better if the flower isn't ever caught on video. Can you imagine how the world would react if everyone knew there was a love-detecting flower on our roof? This probably needs to remain one of The Serendipity's secrets."

"Oh, like the corpse flower," Willa says. "I've heard people buy tickets and stand in line for hours to smell those things."

I definitely don't want people waiting in line to walk through my garden, so as much as I wish Peter could see the flower bloom, I have to agree with Archer and Willa. "Corpse flowers absolutely smell like death," I say. "And I think you're right. The broader public might ruin the magic." What I don't say out loud is that I don't think the magic showed up for everybody else anyway. I'm pretty sure it showed up just for me.

"I wonder if it would work on your mom," Willa says. "Maybe help her find someone she could finally settle down with."

Willa has heard enough of my grumbling when it comes to

my mom's dating habits, I'm not surprised by her suggestion, though I have absolutely no confidence it would ever work.

"I think she'd have to *want* to settle down first," I say, and Willa chuckles.

"Ha. True. Which is why it's absolutely going to work for you," she says. "You want it to." She looks up at Archer. "Sophie has a new dating plan, and it's totally brilliant and amazing. She's calling it Operation Soulmate."

"Do I want to know the details?" he asks dryly.

"Don't sound judgy," Willa says. "It's a good plan."

"I don't know that I would call it brilliant or amazing," I say. "It's actually pretty simple. I opened a dating profile on Swipe Rite, and every time I match with a guy, I'm just going to invite him up here. If the flower doesn't bloom, no date. If it does, well, then I've found my one true love."

Archer frowns. "Sophie, it's not a good idea to invite strange men back to your apartment."

"Not back to my apartment. Just to the garden," I say. "And Peter already promised he would help, so I'll be safe."

"I thought you said Peter can't come on the roof because of his allergies," Archer says, arms folded across his chest.

Goodness, this man's good opinion is hard to earn.

"I already worked that part out," I explain. "I'll be on the roof when my date arrives, and Peter will let him in the building, then walk him up here. He'll hover in the stairwell, out of sight but close enough to hear me should I need him, and stay long enough for me to flower-check the guys."

Archer's frown doesn't budge even the tiniest bit, and I begin to question the merits of my plan. "I know it seems harsh to cancel dates if the flower doesn't open," I add, "and I might have to get creative in how and why I do it since I can't exactly be honest. But I'm most concerned about efficiency, and I'd rather not make a guy buy me dinner when I know I won't say yes to a second date."

Even as I say the words, a smidgen of doubt—or is it guilt?—wriggles in the back of my mind.

I really don't like lying to people. But ending dates before they've even begun will definitely require some lying. I could always tell the truth, but is that truly a better option when it will invariably make my dates think I've completely lost my mind?

"That's generous of Peter," Archer says. "How long will you keep him hovering in the stairwell?"

"That was actually his idea," I say. "I told him he could just prop the door open and leave, but he insisted he wouldn't leave me alone with a man I've only just met. But it shouldn't take long. Just a few minutes of chatting for me to see if the flower blooms."

"Peter's right to stay with you," Archer says. "A lot of things could go wrong."

"They won't, though," I say. "I trust the magic to take care of me. It certainly took care of you and Willa."

His expression softens the slightest bit. "All right. Just don't get yourself hurt," he says, this time with a hint of warmth in his voice that makes me think he cares, even if he does think my plan is completely ridiculous.

Which, I'll be honest.

It might be.

Chapter Eight
Peter

CLEARLY, I am a glutton for punishment.

It's the only logical explanation for why I agreed to help Sophie with her outlandish plan.

Her aptly named Operation Soulmate is in full swing, which means that four nights in a row, I've taken a new date up to the roof to meet Sophie, waited in the stairwell while she talked to each date long enough to test her flower, then watched all four leave a few minutes later looking confused, a little dejected, and in one case, spitting mad.

I followed that guy all the way to the front sidewalk and watched as he climbed into his car and drove away. Just to be safe.

And that's my main motivator here. Sophie is really excited about this flower. She'd be going through with the plan with or without my help. My involvement at least gives me some measure of control over her safety.

I can only hope the pattern will continue—that the flower won't bloom before I find the right moment to tell Sophie how I feel.

I shouldn't be such a coward. But my respect for our

friendship is making me hesitant. I don't want to say anything until I have a better idea whether she'll reciprocate. There's so much at stake—more, probably, in her mind. I'm already a hundred percent certain that if Sophie lets me, I'll love her forever. I won't ever leave. But I'm not sure she's ready to trust that's true—even from me.

It's why I understood the appeal when Sophie first explained Operation Soulmate. Sophie wants love, but she doesn't know how to trust that a man won't eventually leave her and break her heart. According to her logic, the flower eliminates that risk and gives her a guaranteed happily ever after.

I need to see more data before giving the flower that much credit—or any credit at all—but I understand where she's coming from. Sophie has never seen a man stay.

My phone buzzes with a text, and I quickly glance at the screen, already standing from her couch so I can walk down the hall and let in her next victim.

Sure enough, the message is from Sophie, a heads up that her date has arrived and she's ready when I am.

So far, Sophie hasn't mentioned to any of her dates that I'm the one who will let them in the building. The Serendipity stays locked at all times, so someone has to let them in, but I like that they aren't expecting me. Their reaction—and how quickly they recover when they see I'm *not* Sophie—is usually pretty telling.

I reach the heavy front door of The Serendipity and push it open.

Only one guy stands outside, and he is nothing like what I'm expecting.

The rest of Sophie's dates have all fit a certain type. Medium height, average build. Three of the previous four wore glasses. But this guy—he looks like he lives in a gym. He's enormous. Almost as wide as he is tall, with biceps large enough to curl me like a dumbbell. His head is shaved, and he has a snake tattoo that wraps around his neck, then climbs up to his ear. Honestly, it's impressive artwork, and I've never been one to judge based on appearances, so I push my concerns aside and clear my throat.

I glance down at Sophie's text to see the guy's name.

"Uh, Bear?" I ask. Because of course his name is Bear.

He turns. "Yeah?"

"Hey. I'm Peter, Sophie's neighbor. She sent me out to let you in. She's up on the roof in the garden, but I can walk you up there."

He looks me up and down, and I get the impression he's calculating exactly how many muscles he would have to use to break me in half. It must not be too many, because he shrugs, his expression indifferent as he walks toward me. "Cool," he says, his voice so deep, I feel it as much as I hear it. We make small talk as we climb the grand staircase, then head to the back stairwell for the last flight up to the roof.

"You guys have fun tonight," I say, then I watch through the cracked door as Bear makes his way into the garden.

When Sophie first pitched my role to me, I was concerned she'd require me to be *in* the garden with her, and that's something I'm determined to avoid. I won't give my fate over to her flower, if only because of how much I know Sophie believes in it. If we're on the roof together and the flower doesn't bloom, that's it for my chances.

But Sophie made it clear that when Willa and Archer were on the roof with her, the bloom closed up as soon as they stepped into the stairwell. Armed with that knowledge, I feel safe here.

I prop my foot against the door so it can't fully close and lean against the wall, working on the crossword puzzle while I wait for Sophie to do her thing. But I'm barely through the first few clues when she sends me a text.

SOS

PLEASE GET ME OUT OF THIS DATE

My heart starts pounding in my chest. Did the guy hurt her? Why can't she just bow out like she always does?

I push the door open the slightest bit and hear Sophie let out a nervous laugh. "Let's go, then," she says. "That sounds great."

I frown. *She* does not sound great. I see the small wedge of wood Sophie sometimes uses to prop the door open, and I kick it into place before racing down the stairs and down the hall to Archer's apartment. He's a little taller and a little broader than I am, and I'm worried I might need back up.

I bang on his door, breathing out a sigh of relief when he answers. "Hey, you got a minute?" I ask. "Will you come stand in the hallway and look intimidating?"

"What?" Archer asks.

"I'll explain later, but we don't have much time."

He pulls his door closed behind him and steps into the hall. "You just need me to stand here?"

"Probably," I say. "Maybe swing a punch if it comes to that."

"Peter," Archer says. "What are you—"

"They're coming!" I say, cutting him off just as Bear and Sophie emerge from the back stairwell and start down the hall. Sophie's smile is more of a grimace and her eyes are wide as we make eye contact.

Without really thinking about the consequences, I step into their path. "Sophie, can we talk a second?" I say, voice sure and commanding. At least, what I hope is commanding.

She tosses a glance over at Bear. "Um, okay," she says.

"I've been thinking a lot, and I'm just going to come right out and say it." I take a deep breath. "I miss you, pookie pie."

Her eyes widen, and I see the threat of laughter in her expression, but she doesn't break. "You do?"

"I really do," I say. "And when I brought this"—my eyes dart over to Bear—"really handsome man up to meet you, it finally clicked that I never should have broken up with you. I'm still in love with you. I think I'll love you until the day I die."

My skin prickles with awareness as those last words leave my mouth, their truth resonating a little too much.

Sophie takes a step forward. "I love you too, honey cakes."

Ohhhh, I am not going to laugh. I won't. I can't. But seriously. Honey cakes? I press my lips together and clear my throat to kill the threatening laughter, then open my arms. "Come back to me?" I look right at her. "Sugar boo boo bear?"

She runs to cover the distance between us and tosses herself into my arms. I wrap her in an enormous hug, one I hope is big enough to cover her shaking shoulders. Maybe Bear will think she's crying instead of laughing?

I lift a hand to the back of her head and bend down, my lips close to her ear. "You owe me for this," I whisper, and her grip around my waist tightens.

When I look up, Bear is approaching, his face solemn. When he reaches us, he lifts his hands, placing one on Sophie's back and one on mine. "I bless this union," he says, his deep voice serious. "You belong together." Then he turns, steps around us, and walks down the grand staircase.

Sophie and I stay frozen in our embrace for a long moment. If we move, we'll start to laugh, and there's no way we're doing that until we're sure Bear is out of the building.

"I can go now, right?" Archer says from behind me.

I look over my shoulder. "Yes. Thank you. I appreciate your presence."

"I'm glad that's all that was needed," he says. "I would not have punched that guy for you." He turns toward his apartment, but then he stops and looks back. "I would have punched him for Sophie." Then he disappears inside.

Sophie leans back and looks up at me. "Sugar boo boo bear?"

I grin. "I was under duress. It's the best I could come up with. And you're one to talk, honey cakes."

Sophie finally gives into her laughter, her arms falling away from my waist as she practically doubles over. I'm not far behind her, and soon we're laughing so hard, tears run down both our faces.

"What happened?" I ask. "Obviously the flower didn't bloom."

"Definitely not," she says. "But when I tried to extract myself from the date, he said something very weird about trusting the destination, then he mentioned his snake—"

"Please tell me that was not a euphemism."

"No, he has an actual snake," she says. "A python. She's the lockscreen photo on his cell phone."

"I guess the tattoo makes sense, then," I say.

"I guess I just got scared," she says. "I didn't want to make him mad. But maybe my worry was needless. He seemed kinda sweet at the end."

"That was definitely not how I thought things were going to go," I say. "Pookie pie."

This sends Sophie into another fit of laughter. It feels so good to make her laugh like this. To laugh *with* her.

I hold out my hand. "Come on. Let's go downstairs. I cooked."

She lets out a little gasp. "I love it when you cook. You made enough for me?"

"Of course," I say as we start down the stairs.

"I guess my track record indicates you *should* expect me for dinner," she says with a sigh. "I'm five for five, Peter. I might have to take myself out to dinner just to keep my spirits up."

"Don't give up," I say, squeezing her hand. "And you can always go out to dinner with me." The words come from a genuine place of friendship, but as soon as they're out of my mouth, I wonder if they sounded that way to Sophie.

We're talking about dating, after all. Did it seem like I was throwing myself into the mix? We've gone out to dinner together hundreds of times over the years, just as friends. But when Sophie looks over at me, something behind her expression seems different.

Does she feel this too?

Does she feel things shifting?

"I can always count on you, can't I?" she says, her smile warm.

I smile back.

She has no idea how much.

Chapter Nine
Sophie

AFTER A VERY LONG week of unsuccessful dating, Monday morning and a long to-do list for work feels like a welcome respite. I don't have a single date scheduled for the next few days, and I don't plan to until at least Friday, if even then.

I don't know what I expected when I started Operation Soulmate. But I definitely didn't expect it to take this much out of me. I haven't even been on an actual date yet, and it's still been exhausting. I forgot how much I hate the whole song and dance of it. The getting ready. The chatting and planning and making small talk.

I also wasn't prepared for how terrible it feels to tell a man, five seconds after I've met him, that I'm not interested in having dinner with him after all. I'm trying to be kind, to be fully honest about changing my mind or not feeling up to going out after all, but I still don't like it, and it's putting a damper on the whole experience.

The trouble is, I don't really know how else to do it. It would be nice if I could invite fifty men onto the rooftop all at once, but if the flower bloomed, how would I even begin to figure out who the bloom was for?

For now, my only option is to persist. But I'm taking a few days off first.

I sigh and stretch my arms overhead. I've been lounging in bed, reading work emails and building my schedule for the day, but when the smell of coffee reaches my nose, I finally cave and get up. Peter is generally up before me, and he always makes enough coffee for us both.

But he's usually sitting at the table when I emerge, dressed for work and already tackling his day. Which is not what I find when I step into my kitchen.

Peter is standing in the middle of the room in a pair of tiny running shorts and the tightest t-shirt I have ever seen on his six-foot frame. I used to go to Peter's swim meets. I've seen the man in a Speedo.

Except, that's not entirely true.

I saw the *boy* in a Speedo. Then we graduated and went to college, and somewhere along the way he turned into a man, and I maybe forgot to notice.

But I'm certainly noticing now. His shirt clings to his chest and shoulders, revealing unexpected definition. He's still built like a swimmer. Long and lean. Not bulky at all. But *wow*.

"Why are you staring at me?"

My eyes jump to Peter's face. He's not wearing his glasses, and I'm struck by the pale brown color of his eyes. They aren't quite hazel, but they're light enough that it's easy to see flecks of yellow and gold in his irises. "I wasn't staring."

"You *were* staring," he says. "Is there something on my shirt?" He looks down, lifting the fabric away from his body so he can inspect it, which only draws my gaze to his torso.

I force my eyes away and clear my throat. "No, I was just... have you been working out?"

Peter studies me for a long moment before his eyebrows

lift, amusement coloring his expression. "Were you just checking me out?"

From any other man, the question might have sounded flirty. But Peter doesn't know how to flirt, so his question can't be anything but genuine.

That doesn't mean I have to give him a genuine answer.

I roll my eyes and push past him, moving to the fridge so I can hide my face behind the door because yes, yes I was checking him out. The list of thoughts and observations I'm blaming on Willa and her stupid suggestion is getting longer and longer.

I suddenly think of the moment Peter tucked a curl behind my ear right after he wiped Sissy Mayhew's blush from my cheeks, and the same fluttery feeling he triggered then fills my chest.

Okay, maybe it's not *entirely* Willa's fault. But she definitely didn't help.

"I was not checking you out," I say as I inspect a random stick of butter. "My question was more literal. Like, have you been working out *right now*."

I look over my shoulder to see Peter staring at me, arms folded across his chest like he doesn't buy my excuse, and he knows exactly what's going through my mind.

I close the fridge. "Don't look at me like that. You're the one who is suddenly walking around my apartment looking all toned and muscly. I don't know what to do with this version of you."

He walks to where I'm standing and reaches over my head, pulling a box of granola bars out of the cabinet just to the right of me. It brings him close enough for me to feel the heat emanating from his body and catch the musky scent of his skin.

"This version of me?" he says. "How is this different? I run. I swim. That's always been my exercise routine."

I lift my hands in surrender. "Fine. Forget I said anything."

The man is standing impossibly close to me, but he doesn't step away. Instead he puts the box down on the counter and leans even closer. A part of me thinks he's doing this on purpose. Standing this close because he *wants* to get a rise out of me.

"I haven't changed, Sophie. Maybe you've just never noticed."

I purse my lips to the side and study him. Objectively, he's probably right. At least in the last few years. Since he got through puberty and grew into an adult, he pretty much *has* stayed the same.

So if Peter hasn't changed...have I?

"Have *you* ever noticed?" I hear myself ask.

I wish I could pull back the question the second it's out of my mouth. I've *never* talked to Peter like this. But it's too late now. I'm already committed. He's watching me intently, his gaze serious, but his expression holds curiosity too.

"Have you ever noticed me?" I add. "Like..." I shrug and push my hands into my back pockets, needing to put them somewhere just to keep them from fidgeting. "You know. Like that."

Peter looks at me for a long moment, his expression darkening before he puts one hand on the fridge directly behind me and leans forward, his face mere inches from mine. "I've noticed," he finally says. "You're beautiful, Sophie. And I'm not blind."

His words feel like an actual caress, and for a split second, I can't pull *any* air into my lungs. My heart pounds harder and harder until I finally inhale, heat spreading through my belly like warm honey.

This is Peter, a part of me thinks. My *best friend*. Except he is not looking at me like I am just his friend.

"Hey, listen," he says, his body still close, his eyes fixed on my face. "Remember when I asked if you'd come home with me to pick up the rest of my stuff?"

I swallow and force myself to nod. "Yeah," I say, my voice much too breathy.

Peter's lips lift on one side, his eyes flashing with something I can't quite read before he says, "Are you free on Saturday? I could really use the help."

"Of course," I say. "I'd love to help. But I might have a date."

I don't know why I say it. I do not have a date planned, and even if I did, I'd cancel it to go home with Peter. His family is *moving.* This is exactly the kind of thing his best friend is supposed to do.

But he's making me feel *so much* right now. With his intense looks and his soft words and the unexplained fluttering that keeps skittering behind my ribs.

Mentioning the possibility of a date is my only defense. The only way to land us back in the friendzone.

Peter's lips twitch the slightest bit, but that's his only reaction before he says, "I guess you can check and let me know?"

"I will. Definitely. I could text you, maybe."

I could text him? What am I even saying right now? Why am I making things so weird?

"That would be great," he says, like we're making some formal arrangement. Like he isn't currently sharing my apartment, and we haven't been *best friends* for the past decade.

"I'll look forward to hearing from you then," Peter says. He finally pushes away from the fridge and turns to walk away, but then he pauses and spins around to face me again. "Can I ask you one more question?"

I nod. "Of course. Anything."

"What are you going to do if you keep dating, keep taking man after man up to the roof, and the flower never blooms?"

A knot of dread forms in my gut. So far, I've only thought of this plan in positive terms. The flower feels like my own personal gift, a way to bypass my initially crappy instincts and find a guy who's truly meant just for me.

But what if it doesn't work? How many men am I willing to parade across The Serendipity's roof before I give up?

"That isn't going to happen," I say. "The flower appeared in *my* garden. I have to believe it's here to help me."

He nods. "And you're sure you'll find the right guy just... randomly dating like this?"

"It's not random," I argue. "I match with their profile first."

"Right. Match with guys like Bear," he says, the words stinging despite his gentle tone. "He really seemed like your type."

"Okay, to be fair, Bear's profile picture was completely different from how he looked in person."

Peter runs his hand through his hair, and for the first time, I sense a little wariness from him, like there are things he isn't saying. Whether about me or Operation Soulmate, I'm not sure.

He opens his mouth, like he's going to say something, but then he stops, swallowing his words as he shakes his head.

"Just say it, Peter," I say. "I can tell you're clearly thinking something."

He breathes out a sigh, his hands moving to his hips. "I just—Sophie, you know I want you to be happy. And if you want to keep up this dating thing, I'll keep helping you. I promised I would, and I won't go back on my word. But..." He hesitates, his jaw flexing before he looks me right in the eye. "I don't think you're looking in the right place. I don't think this is going to work for you."

"Well, I do," I say, feeling a need to defend myself. What does Peter know about where I should be looking for dates?

"The flower appeared for me, Peter. It appeared now, this season. Not last fall. Not when I first started tending the garden. I have to think the timing matters here." I fold my arms across my chest. "And I don't exactly think you're in a position to give me dating advice." The words sound sharper than I intend, and they must hit their mark, because Peter flinches, making me immediately regret them.

But a part of me also doesn't like that Peter is judging, so I hold my ground, lifting my chin the slightest bit as if to say, *yeah, that's what I said. And I meant every word.*

"You're definitely right about that," he finally says, his words heavy, his tone holding an element of defeat. "I just know you, Soph. I know what you need. And these guys you're matching with—they aren't it." He turns to leave but pauses before he enters the hall and motions toward a coffee mug sitting on the counter. "It's probably still warm," he says. "I poured it right before you showed up. I was going to bring it to you."

As soon as he's gone, I slide down the fridge until I'm sitting against it and drop my face into my hands.

I have no idea what just happened.

One minute, Peter was taking my breath away, melting my insides with the intensity of a single look, then the next, he was calling me out, questioning my dating tactics, poking holes in Operation Soulmate.

I could be making something out of nothing. Seeing things that aren't really there. Peter could be annoyed with my dating plan simply because he's my friend, and he cares about me. Doesn't want to see me get hurt.

Or he could be annoyed because Willa was right. And he'd rather be dating me himself.

I groan into my palms. What is happening to me? I have a plan. A purpose. All this overthinking is only going to mess with my headspace.

I just need to focus. Schedule more dates. Trust the process.

Still. The way Peter looked at me—I don't think I made that up.

Even more concerning: I think I might have liked it.

Chapter Ten
Peter

My parents have done a lot since I was last home.

I barely recognize the place. The entryway is lined with boxes, the pictures are off the walls, and it looks like they're repainting the living room. All the furniture is covered with plastic, and cans of paint are stacked under the window.

I stand in the entryway, eyes surveying the scene, heart somewhere on the floor. I love my apartment at The Serendipity, but this house was home for so long, and now it isn't anymore. At least, it won't be in a couple of weeks.

Sophie steps up beside me and slips her arm through mine, giving it a little squeeze. "This is pretty wild."

Despite our slightly tense conversation on Monday morning, things were fine for the rest of the week. Though I did notice Sophie didn't schedule any more dates. I won't ask her if it's because of anything I said, but I won't deny how much I enjoyed having her around without having to worry about playing chaperone.

It's a selfish thought, but I like having Sophie all to myself.

I'm also glad she's here with me today. She's maybe the only person who understands what this feels like for me.

I take a steadying breath. "Yeah. I didn't expect it to hit me so hard."

"You lived here your entire life, Peter," she says gently. "It's a big deal."

Mom appears on the opposite side of the living room, and she smiles wide. "If it isn't two of my favorite people." She walks toward us, pulling both of us into a crushing group hug, one arm looped around each of our necks.

"Oof," Sophie says, her face smooshed into my ribcage. "So good to see you, Mrs. Stone."

"Stop calling me that," she says to Sophie. "Once you're out of college, you get to call me Evelyn. How are you? How's life?"

"Good. Lots of the same. Work. Work. A little more work."

"How's your mother?" Mom asks.

Sophie's eyes shift to mine for the briefest second. "On a cruise, actually. With Pierre. Or, wait. I think it's Jean-Luc, now."

"Jean-Luc?" I say, looking at Sophie. "What happened to Pierre?"

"Good question," she says.

"Someone new?" Mom asks.

Sophie grimaces. "It's always someone new, Evelyn."

Mom takes Sophie's hand, patting it gently. "Well, if she's happy, that's all that matters, right?"

It's hard to guess what my mom really thinks about Isabella Stewart's dating habits. My parents have been married for twenty-seven years, and they've never seemed happier. When Allison and I were teenagers, we decided it was pointless to ever hope we'd find a love as good as what our parents have. They're *that* perfect for each other.

"What about you?" Mom says, turning to face me. She

reaches up and cups a hand around my cheek. "What's new with you?" I sense a level of worry in her voice, and I don't like it. I know she's stressed about leaving me, so even though I'm gutted by the sight of their house all packed up, I force myself to smile.

"Since I was here last week?" I ask.

"A week is a long time," she says.

"I'm good, Mom," I tell her. "Everything is good."

Mom smiles, but it doesn't quite reach her eyes. I'm not sure she believes me.

"Actually, Peter might be getting a promotion," Sophie says, and I shoot her a surprised look. Her eyes widen the slightest bit, like she's begging me to just go along with it. "A management position," she adds. "Corner office, a pay raise, it's a pretty big deal."

There is no corner office connected to the job offer I'm still waiting to hear about, but I understand what Sophie is trying to do. As much as Mom worries about me, it will be a lot easier for her to leave me behind if she thinks great things are happening for me in Serendipity Springs.

"Oh, Peter, I'm so proud of you," Mom says.

"I am too," Sophie says. "I'm planning a big party to celebrate as soon as we get the news." A party is the last thing I'd want, and Sophie knows it, but she has my mother eating out of her hand right now, so I don't protest.

"See?" Mom says, looking at Sophie. "This is the main reason I feel okay about moving and leaving Peter here all alone. Whenever I think about it, and I start to worry, I just think to myself: he'll still have Sophie. Sophie has always taken care of him."

"And you know I always will," Sophie says, then she gives my mom another hug.

Will she, though? If Sophie's dating plan works and she falls in love with someone else, our relationship will have to change. I wonder if that thought keeps her up at night like it does me.

Mom leads us into the kitchen, where lunch is already waiting for us. Homemade chicken salad, fresh croissants, fruit. And Allison's favorite brownies. In preparation for the move, Allison already moved out of her apartment, and she's been living with Mom and Dad ever since.

I hold up a brownie. "Where's Allison?" I ask before taking a bite.

"She and your father went to the hardware store to get some putty to patch the walls. They should be back any minute."

"How's she doing?" Sophie asks.

"Better every day," Mom says. "She hasn't mentioned Chase in a week, at least."

I grumble at the thought of my little sister's ex-fiancé. He's the one reason I'm glad Allison is moving to South Carolina. She needs a fresh start where there's no risk of her ever running into his sorry, cheating—

"That makes me really happy," Sophie says, cutting off my wayward thoughts. "She deserves so much better."

"I do, don't I?"

We all turn to see Allison coming in the door from the garage. Sophie squeals and stands up, rushing over to give Allison an enormous hug. Only a year younger than us, Allison always looked up to Sophie. By the time we graduated from high school, the two of them were almost as close as Sophie and me.

"You deserve the world," Sophie says. "I hope I run into that pig of a man just so I can kick him in the shins for you."

"Don't do it," Allison says. "He's not worth the bruised toe."

When Sophie finally lets her go, I stand and pull my little

sister into an embrace. "Hey, Allie," I say. "Good to see you. How's the South Carolina job hunt going?"

"I have a virtual interview on Monday," she says, "and it's the final one. Seems like a good firm."

"That's good news," I say.

"Yeah, I think so. How about you?" She looks over at Sophie with a smirk. "Have you two fallen in love yet?"

My gut tightens, but Sophie only rolls her eyes and laughs. This has been a running joke for years now. Growing up, Allison always talked about wanting Sophie as an actual, for real sister, and the two of us getting married was the obvious way for that to happen. Every time she saw us together, she'd make some kind of joke, suggesting we try different romantic dates to take our relationship to the next level. Stargazing. Ice-skating. Horse-drawn carriage rides. The longer the joke went on, the more elaborate her suggestions became.

"Sorry, Allison," Sophie says. "Your parents are just going to have to adopt me the old-fashioned way."

"You're already one of us," Mom says, raising her glass to Sophie. "You know that."

Dad steps into the kitchen next, and we go through the same thing. Hugs all around. Greetings and questions for Sophie that are just as thorough as the ones asked of me.

She really *is* a part of us.

More than anyone else who *isn't* us.

After lunch, Sophie and I head up to my room. It's mostly packed up, but the closet is still full of LEGO bricks, enormous bins sorted by size, shape, and color stacked from the floor to the ceiling.

"Wow," Sophie says. "You really don't have room for all these."

"Do I even need to keep them?" I say. "I have the assembled sets. What do I need these for?"

"They're probably worth something," Sophie says. "And

you might have kids one day. What kid wouldn't love this collection?"

I tug open the top drawer of one of the plastic storage units on the left side of the closet. It's filled with instruction manuals for unbuilt models, the ones I didn't have space to display in my room.

It's stupid to feel emotional over LEGO bricks. They're just toys. Building blocks. But when I was a kid, they got me through a lot of lonely years. The thing is, I didn't really know I was lonely until Sophie blasted her way into my life and showed me what it feels like to have a friend.

She's the one who taught me that just because I'm happy keeping my own company, I don't have to *always* be that way. I resisted for a long time, mostly because she was the most beautiful girl I'd ever seen, and I had no idea how to talk to her. But she didn't give up.

She asked and she asked and she laughed at my rejections and joked about how many times it would take before I finally said yes.

Fourteen.

That's how many times it took. Once I said yes, everything changed for the better.

"Hey, what's with the face?" Sophie asks from beside me, her voice gentle. "What are you thinking?"

I look over at her. "Nothing. Just...I don't know. It's stupid."

"No feeling is stupid, Peter. Talk to me."

I run a hand down my face. "Just memories," I say.

She nods, but I'm not sure she's convinced that's all that's going on.

Needing a distraction, I dig through the drawer of instructions, looking for one booklet in particular. As soon as I find it, I tug it out and hand it to Sophie. "Here. Build this with me."

"Really? Right now?"

"I don't want to do this yet," I say, motioning my head toward the closet behind me. "And this one won't take long. It's an easy one."

"A greenhouse," she says as she looks at the booklet. She flips through the pages while I pull out the bins I'm pretty sure hold most of the pieces we need. "Oh, my gosh. And the inside is full of flowers."

"I thought you'd like it." I set the bin down in the center of my mostly empty childhood bedroom and sit down beside it, holding a hand up and offering it to Sophie.

She shakes her head, chuckling as she lets me tug her onto the floor. "Hey, so sorry about spilling the beans about your promotion," she says as she tucks her feet under her. "I don't know what I was thinking, just blurting it out like that. I could see the worry in your mom's eyes, and I thought it might make her feel better."

"I didn't mind you saying something," I say as I riffle through the pieces, pulling out the ones we need. "It was a good idea."

She smiles. "Good. I worried you still might not get it, and then you'd be mad that we gave your mom false hope," she says. "When will you find out for sure?"

"Any day now," I say. "Actually, I expected a call yesterday, but it never came."

"Does that worry you?" Sophie asks, and I scoff, breathing out a little chuckle.

"Oh, I see how it is," she says, her tone playful. "The master data scientist is very confident."

My cheeks heat the slightest bit. I *am* confident, but my boss also told me I'd all but gotten the job. He's waiting for our corporate offices down in Charlotte to make things official, but that's more a formality than anything else.

"They pretty much told me the job is mine," I say. "That's all I'm saying."

"You don't have to justify it to me," she says. "I already think you're fabulous. You deserve all the promotions."

I set a thin green plate on the carpet to act as our base, then give Sophie several pieces we'll need to assemble the foundation of the greenhouse.

"How long has it been since you've done this?" she asks, lining the pieces up in front of her.

"Years," I say. "This one is actually the last one I built. During our senior year of high school. I built it for you."

Her gaze jumps to mine. "What?"

I shrug. "You'd just gotten into UMass, and you were so excited about the botany program. I bought it for you, built it thinking I would give it to you, but then..."

"Why didn't you?" she asks. "Peter, I would have loved it."

I reach up and adjust my glasses. A part of me wants to just tell her everything. How I felt about her then. How I *still* feel about her now.

But I told myself I wouldn't risk it until I'm sure she feels the same way.

For a split-second last Monday, when I admitted I thought Sophie was beautiful, I wondered if she might. I saw a spark in her eyes, and the way her breath hitched—I did that to her. I know I did.

But then we argued about Operation Soulmate, and she insisted she believes it's going to work—that her soulmate is out there somewhere.

I'm sure it's fear holding me back. But how can I not be scared?

I'm right here. Around Sophie all the time. And she still feels the need to orchestrate an elaborate scheme to find someone else. It isn't exactly a confidence booster.

"I don't know why I didn't," I finally answer. "I maybe thought it would give you the wrong impression."

"Whatever. It absolutely wouldn't have."

I snap a few pieces onto the LEGO plate, then nudge it toward Sophie, turning the instruction booklet so she can see where her pieces go. "Maybe not," I concede, "but I wasn't good at stuff like this, especially not back then."

"At LEGO sets?" she teases. "Pretty sure you were an expert."

"At people," I say. "At friendships."

"What are you talking about?" Sophie clicks her pieces in, then slides the plate back to me. "You were a great friend."

"Because *you* made me one," I say. "You have to admit, Sophie, we never would have been friends had you not tried so hard to wear me down."

She huffs out a little chuckle. "True. You were one tough nut to crack."

"Why did you try so hard?" I ask. "What did you see in me?"

"What didn't I see in you?" she answers, the words coming so quickly I know she has to mean them. "You were smart and confident, and you didn't care what anyone else thought. High school was silly in so many ways, but you never were. You were serious and studious and so mature. Like you were completely ready for the world." She shrugs. "I envied you, really. I think I thought if we hung out together, you might help me feel less lost."

It's weird to hear her talk about how she perceived me in high school because it's so far from how I truly felt. "I was the one who was lost," I say. "I had no friends. I had no idea how to relate to people." I add another piece to the model, and my hand collides with Sophie's. But instead of pulling back, I grab her hand, holding it in mine. "Not until I met you." My heart climbs into my throat as I slowly rub my thumb across the back of her hand.

For all the times I've touched Sophie, hugged her, sat with my arm around her, nothing has ever felt so charged as this. Even that moment in Sophie's kitchen doesn't quite compare. Maybe because nothing has ever been so intentional.

Sophie lifts her gaze to meet mine, a question clear in her eyes.

I turn her palm, pressing it flat against mine and thread our fingers together.

It could be a friendly gesture. Friends hold hands all the time.

But I hope she senses that I don't want it to be.

Behind us, the bedroom door flies open and Allison steps inside.

Sophie yanks her hand away and scoots several feet away from me, like we're teenagers who just got caught making out.

Allison's eyes go wide. "Uh, sorry, I...I didn't mean to interrupt."

"You weren't interrupting anything," Sophie says, the words a little too rushed.

"Right," Allison says, her eyes darting from me, to Sophie, then back again. "I was just wondering if Sophie wants to run down to Cookie's with me to get a latte. Mom has me packing dishes, and it's totally boring, and I could really use a pick-me-up."

"Yes! Definitely!" Sophie says, jumping up with a ridiculous amount of enthusiasm. "Let me just run to the bathroom really quick."

As soon as she's out of the room, Allison closes the door and kicks the side of my leg. "Oh my gosh! Were you seriously just holding her hand right then? Is something happening? Please tell me something is happening!"

"Chill, please," I say. "And lower your voice. Nothing is happening."

"Um, then why were you holding her hand?"

"Allison, please don't," I say. "There's nothing going on. There is never going to be anything going on."

"I don't understand," Allison says. "It really looked like something was happening."

"It doesn't mean anything to *her*," I say. "It's just friendly. It has to be, because she's right in the middle of this big dating experiment thing, and I'm not a part of it."

"A dating experiment?" Allison asks.

I glance at the door behind her. Sophie will probably be back any minute. "It's a long story that I'm sure she'll tell you if you ask. The point is, she isn't interested in me like that. She never has been."

"But you still are, aren't you?"

My jaw tightens. *Still.* Allison is the only person in the entire world who knows exactly how I feel about Sophie. My senior year, when Allison was a junior, I decided it was time to finally shoot my shot. I had no idea what to do or how to do it, so I went to my sister for help, and together, we came up with a plan. I ordered a cake from a local bakery decorated with the words "*Will you go to prom with me?*" then spent three hours making a simple cypher out of letters and numbers, explaining to Sophie how I felt about her. How I'd *always* felt.

I had never done anything so bold, and I was sick for days leading up to the Saturday when I was finally going to ask her.

But then, Friday night, while the cake was already in my refrigerator, Sophie texted and said she was coming over to tell me the "best news ever."

She'd been asked to prom.

By Jack Larson, the captain of the swim team and the one guy in the entire county who could beat me in the two-hundred-meter freestyle.

I pasted a smile on my face and told her how happy I was for her, then, once she left, I threw the entire cake in the trash.

Sophie and Jack went to prom together and dated through the end of high school, but they broke up not long after.

Allison pushed me to try again, but I'd already decided it wasn't worth the risk. Even though Sophie never knew I planned to ask, and it was probably my fault for waiting so long, prom still felt like a rejection, and it wasn't one I wanted to repeat. Our friendship was good. Great, even. Why screw it up? So I boxed up my feelings and tucked them away and left them alone until I moved into The Serendipity.

"It doesn't matter," I say. "She doesn't see me that way, and she never will."

Allison scoffs. "She definitely won't if you never tell her how you feel. It's not fair to her, Peter. You can't be mad that she isn't reciprocating if you aren't being honest with her."

Down the hallway, the toilet flushes, and I shoot Allison one final warning look. "Please don't say anything to her," I say, and Allison rolls her eyes.

"Who do you take me for? But I still think you're being dumb."

Sophie doesn't even come back into the room before she and Allison leave to get coffee, and I try not to read into it. Was she freaked out by what happened? When she jumped away, she seemed like she didn't want Allison to get the wrong impression.

And then she practically ran to get out of here.

Was she running from me?

And if Allison hadn't come in when she did, what would have happened next?

Chapter Eleven
Sophie

OKAY, so it's fine, right?

Friends hold friends' hands all the time. That's all that was. Just friendly, totally benign handholding.

Handholding that made my breath catch and my skin tingle and my heart flip somersaults in my chest. But that's fine!

All of this is absolutely fine.

"You're awfully quiet over there," Allison says as we make our way down the sidewalk. The weather is nice enough that we decided to walk the half mile to Cookie's Coffee House, something I'm grateful for because I could really use some time to clear my head.

"Am I?" I say as I step around a puddle. "Just enjoying the sun."

"Uh-huh," Allison says. "I'm sure that's all it is."

I stop. "What?" I ask. "Just say it. You're clearly thinking something."

She bites her lip and looks over at me. "I'm not thinking anything," she says. "I'm definitely not thinking about you darting away from my brother like you were caught doing something sneaky."

I shoot her a look. "You just startled me. Don't make this a thing."

She chuckles. "Funny. He said the same thing."

My ears perk up. "He did? What did he say? What did you ask him?"

Allison stops in her tracks and spins to face me. "So it *is* a thing. You wouldn't have just asked all those questions if it wasn't."

I scoff and put my hands on my hips. "You tricked me."

"You're avoiding my questions."

I huff out a breath and start walking again, hugging my arms around my sides. I *am* avoiding her questions. Because I have no idea how to answer them.

Was holding Peter's hand a thing? Or was it totally innocuous and friendly? Do I want it to be more?

It's not lost on me that in the past two weeks, I've spent *a lot* of minutes noticing things about Peter that I've never noticed before. But when he held my hand—that's the first time I've truly recognized how good of a boyfriend he would actually be. There was a spark, a real connection, and a potent awareness that he's pretty much everything I want in a man.

The thought hit me like a brick to the forehead, but it was quickly eclipsed by an overwhelming sense of fear.

I don't remember much about when my dad left. But when my stepdad left, my mom and I both fell apart, and it was Peter who held us together. Peter who promised I would still go to college even though Mom's savings were gone. Peter who let me cry on his shoulder. Peter who listened to us both lament over my stepdad's betrayal, over his careful paper trail that made it look as though his actions weren't criminal.

Through it all, I was okay because Peter was there to keep me grounded. To take care of me. But if *Peter* is my boyfriend, and things don't work out, who will be there for me? Not my mom—we haven't been that kind of close in years. Willa, of course, but she's got so much on her own plate, and she has Archer to focus on now.

It's always been Peter for me. He's always been my safety net.

I don't know if I can give that up.

Allison falls into step beside me, her expression worried. She nudges me with her elbow. "I'm sorry, okay? I'll let it go."

I give my head a little shake. "It's okay. I know how much you would love for us to get together for real. But it would be so complicated," I say. "We've been best friends for so long. I don't want to lose that."

"Who says you would have to?" she asks.

History. Time immemorial. My own crappy dating history that indicates I am a master at torching relationships.

Instead of answering, I steer the conversation to safer territory. "Let's talk about you, okay? How are you feeling about the move?"

She shoots me a knowing look. "I'll allow the deflection, but only because of how much I love you."

I loop my arm through hers. "Come on. Spill. Are you excited about South Carolina?"

She's quiet for a long moment, so long that I start to worry there's something really wrong. Finally, she breathes out a sigh. "Yeah. I guess so."

"Wow. Way to really sell it," I say, and Allison rolls her eyes.

"I am!" she says. "I promise I am. I'm just worried about Peter."

"Peter is a grownup, honey. He'll be okay." I eye her, suddenly wondering if there's more to Allison's hesitation than meets the eye. "Is Peter really your *only* reason for hesitating? You know you don't have to move, right? If you wanted to stay in Serendipity Springs, I'm sure your parents would understand."

We walk in silence for almost a minute before she finally says, "I think my logical brain knows that, and it also knows a fresh start is what I need. But a tiny part of me is still clinging to the possibility that if I stick around, Chase might change his mind." She winces as she says the words, like she knows exactly how ridiculous they are.

"Oh, you are definitely going to South Carolina," I say as we finally reach Cookie's. "You will not take that man back."

"I know. I *know*," Allison says. "But—"

"Nope," I say. "No buts. And no using Peter as an excuse to stay. You're going to move to South Carolina, meet a gorgeous, rich Southern gentleman, then you can come back to Serendipity Springs for vacation and rub your happiness in Chase's smarmy face."

This finally makes Allison laugh. "I like the sound of this plan."

I open the coffee shop door for Allison, then follow her inside. Cookie's Coffee House doesn't quite compare to Serendipi-Tea, but it makes a mean cappuccino, and they make the best oatmeal cookies in the city, so it was always a favorite hangout spot when I was in high school.

"So," Allison says as we step into line, "will you tell any of the men in your dating experiment about the handholding that happened earlier?"

I roll my eyes. "Stop it with the handholding talk. You're turning it into something it wasn't."

I think.

Something it *probably* wasn't?

Something I think I'd like to do again, despite my better judgement.

"Besides, what do you know about my dating experiment?"

"Nothing at all. Peter mentioned it, but he didn't give me specifics," Allison says. "You should tell me everything. I'm already intrigued."

As skeptical as Peter is himself, I doubt he mentioned the love flower as a part of my experiment, so I give Allison a modified version of the truth, mentioning the dating app, and my determination to date with a little more intention. I even give her a quick rundown of the newest guy I matched with—a pediatrician named Jake who, at least inside the app, seems like an actual possibility.

"We haven't made plans to get together or anything—his schedule is insanely busy—but we've been talking back and forth, getting to know each other, and he seems really great." Allison must pick up on the slight phoniness to my tone because she offers me a pained smile before saying, "I can't decide if you're trying to convince *me* that Jake is great or yourself."

"He's great," I say. "Of course he's great."

"Okay," Allison says. "Well, if that's the case, then I hope it goes well."

When it's my turn to order, I order two cookies, one for me and one for Peter, tucking his into the outside pocket of my purse.

Allison eyes the plastic-wrapped treat and shoots me a knowing look.

"What?" I ask. "I buy Peter a cookie every time I'm here."

"You do, don't you?"

"Because we're *friends*," I say.

"Mm-hmm," she says, but her tone doesn't sound at all like she believes me. "That's why he's staying at your place right now."

"Because the wiring at his place is all messed up. And. We're. *Friends*," I say, enunciating each word.

The barista behind the counter finishes our drinks and

hands them over to Allison, who passes mine to me. "A friend who you think is hot," she says.

"I do not," I say, but that doesn't stop my brain from conjuring an image of Peter in his running clothes. I try to shove the image away, but it's too late. I can already feel the heat climbing up my neck, flushing my face, making my cheeks bright red.

Allison smirks. "That's what I thought."

———

Peter is in the driveway when we get back, loading bins of LEGO bricks into the back of his SUV.

"Are they all going to fit?" I ask as I step up beside him.

"Barely," he says. "But I still don't think they'll all fit in the basement."

"We'll figure it out," I say. "Between your place and mine. Speaking of your place, any word on the wiring?"

Peter runs a hand through his hair. "I just got a text from Steve, actually. He says the electricians just finished up this afternoon."

"Oh that's great news," I say.

"Is it?" he asks dryly. "Because even though they cut out half my walls, ripped out insulation, and replaced the wiring in the entire apartment, the lights are still flickering."

"You're kidding," I say.

"I wish I was."

"Peter. That doesn't make any sense."

"Steve's last piece of advice was that the building usually chills after someone falls in love, so maybe I should amp up my dating life."

"You could join Operation Soulmate," I say, though the thought of Peter taking women up on the rooftop to see if the flower blooms makes me immediately stabby. "I'm sure the flower would work for you, too."

"I don't think Steve was serious, Soph," Peter says, and a weird sense of relief washes over me. I should not hate the idea of Peter dating someone else.

I shouldn't.

But I absolutely do.

"So what are you going to do?" I ask.

"I have no idea," he says. "I just know I can't sleep on your couch forever. But I also can't live in an apartment that's somehow both disco night at the dance club and a hallucinogenic fever dream, all at the same time."

I'm not sure where the laugh comes from, but hearing Peter talk about his finicky electricity suddenly sends me into a fit of giggles. Once I start, I have a really hard time stopping.

Peter looks at me, his expression annoyed, but the longer I laugh, the more he smiles.

"Stop laughing," he finally says, his shoulders shaking because now, he's laughing too. "It's not funny."

"Then why are you laughing?"

"Because *you're* laughing."

I don't stop until my phone buzzes with a text that I do not expect. "Whoa," I say, and Peter frowns, the traces of his laughter gone right along with mine.

"What is it?" he asks.

I hold up my phone. "A text from my dad."

"But it isn't Christmas or your birthday," Peter says.

"I know, right?" I turn and sit down on the bumper of Peter's SUV and open the text thread, and Peter sits down beside me.

"What does it say?" Peter asks, and I hand my phone over. He's quiet while he reads, then he hands it back. "That's not too bad, is it?"

It isn't, but it still leaves me feeling hollow. "Not really. But..."

When my words trail off, he nudges my shoulder with his. "But what?"

"I don't know. It's just...weird to see him being a dad, I guess?"

It's not like I think my dad is a terrible person. He's not— not like Charles Crooksley is. He's just always been absent, at least when it comes to me. He checks the boxes, sends two hundred dollars every birthday, and I get the family e-greeting his wife sends out every Christmas. But that's it. We've never been close, and I've never felt like more than an obligation.

Which is fine with me, honestly. I don't want to be close to him, because I know how badly his leaving broke my mom.

"I didn't know you had your grandmother's journals," Peter says.

"Yeah, he gave them to me when I was in middle school. Eighth grade, maybe? His mom died before I was born, so I never met her, which made it all feel very weird to me. I barely knew *him,* so it seemed strange he'd want me to get to know his mom."

"He just randomly showed up with them one day?" Peter asks.

"Not entirely," I say. "He got into a fight with my mom, I think. Probably because he was never around. I overheard them on the phone, and she said all this stuff to him, listed off all the things that were going on in my life. I'd planted a garden all by myself, and I'd won the science fair at school and gotten straight A's and started my period for the first time. I really loved that part—that she felt like she needed to include *that,* talking to a man I rarely even saw. Anyway, it must have triggered some kind of guilt trip because he showed up the next day with a box of his mom's things and took me to get ice cream."

"Wow," Peter says. "That's...was it awful?"

"Totally awful," I say. "The only thing he asked about was my period."

"Not the science fair?" Peter asks. "That would have been so easy."

"He was nervous," I say. "And I could tell he was trying, it was just...I don't know."

"Too little, too late?"

I shrug. "Yeah, maybe."

"It had to be hard," Peter says, his tone gentle. "Seeing you grow up. Knowing he wasn't a part of your life."

"I'm sure," I say. "But he could have been. Until we moved to Serendipity Springs, he lived on the other side of town. It was a thirty-minute drive, Peter. That's nothing. I know he couldn't be my mom's husband, but he could have still been my dad." Familiar tension claws at my throat, and I shove it away, just like I always do. "It's honestly fine though," I say. "I got over it a long time ago."

Peter slips an arm around my back and tugs me toward him. I fall against his side, breathing in his familiar scent, and my nerves immediately start to settle. "Even if you aren't over it," he says, "it's okay. It sucks. You don't have to pretend like it doesn't suck."

I take a deep breath. "Yeah, it does suck, doesn't it?"

"So what do you do now?" he says. "Do you still have the journals?"

"I'm sure they're still at Mom's," I say. "Probably in her attic. So I guess that means I get to go see her."

"When does she get home from her cruise?" Peter asks.

"Any day now, I think," I say. "She texted yesterday and said she was back in the states."

Peter gives my shoulders a squeeze. "Let me know if you want me to go with you," he says. "It's the least I can do after you came here with me."

I will let him come with me. Of course I will.

And I will carefully file away any thought or feeling about Peter being more than just my friend.

This, right here, this is why I need him in my life.

This is why I can't risk losing him.

Chapter Twelve

Peter

STEVE HANDS me one more container of LEGO pieces and I add it to the very tall stack of storage bins in the basement of The Serendipity.

"I think that's the last one," Steve says as he slides his hands down his sweater vest. Steve and I are relatively new acquaintances, but I immediately liked his mild manner and no-nonsense approach to running things. "You have *a lot* of LEGO sets, Peter."

"I was kind of a lonely kid," I say, and Steve nods his head in understanding.

"Ahh. I get it," he says.

"Thanks for your help." I close the metal caging that surrounds my small section of storage space. Up until an hour ago, the only things down here were my bicycle and the luggage set my parents gave me when I graduated from college. Now, it's full of bins of LEGO bricks...stacked, well, like LEGO bricks. I still have no idea what I'm going to do with them all. I probably could sell them. But Sophie was right. If I eventually get married and have kids, it might be nice to hang onto them.

"Anytime," Steve says. "It's the least I can do, seeing as how I can't seem to fix your apartment."

I turn and follow him through the basement and toward the elevator. "Have you talked to Archer about it? Does he have any suggestions?"

"Not useful ones," Steve says. "Unless you also think it's a good idea to call the Ghostbusters."

I chuckle. "You sure that suggestion didn't come from Willa?"

His lips quirk up the slightest bit. "I wondered the same thing."

"I know you're trying, Steve, but I can't stay with Sophie forever," I say as Steve presses the button for the elevator.

He holds up his hands. "I know. I promise this is at the top of my priority list right now. I'm just not used to the *outside-the-box* thinking this building requires of me."

The elevator dings, and we step into the first-floor lobby of The Serendipity.

"I'll keep you posted on your apartment," Steve says as he heads toward the grand staircase. "Thanks again for your patience."

I lift a hand and wave it in acknowledgement. "It's not like I have much choice in the matter," I mutter under my breath. Before I reach Sophie's apartment door, my phone buzzes with an incoming call.

Sophie left me to unload the LEGO bins on my own, saying she needed to water the garden before it got dark, but she might be back in her apartment by now, and I definitely don't want to answer this phone call with company.

Because it's my boss.

Calling me on a Saturday.

That's never happened before.

Instead of heading left toward Sophie's apartment, I turn right and duck into the library. It's blessedly empty at the moment, so I quickly answer the call just before it gets sent to voicemail.

"Dr. Conway," I say. "How are you?"

"Good. Thanks for answering. Sorry to bother you on a Saturday," my boss says.

Dr. Conway is a good boss. A *great* boss, really. He's patient and respectful of my intelligence, and he doesn't micromanage. As long as I get my work done, he lets me manage my time working from home however I see fit, whether it's two in the morning or two in the afternoon.

"That's okay, sir. You caught me at a good time. How can I help you?"

"Well, I just got out of a very long meeting with the executives down at corporate, and we had a conversation I think is going to interest you."

"Okay," I say, nerves making my gut tighten. Is this about the promotion? Have they decided not to give it to me?

"I know you're expecting the lead data position here in Serendipity Springs."

"I wouldn't say expecting," I say, rolling back some of my earlier confidence. "Hoping, but I know I'm not the only one qualified—"

"You're the best man for the job, Peter," he says, his tone perfunctory. "Everyone knows that. Unfortunately—or fortunately, depending on how you look at it—corporate is also impressed with your work, and they've got another job offer they'd like you to consider."

"A job?" I ask. "At corporate?"

"If I were selfish, I'd discourage you from taking it," he says, "because I hate to lose you. But they need a new chief data scientist, and they want you. It's one heck of a promotion, kid. You'll be making what I make. Executive salary, full benefits, retirement, all of it."

I drop onto the nearest chair, heart pounding.

Chief Data Scientist for IronKey Cybersecurity.

It really *is* a promotion. One I wouldn't expect to get for at least another ten years.

"Why not you, sir?" I ask. "You know so much more than I do."

"Nah," Dr. Conway says. "I don't, and we both know it. I might have more experience, but you've got the brain power. Besides, they offered me the job already. My wife would leave me if I tried to move her out of Serendipity Springs, and my kids would help. But you're young. And Charlotte's a great city."

Charlotte.

North Carolina, but right on the border with South Carolina. I'd probably be within just a few hours of the rest of my family.

"I don't know what to say," I say. "Moving...that's..." My words trail off because what can I really say? I don't particularly want to move. I like where I live. Where I work. I like being close to Sophie.

But I don't know how to say no to an opportunity like this.

"Just think about it," Dr. Conway says. "No reason to make a decision right now. HR will email over the official offer so you can take a look at the salary and benefits package. You've got a couple of weeks to think it over, but I expect they'll want a firm yes or no by the end of the month."

"Right. That makes sense. I'll look for the email."

"Good. Enjoy the rest of your weekend."

"Wait, Dr. Conway. One more question."

"Sure."

"If I don't take it, will there still be the possibility of the lead scientist position here?"

"Absolutely. And I'd love to have you. But it might mean

you miss out on future opportunities. Corporate likes people who want to play the game."

"Understandable," I say. "I appreciate your honesty."

"Congratulations, Peter. This is a big deal."

He hangs up, and I drop my phone into my lap, letting the silence of the peaceful library wash over me.

I have no idea what to make of the job offer. I wasn't expecting it. And if my family were staying in Massachusetts, I probably wouldn't even consider it.

But now, maybe I should.

Leaving Sophie, though. Even just the thought is absolutely gutting.

Then again, if Sophie winds up finding someone through her dating experiment, moving might be exactly what I need. A fresh start just like Allison is getting. Somewhere I won't have to be confronted with a daily reminder that Sophie didn't choose me.

I pocket my phone and leave the library, walking the short distance down the hall to Sophie's apartment. I open the door and find her standing in her kitchen, phone in hand.

She looks up, her expression wide-eyed like I startled her, and tucks her phone behind her back. "Hi," she says.

"Hey. Are you okay?"

"Yeah. I'm good. Great."

"Why do you seem like you're hiding something?"

She pulls her phone out from behind her back and looks at it, like she's angry it incriminated her. "Oh. I, um..." She swallows and tugs her bottom lip into her teeth. "It's nothing. I was just...scheduling another date." She says this with a measure of caution she wouldn't have used yesterday or the day before.

She's only using it now because of what happened at my house.

Because she's letting me down gently.

A million emotions pass through me at once, but I have handled this kind of rejection before, and I will handle it again. "That's great," I manage to say. "Maybe this will be the one that finally works out."

Chapter Thirteen
Sophie

"Okay, so I'm dropping you off, then going to the nursery to pick up your plant order, then coming back to your Mom's to rescue you?" Peter says from the driver's seat of his SUV.

I buckle my seatbelt. "Is that okay? I might not need an escape route, but I'd like to have one just in case. I have no idea how Mom is going to handle hearing about this thing with Dad. If she just wants to rant all afternoon, I'd rather not stick around for it."

"I'm here for you however you need me," Peter says. "And the plant order will be ready to go?"

"Yes! I already talked to Miranda. She's expecting you."

Peter lifts an eyebrow. "Miranda, huh?"

"What?" I say, as innocently as possible. "She works there."

"Right," Peter says as he backs out of his parking space. "Doesn't the nursery usually deliver your orders?"

I clear my throat. "But it's so close to my mom's house. Seems silly to make a box truck drive all the way to The Serendipity when we'll be less than a mile away and you have all this perfectly good space in the back of your SUV."

I'm pretty sure Peter sees right through me, but I'm desperate. After what happened at his parents' house, I need him to start dating someone, and Miranda is perfect. She's funny and pretty and likable and we're just going to ignore the fact that every time I think about her with Peter, I want to punch someone.

It's fine. A phase. Whatever this weird feeling is, it'll pass, and then everything will go back to normal.

"Does your mom know you're coming?" Peter asks.

"Yeah, I texted her. But she doesn't know why. She thinks I'm just dropping in to catch up after the cruise."

Dropping in on my mom is not my usual style. It's not that we have a bad relationship. I just tend to need a little bit of preparation before we hang out...*and* then also a little time to recover after. I love my mom. But I don't always understand her, and that leaves me feeling unsettled, unmoored somehow whenever we've been together. It's gotten easier as I've gotten older, but mostly because I've gotten better at protecting myself. I retreat when I need to retreat. And I lean on Peter when I need someone to ground me again.

Peter pulls into my mother's driveway but leaves the engine running. "All right," he says. "I'll come straight back here, so I won't be long."

I nod. "Okay, but don't hurry. If you happen to start up any interesting conversations you don't want to end, I won't mind."

"Not subtle, Soph," Peter says dryly.

I smirk. "Who says I was trying to be subtle?"

Fake it till you make it, I think as I climb out of Peter's SUV. I wave as he pulls away, then make my way onto Mom's front porch.

She opens her front door wearing a gauzy white dress that looks more like a swimsuit coverup, sunglasses, and bedazzled flip-flops. As is typical, her hair falls in loose waves over her shoulders, and her makeup is perfect.

She looks exactly like how someone who has been cruising around the globe for the past three months should look: sunkissed and relaxed and perfectly happy.

I look down at my own cutoffs and oversized v-neck t-shirt. Ninety-nine percent of the time, I'm pretty comfortable with my crazy curly hair and freckled skin, with my mostly casual wardrobe and understated vibe. But sometimes I look at my mom and wonder how I ever came *from her*.

No one has ever made being beautiful look so effortless.

"Oh, my gosh! It's so good to see you!" Mom says, pulling me into a hug. She smells like coconuts and sunscreen and Chanel N°5. She leans back, giving my shoulders a quick squeeze. "I'm so glad you came. Come sit by the pool. I made mimosas, and I can't wait to tell you all about my trip."

"Did you just say *pool?*" I ask. Because last I checked, my mom did not have a pool in her backyard.

"Yes! Did I forget to mention it? It was installed while I was on the cruise." She sashays through her kitchen, stopping at the double French doors that used to lead to a fairly boring backyard. Grass. A few trees. A concrete patio. I did more than one design for her while I was in school, but mom never seemed all that concerned about improving the space. Maybe I should have included a pool.

"Aren't pools expensive?" I ask. By nature, my mother has always been a little more "live in the moment" than "save for a rainy day," but after Charles cleaned her out, she's been much more frugal, so splurging on a pool feels way out of character, even for her.

"A hundred and twenty grand for this one," she says, "because of the water feature and the fire bowls."

I step up beside her and look through the glass patio door. The backyard is completely different. And it's *stunning*.

Concrete decking, a gorgeous pool with a fountain situated at the far end, flanked by stone pillars holding bronze fire bowls. The landscaping lining the edge of the pool space is intentional and tasteful, as pretty as anything I would have designed myself.

"Mom, it's incredible," I say. "I can't believe I didn't know this was happening."

"It was all rather sudden," she says. "Pierre got a whim and thought it would be fun if the entire project happened while we were on our cruise." She slides open the door, flashing me a dazzling smile. "Come see. It's so much more gorgeous than I thought it would be."

"Wait," I say as I follow behind her. "*Pierre* got a whim? Mom, did he pay for this pool?"

"I mean, technically yes, but I'll have to cover the upkeep and cleaning."

She pours a mimosa into a tall champagne flute and hands it over.

"How generous of him," I say, taking the glass. I look over my shoulder. "But didn't you break up? What happened to Jean-Luc?"

She waves a dismissive hand. "Jean-Luc was just a cruise fling. But Pierre and I did break up."

I take a sip of my mimosa, not fully believing what I'm hearing. "So, he paid for your pool, and then you *broke up*? Do you have to pay him back?"

"Honey, this pool was pocket change for him. He's probably already forgotten about it." She settles onto a lounge chair with her own mimosa and pulls her sunglasses down, tilting her face toward the warm, spring sunshine. "If the leggy brunette he met on the boat is any indication, he's not thinking about me at all."

I lower myself onto the deck chair beside hers. I hate to admit it, but with the sound of the water feature splashing into the pool, the warm spring breeze, the birds chirping overhead, it really does feel pretty magical out here.

Mom spends the next ten minutes giving me a rundown of her favorite moments from her trans-Pacific cruise. Tokyo, Bali, Singapore. She mentions Pierre multiple times, and every time, she speaks of him with affection and humor.

I don't know how she does it. How she transfers her affection so easily. How she isn't seething over the breakup. Maybe coming home to a brand-new backyard pool eased the sting a little?

"Can I ask you a question?" I say when Mom's travelogue finally comes to an end.

She turns her head and smiles at me. "You can ask me anything."

"Do you actually fall in love with all the men you date?"

"Of course I do," she says easily, like it's hardly a question worth asking.

"Really? All of them?"

"Sure," she says. "Why would I date them if I didn't?"

"But you don't seem all that heartbroken over Pierre," I say, still struggling to understand. "And you were with Jean-Luc, what, five minutes after you broke up? How could it have been real love if you aren't sad about the relationship ending?"

She's quiet for a long moment, eyes toward the sky. I start to wonder if she's going to answer at all, but then she takes a deep breath and lifts her sunglasses from her face, pushing them up into her long auburn hair. "Look. I know some relationships last decades. Lifetimes. I saw clients married for twenty, thirty, forty years work through hardships and come out the other side even stronger. I know it's possible. But that's not how I'm built, Sophie. I did love Pierre. I loved our time together. I loved how much he made me laugh, how sweet he is with his grandkids. But it was time to move on. I knew it. He knew it. I loved him while it lasted, and I'll love the next one, too."

Mom pulls her glasses down and looks back up at the sun with an air of finality, like she has nothing more to say on the subject. But I'm not ready to leave it alone. She's a *therapist*. She made a career out of helping people stay connected and weather life's storms. It feels counterintuitive that she's the one who keeps moving from man to man.

"But what if there *is* a man out there who you're supposed to love forever?" I ask. "What if there's someone so much better than all the other men you've been with?"

Mom lifts her glasses one more time and smirks. "If there is, I doubt he could afford this pool."

I drop back onto my chair and drape an arm over my eyes to shield them from the sun. I didn't wear sunglasses today, *or* bring a swimsuit, two things I might have done differently had I known Mom's backyard had morphed into a tropical oasis.

I don't want to think my mom is a liar. But if she really *did* love Pierre and Jean-Luc and Frank and Tom and Leonardo and all the others, I don't think it's the same kind of love the Hathaways have—the kind that makes my flower bloom.

I have to believe it isn't. I have to believe that what I'm searching for is bigger than anything that fades or passes so quickly.

I'm also not naive enough to miss the layers hiding behind my mother's casual assertions. I see the way she's protecting herself from the heartache that scorned her not once, but twice.

"I just think it looks like you're scared, Mom," I say. "Like you're hiding behind all these shallow relationships because you don't want to get your heart broken again."

Mom scoffs. "Well that's quite a judgment coming from you."

"What's that supposed to mean?" I ask.

She gives me a pointed look. "I don't see *you* settling down."

I huff out a breath and reach for my mimosa, draining it in two long swallows. "Are you serious?" I say. "I'm only twenty-five. This is not the same thing."

"Are you sure?" she shoots back. "I know a little more about relationships than you do, Sophie, and from where I'm standing, you're the one hiding here. Not me."

It's not often that Mom uses her therapist voice on me, but that was it, and her words hit me harder than I expect.

She thinks *I'm* hiding? From what? And what does she know about my dating life? I'm actively trying to find someone, to settle down. She doesn't know what she's talking about.

"I heard from Dad," I say, my words pointed and sharp. "That's why I'm here."

Mom tilts her head toward me. She's still on her lounge chair, but her body language has completely shifted. "What?"

"I need to pick up the box of journals he gave me when I was in middle school."

"His mother's journals?" Mom asks. "But he gave those to you."

"He did. But now Callie is working on a family history project at school, and he thinks she'd like to read them."

Mom scoffs. "*Callie*, huh? Is she his oldest?"

"Yeah," I say. "She's a freshman this year. Almost fifteen."

"Wow," Mom says, almost more to herself than to me. "Time goes by fast." She sits up a little taller. "You know, those are *your* journals, Sophie. Your father can't just pry a gift out of one daughter's hands and give it to another. You can say no," she says.

I fight to contain my sigh. I *did* say I wanted to needle her, but I clearly forgot how much her anger drains me. "It's not a big deal, Mom. I haven't looked at those journals in years."

She purses her lips, her frustration clear on her face. "Well. Still," she huffs. "I think it's rude that he just expects—"

"Knock, knock," Peter says from behind me, and I sit up, spinning to face him, relief washing over me like a cool breeze. "Hey! You're here."

"Sorry for just letting myself in," he says. "No one answered when I knocked, so I took a gamble and found the door unlocked."

"I'm so glad you did," Mom says, standing from her chair and moving toward Peter. Whatever anger she had simmering beneath the surface moments ago is completely gone now, but that doesn't surprise me.

Mom will never pass up an opportunity to be beautiful and charming.

"Hi, Peter," she says, pulling him into a hug. "How are you?"

"Good, Mrs. Stewart. It's nice to see you." He looks around the backyard. "You have a pool now."

"Isn't it gorgeous?" she says. "Want to swim? I still have a ton of Pierre's clothes. I'm sure there's some trunks you could borrow."

Peter's eyes dart to mine, and I do my best to communicate how much I *don't* want that to happen. "Oh, um, that's okay," he says. "I think...Sophie and I actually have somewhere to be."

I give him a quick thumbs up before my mother turns around to face me. "But you just got here."

"I know. I'm sorry. It's just a...thing. It's been scheduled a while," I say. "But I'll come back soon when I have more time." I stand and move toward the patio doors. "I'm just going to go upstairs to find the journals."

"I'll come too," Peter says, but my mother intercepts him.

"You'll do no such thing," she says. "You sit here and chat with me a while. Sophie can manage one small box on her own."

Peter shoots me another look.

"I'll be fast," I say, and he nods.

The journals are exactly where I expect them to be. I open the box and pull the top one out, flipping through the first few pages. I read them all when I was younger, anxious to feel some connection to the paternal grandmother I would never know. She was a gardener, like me, and wrote a lot about her heirloom tomatoes and her prize-winning pumpkins. It didn't mean a lot to me then, but I feel a sudden desire to read them again now. Maybe I will before I give them back to Dad.

Peter stands the minute I appear in the kitchen and lets himself in through the back door. "Ready to go?" he says, and I suddenly wonder what Mom said to make him so jumpy.

"Yeah," I say. "You okay?"

"Good," he says. "All good."

I say goodbye to my mom, promising to text her so we can make plans to have lunch, then follow Peter out to his car.

"You sure everything is okay?" I say after I've dropped the box into the back seat and climbed in. "What did my mother say to you?"

He clears his throat. "Nothing. I'm fine."

"Peter," I say. "You clearly aren't."

His eyes dart to mine. "I am. It was just a lot of stuff about you and...me. How she wishes *we* would just date."

"Oh. Well that's—" My words cut off even as heat climbs my face. "Well that's just silly."

"Did you tell her I have a date tonight?" I say, though the tone of my voice is all wrong. It sounds artificial, even a little squeaky, like I'm trying really hard.

Peter's jaw tenses. "I didn't mention it," he says without taking his eyes off the road. "But I guess I should have."

Most of the time, when Mom asks about my dating life, she makes a joke about Peter being my backup plan, then volunteers to set me up with the son or the nephew or the distant second cousin of her latest conquest. It's odd to know she was this pointed with Peter, if only because it's a shift from the norm.

But then her earlier accusation pops into the front of my mind. *You're the one hiding here. Not me.*

Hiding from what?

From a serious relationship? And then she turns around and tells Peter she thinks we should date.

There is truth buried somewhere in my fragmented thoughts. Some kernel of wisdom that I sense lurking, hiding just beyond reach, but I can't grasp it. I can't see it clearly.

But as I think about my dad living his life with his family, helping his daughter with her family history project or my mom, lounging by her pool or cruising the world with beautiful men, I do start to wonder.

What if the person most damaged by my parents' divorce was *me*?

Chapter Fourteen
Peter

I'M REELING HERE. It's been a solid week since I learned about the job in Charlotte, and I'm no closer to knowing what to do. I haven't even told anyone about the offer. Not Sophie. Not Allison. Not my parents.

Professionally, it would be an incredible move. *Mostly* an incredible move. I have concerns about how I would fit in a corporate culture. I like wearing a suit every once in a while, but it's hard to imagine doing it every day. And I have so much freedom working in Serendipity Springs. Dr. Conway is an excellent boss, and while I don't make as much money as I could, I make enough.

I'm not sure what I'd gain would compensate for what I'd be giving up.

On a personal level, part of me wants to take it just to get away from Sophie. To make it a little easier to box up my feelings like I did last time. It got easier when we were in college. The distance helped.

But another part can't stop thinking about my sister's assertion last weekend that I'm not being fair to Sophie if I don't tell her how I feel. Even Sophie's mom thinks we're meant to be together.

Even if that's true, *how* do I broach the subject when Sophie seems so excited about dating other people?

My thoughts are not less jumbled when I find Sophie's date standing on the stoop outside The Serendipity's front door at seven p.m. on the nose, and for the first time, I'm faced with a guy who looks like he actually *could* be Sophie's soulmate.

"Jake?" I say, as I hold open the front door.

"Yes?" he says, his confusion reasonable since he's expecting Sophie, and I'm not half as beautiful as she is.

Jake, though. He *is* beautiful. Stupidly so. He's an inch or two taller than I am with broad shoulders and really good hair. Thick and full. His teeth are straight, his eyes are bright blue. He looks like he belongs in a car commercial. Or in a print ad selling cologne.

I immediately hate the guy.

Which is stupid and wrong, and I do my best to swallow the emotion. Because it isn't hatred. It's jealousy. And I'm enough of a man to admit it, even just to myself.

"Hey, Sophie sent me down to let you in. She's up on the rooftop watering her garden, but you're welcome to wait for her up there."

"Oh, awesome," Jake says. "Sounds good." He walks toward me, and I lean back, holding the door open so he can cross in front of me into the building.

"Cool place," he says. "Are you and Sophie neighbors?"

"And friends," I say. "We went to high school together."

"Oh, cool. Locally?" Jake asks. "Sophie and I haven't talked about where she's from."

"Yeah. Sweethaven High." I motion toward the stairs. "You want the stairs? Or a really old elevator? It's four flights."

"Stairs are cool," Jake says. "I skipped my workout today. It'll be good for me."

I try my best to take the stairs at a reasonable pace, but it's possible I take them a little faster than usual, and by the time we reach the top of the third floor, Jake's huffing, his breath coming in short bursts.

I am only slightly ashamed of how happy this makes me. I rarely have the opportunity to be that guy. I can never bench the most or run the fastest. But I swam distance in high school—still swim at the gym when I have the chance—and I'm built for endurance. I can climb stairs all day.

"What about you?" I say to Jake. "Are you from around here?"

"Nah, from Charlotte, actually," Jake says. "I'm just here for my residency."

My ears perk up when he mentions Charlotte. Would it be weird if I asked him how he liked the city? "Residency?" I ask instead. "You're a doctor?"

He takes a deep breath as we finally reach the top of the fourth floor. "Yeah. A pediatrician over at Springs Memorial." He looks over his shoulder and glances down the stairs. "Man, apparently I need to work on my cardio."

I fight a groan. The guy isn't just a pediatrician. He's a self-deprecating one who is making it harder and harder for me to hate him.

"Just one more flight," I say as I lead him down the hall and to the back stairwell that accesses the roof. I wait just inside the door just like always, but Sophie won't need me this time. Not with this guy. Her *ick* detector might be broken, but mine isn't, and Jake seems like the real deal.

Still. What are the odds any one of the men Sophie brings up here will actually trigger a bloom? I lean against the brick wall behind me and think about the data I'd need to figure it out. The numbers will change depending on a few different factors. Age limitations, proximity, relationship status. But the biggest factor is something unknown, and that's a major hindrance to me finding an actual statistic.

Does the flower bloom for one single soulmate?

Or could there be multiple possibilities?

Does it guarantee a happy ending? Or does it just promise the potential for one?

I'm still thinking through the different variables, forming potential equations, when the door squeaks and Sophie and Jake appear.

My heart starts pounding as I take in her expression. She looks happy, comfortable, but she doesn't look as starry-eyed as I would expect had the flower officially bloomed for her and Jake. But they're leaving together, so...does that mean it did?

Maybe she's just walking him out?

Jake eyes me as he passes by, but I'm not going to apologize for still being here, no matter how genuine he seemed when we first met. Sophie is my best friend, and he's a stranger. I won't take chances.

I make eye contact with Sophie, and she offers me a hesitant smile.

"You okay?" I ask, and she quickly nods.

"Yep. Just headed to dinner." She starts down the stairs, hand gripping the railing, but I call her back.

"Sophie."

She turns and looks over her shoulder. "We'll talk later, okay?"

Then she's gone.

I breathe through my nose, slow and steady, and count to ten. When the fourth-floor access door opens, then clicks closed, I count to ten *again*. They're either taking the grand staircase or the elevator down to the first floor. Either way, I want them well and truly gone before I leave the stairwell.

So that's it, then. She's met her soulmate. That's all it took.

Of course, I knew it was a possibility, but I didn't think it would happen before I took my shot, told Sophie how I feel.

I finally make my way down the stairs, twitchy and agitated, and push through the fourth-floor access door. Without really thinking about what I'm doing, I charge down the hallway to Archer's penthouse apartment. It's not a true penthouse because it doesn't take up the entire fourth floor. But it does fill the entire front of the building, which means you could fit my place inside his place many times over.

I knock on the door, trusting that this late in the day, Willa will probably be there.

Luckily, it's Willa who opens the door.

"Hey, Peter," she says. "What's up?"

I push into the apartment without waiting for an invitation.

"Sure. Come on in," she says dryly.

I spin around in Archer's entryway. "Sorry. I'm sorry."

"It's okay. What's going on?"

"Sophie is out on a date."

"Oh, right. Jake? The pediatrician?"

I nod, hands propped on my hips. Jaw clenched.

"Is everything okay? He seemed nice. At least from all the DMs she let me read."

"He was very nice. That's the problem."

She frowns. "I still don't understand."

"They went to dinner," I say more pointedly. "She was only supposed to go to dinner if the flower bloomed, Willa. And they went."

Her eyes widen. "Oh. Oh! Oh, my gosh. That's great news."

I shake my head, letting out a disheartened laugh.

"Or it's...not great news?" Willa asks. "Peter, what are you not saying right now? Why is this a bad thing?"

I have no idea why I'm here. What I'm even supposed to say. I knew this was a possibility. I can't be upset about it now. But I just thought I had more time to figure out what to say and how to say it.

When I finally look up to meet Willa's eye, her expression is full of compassion and understanding.

"You're in love with her," she says gently.

When I don't object, she lets out a sigh to match mine.

"Oh, Peter."

Before I can respond, Archer appears in the entryway and wordlessly hands me a heavy crystal glass, then turns and heads into the living room.

"That was an invitation to stay," Willa whispers.

I lift the glass to my nose. "Bourbon?"

She nods. "Worth more than your rent, probably." She gestures for me to follow her into the living room. "Come on. Sit. Drink. Tell me everything."

Chapter Fifteen
Sophie

HONESTLY. Jake is so much prettier in person than he is in his photo.

Tall and broad—and *that smile*. He could stop traffic with that smile. He's wearing jeans and a nice button down over a white henley, the buttons at the top revealing a nice triangle of tan skin. I bet the nurses *love it* when Dr. Jake is on rotation.

Which is why I should have been disappointed when the flower didn't bloom.

I tried. *Really* tried. Gave him a complete tour of the garden, visited every planter and spent five solid minutes standing next to the Japanese maple, my mystery flower climbing the trunk, just to make sure it knew we were there.

But it didn't so much as tremble in the breeze.

Not when Jake complimented my garden or told me a story about one of his patients or showed me a picture of his puppy. I even tried touching him, thinking that might trigger something, but nothing happened.

Except the realization that touching Jake wasn't even a little bit thrilling. No spark. No thrill. No flutters. I knew right then that the flower was right, and Jake is not the man for me.

Telling him wasn't fun.

He seemed too nice to lie, so I went for the truth and just told him I tend to trust my gut and first impressions are huge, and I didn't think we had any chemistry.

I could tell he was surprised, but then he surprised *me*.

"Okay. What about this?" he said. "Just have dinner with me. My treat. If you still feel the same way after we eat, I won't ask any questions." He shrugged his shoulders. "I mean, a woman has to eat, right? Worst case, we get a nice meal out of the deal, and we've each made a new friend."

I *did* need to eat. And since I'm desperately in need of groceries, I would have had to order takeout had I just gone home. Or mooched off of Peter, which a girl can only do that so many times.

So here we are.

At dinner.

Talking and joking with a very easy vibe between us, and I feel like I really *have* made a new friend. This guy is amazing. A gentleman in every way. I want to start having kids just so he can be their doctor.

But I really *don't* feel that spark—something I feel empowered to acknowledge now that I have a little bit of magic to back me up.

"So, plants—that's your job, right? Landscape architecture?" Jake asks as he spoons up a bite of his dessert.

"A little," I say. "I'm more on the computer design side of landscape architecture. I *talk* about plants at work a lot, but I don't usually see them go in the ground. I guess that's why I love having the rooftop garden. It's like therapy."

"I love that," Jake says. "You turned it into a beautiful space."

"Thanks."

"And your friend, Peter?" he says next, and I lift my eyes to his. "He's *just* a friend?"

I smile and huff out a little laugh. "I know it seems weird that he hovered in the stairwell, but you were a stranger. He just wanted to make sure I was safe."

"No, I liked that about him," Jake says. "I would have done the same thing. It was more just the way he looked at you."

I wrinkle my eyebrows. "How did he look at me?"

Jake's expression turns wry. "Come on, Sophie. You know what I mean."

I sigh because how many people are going to try to convince me that Peter likes me? "It's definitely not like that," I say, like it's a reflex. It *is* a reflex because I've been saying it for years. "We've just known each other for a long time. Since high school."

"Yeah, he told me," Jake says. "And I get it. I had a best friend like that, too."

"Had?" I ask, and Jake winces.

"Uh, yeah. We finally got together after our freshman year of college, and it didn't work out."

I frown. "And now you're not friends?"

He shrugs. "We tried to be. And we're still nice when we see each other. But it's hard to go back, you know?"

"This is what I keep telling people," I say, emphatic enough that Jake jolts a little at my sudden response. "Sorry," I say, dialing it back just a bit. "It's just that so many people keep telling me we're perfect for each other and we should date already, but I don't want to screw up our friendship. Why is that so hard for people to understand?"

"I get it," Jake says. "We got a lot of the same pressure." He shrugs easily. "Sometimes it works out though. It would suck to miss out on something amazing just because you want to protect something slightly *less* amazing."

I shove a huge bite of crème brûlée into my mouth. "How do I know though? How do I know a relationship would be more amazing?"

"Come on," he says. "How could it not be? If you have good physical chemistry, and you're both committed, why wouldn't a relationship be better? It's just friendship with more perks, right?"

When the night is finally over, Jake walks me back to The Serendipity, pausing once we reach the front door.

"I'd ask you if I changed your mind about another date, but I think I already know the answer to that question."

I grimace. "You're amazing, Jake. Truly. But..."

"I get it," he says as he pushes his hands into his pockets. "But for the record, I think you should go for it with Peter."

"For real?" I say. "You too? Even after you lost a friendship in the same kind of scenario?"

He lifts his hands and chuckles. "You do you," he says. "But I feel like it's worth noting that I mostly lost my friendship with Sarah because she got married, and it was no longer cool for us to hang out all the time. That might be something else for you to think about. If you like hanging out with Peter, you might have to marry him to keep things the way they are."

My mouth drops. "I can't believe we're having this conversation right now. Can no one leave my friendship in peace?"

"Okay, okay. I won't say another word," Jake says. He pulls me into a friendly hug. "I'm glad I got to meet you, Sophie."

As he walks down the sidewalk, it occurs to me that Jake would be perfect for Allison. If only she wasn't moving in a couple of weeks.

Peter is sitting at my kitchen table when I enter my apartment.

In the dark.

Doing nothing.

"Peter?" I ask as I turn on the light. "Are you okay?"

He looks up, a blank expression on his face. "Hey. You're back," he says. His words are a little slow, a little soft around the edges.

"Yeah, I am. Have you been drinking?"

He holds up his thumb and forefinger an inch apart. "Tiny bit." He swallows, and I watch his Adam's apple bob up and down.

I drop into the chair across from him. I've actually never seen Peter drunk or even tipsy, so this version of him is a little foreign. "Were you drinking alone?"

He shakes his head. "With Archer. That man has good bourbon."

I huff out a tiny laugh. "Yeah. I bet. Have you eaten?" I slide my leftovers across the table. "I have some pasta."

He reaches for the container and lifts the lid. "What kind?"

"You'll like it. Chicken, sundried tomatoes, lots of parmesan." I stand and grab him a fork, then fill a glass of water and set it down next to the open to-go container. "Why were you drinking with Archer?"

Peter shrugs as he digs into my leftovers. "No reason. Just that he offered." He chews slowly, keeping his eyes down as he asks, "So, do you want to tell me about it? About meeting him?"

I furrow my brow. "About meeting Jake? I guess I *can*. What do you want to know?"

He looks at me like I'm missing something important.

"You don't *want* to tell me about it? If this guy is your soulmate, I figured you'd be eager to fill me in on all the details."

Understanding finally dawns.

Of course Peter thinks Jake is my soulmate. Because I *went* to dinner. And that was only supposed to happen if the flower bloomed.

"Peter, Jake's not my soulmate," I say quickly. "The flower didn't bloom."

He pauses, hand frozen over the pasta for a few seconds before he puts his fork down with slow, deliberate movements.

"Then why did you go to dinner?"

"Because Jake was nice, and he asked me to. When I saw that the flower wasn't going to bloom, I told him I didn't think we had any chemistry, but he asked if he could buy me dinner anyway."

Peter blows out a breath. "Wow. Nice guy." There's a lightness to his tone that wasn't there before, and I get the distinct impression that he's relieved.

I let out a little laugh. "Honestly, he's the nicest. Had I not flower-checked him, I definitely would have agreed to go out with him again. He's basically perfect."

"So why don't you?" Peter asks. "What if the flower is wrong?"

I lift my shoulders. "It wasn't wrong. We had good energy, but it was total friend energy. I meant what I said about not feeling much chemistry."

Peter takes another huge bite of pasta, and I wait for him to finish chewing before asking, "Why were you relieved to know the flower didn't bloom?"

"I wasn't relieved."

"Yes, you were, Peter. I know you too well."

He breathes out a sigh. "Just because..." His words trail off, and his jaw clenches. "I guess because I know things will change once it does."

"No, they won't," I say. "Of course they won't." But I just

had this conversation with Jake, and he warned me of the same thing.

"I'm not saying we won't still be friends," Peter says. "But things will be different. They'll have to be. You can't sit on the couch and snuggle with *me,* then go home to your boyfriend and snuggle with *him.*"

He's right.

I know he's right.

I just don't know what to do about it.

"Do you want brownies?" I suddenly ask.

When in doubt, eat chocolate. One of life's many mottos.

"Oh! And some caramel sauce!" I add. "I have vanilla ice cream in the freezer. We could have brownie sundaes while we watch a little more *Ted Lasso?*"

I already had crème brûlée at the restaurant, and I don't need a second dessert. But I do need to feed my denial. And what better way to do that than brownies?

Chapter Sixteen
Peter

IF I THOUGHT I was having a hard time falling asleep before, the night after Sophie's date with Jake is something else entirely.

After confessing nearly a decade of feelings for Sophie to Willa and Archer—and drinking Archer's very expensive bourbon—I came back to Sophie's to sulk on my own, sure that her Jake the pediatrician with the wavy hair and perfect smile was her soulmate.

I'm relieved now that I know it's not true, but I can't keep doing this to myself over and over.

I was completely useless tonight. I had work I needed to do, but I just sat around. Sat and thought and felt sorry for myself because the woman I love is actively trying to love someone else—*anyone* else. And I'm supposed to be her trusty sidekick in making it happen.

I punch my pillow and roll over so I'm facing the back of Sophie's couch. It really *is* a comfortable couch. I should be sleeping like a baby. But my thoughts are my biggest enemy, and I cannot figure out how to turn them off.

I could just be honest with her. I *should* just be honest with her.

I shift again, rolling onto my back and stare into the darkness. Maybe if I intentionally try to keep my eyes open, a little self-imposed reverse psychology, I'll start to feel tired.

I'm almost convinced it's working, but then a crash sounds outside, and I sit up, heart pounding as I lean toward the window, straining my ears to hear whatever is on the other side of the glass.

"Peter!" Sophie whisper yells from her room. "Did you hear that?"

I stand and slowly creep through the kitchen and down the hall to Sophie's bedroom.

"Hey," I say from the doorway. "You okay?"

Even with the nightlight in the corner of Sophie's room, the room is too heavily shadowed for me to make out her face. I can only see the shape of her sitting up in the center of her bed.

"I'm okay," she says, her voice shaky, "but I think I heard something scratching at the glass."

I move across her room, stopping in front of her window. Sophie has curtains instead of blinds, and they're currently drawn, so I slowly pull one to the side to peek into the alley on the other side of the glass.

"Don't!" Sophie says, startling me enough that I drop the curtain, and it falls back into place. "They'll see you!"

"Who's *they*?" I whisper back.

"Whoever is trying to get in my window."

"It's probably just the possums Archer dealt with," I say as I reach for the curtains a second time. But then I hear the noise again, and it definitely sounds more human than possum.

I lean toward the window. Footsteps, a grunt, a low

rumble of laughter. More footsteps. Then the sound of a window sliding up on its rickety frame.

Sophie lets out a gasp. "Was that in my apartment? Please tell me it isn't my apartment."

"All your windows are locked," I say, something I'm sure about because I checked them before I went to sleep. I even came in here and checked the ones in Sophie's room while she was in the shower.

"Are you sure?"

"Of course I'm sure," I say. "I checked them myself." I peek around the curtain one more time, but from this angle, I can't see anything but the empty alleyway.

"Stay here, okay?" I say to Sophie. "I'm going to check through the living room windows."

"Okay, but come straight back," Sophie says, her voice sounding smaller than I've ever heard it before.

The living room is darker than Sophie's bedroom, so it's actually easier to see more outside. Someone *is* there, but it's not anyone we need to be afraid of. I unlock Sophie's window and slide it up, the old wood sticking in multiple places.

"Hey! Reggie," I call once the window is open enough for me to lean through. "What are you doing out here, man?"

Reggie, a college-aged guy who lives directly next door to Sophie, turns and looks at me. "Peter? Is that you?"

"Yeah. It's me. You know it's one in the morning, right?"

"Dude, I'm so happy to see you," he says, like he didn't even hear my complaint about the late hour. "I'm locked out of the building, and I lost my key. I'm pretty sure I left my window open, but I couldn't figure out which one was mine." He points. "That one is Sophie's?"

I breathe out a sigh. "Yeah. Which means the one right in front of you is yours."

He leans toward the window and hoists it a little further up.

"Sweet," Reggie says. "Thanks, man. I owe you one." He's halfway through his window when he leans back out, one leg inside and one leg out, and says, "Should we have a conversation about what you're doing at Sophie's in the middle of the night? Shirtless?"

"We should not, Reggie," I say, and the younger man chuckles.

"Got it. Understood, man. I'll stop hitting on her so much."

I frown. Reggie has been hitting on Sophie?

"Goodnight, Reggie," I say as he disappears inside his apartment. I wait until I hear the sound of his window closing, then I shut Sophie's window and make sure it's locked.

I'm not sure how much of our conversation Sophie was able to hear, so I head back to her bedroom to tell her everything is okay.

"What was it?" she asks when I appear in her doorway.

"It was Reggie," I say. "Trying to break into his own apartment."

"Oh, my gosh. Stupid Reggie," she says. "I thought I was going to have a heart attack."

I move over to her bed. "It's okay. Everything's okay."

She holds her hands up in front of her. "I'm still shaking."

Sure enough, her hands are both trembling. I take them in mine, pressing her palms together and rubbing the backs of them. "Just breathe," I say. "You're safe."

She takes another deep breath, holding it for a few seconds before she blows it out. "Logically, I know that, but..." She hesitates and clears her throat. "Geez, I don't know why I got so worked up. That really scared me."

"Understandably," I say. "What do you need? What can I get you? Some water? Tea? Just name it."

"Nothing," she says. "But...can you just stay with me a minute? I don't really want to be alone right now."

"Sure," I say, not really thinking about the implications of what this means. Because of course I'll stay with her. I'll give her whatever she needs.

Sophie scoots over, making room for me on her bed, and I recline into her pillows. She throws the blankets back then tugs them up and over me before nestling herself into the crook of my shoulder, her arm draped over my midsection.

I drop my arm across her back, rubbing smooth circles up and down.

"Is this weird?" Sophie says, her voice soft. "I don't want this to be weird. I just...need an anchor right now."

"It's not weird," I say. And it's not a lie. Weird is not the word I would use for what this is right now.

Magical. Amazing. Incredible. Blissful.

Those all feel a lot more applicable than *weird*.

"I'm here," I say, trying to keep my tone gentle. "Maybe try to match your breathing with mine? It might help you relax."

We breathe silently for a few moments before Sophie says, "I think that's helping."

"Really? I was pretty much shooting in the dark."

She chuckles, and her grip around my waist tightens. "Shut up."

"Hey, does Reggie really hit on you all the time?"

"Daily," she says without hesitation. "But it's harmless. I think he's on a mission to find the most ridiculous pickup lines ever. It's turned into a joke between us now."

"Yeah, um, he might not do that anymore," I say.

"Really?" Sophie yawns, which has to be a good sign. That she's relaxed enough to feel sleepy.

"I mean, he saw me in your window, in your apartment, in the middle of the night."

She lifts her hand and pats it against my chest. "Shirtless."

"Exactly. He told me he'd stop the flirting."

I wait to see how she'll respond, if she'll protest against the idea of her neighbor thinking we're together.

But she doesn't respond at all. Instead, her breathing settles and falls into an easy, peaceful rhythm.

It's funny. As much as I was struggling to fall asleep before, with Sophie beside me, it's only a matter of minutes before I drift off as well.

Chapter Seventeen
Sophie

IT TAKES me a minute to figure out what, exactly, is going on when I wake up on Friday morning.

Because Peter is in my bed.

Sound asleep. One arm thrown over his head. Bare, muscular chest on full display.

What's more, I didn't just wake up *beside* Peter. I woke up practically *on him*. One arm draped over his chest. One leg hooked over his leg. Head pressed against his chest.

I slowly inch away, not wanting to wake him up, but needing to get away from how deliciously manly he smells long enough to gather my wits about me.

I did *ask* Peter to stay with me last night. After the whole Reggie thing happened, I'm pretty sure I would have had a panic attack had I *not* asked him to stay.

But now, in the clear morning light streaming in through the curtains, having Peter in my bed feels like a much bigger deal.

Also, *when* did he get those pectoral muscles?

I slowly lift the covers and glance down at my own wardrobe. Pajama pants. Enormous t-shirt. At least I have that much going for me. I've been known to lose the pajama pants and sleep in my underwear when I get too hot, so I guess I should be grateful it was a relatively cool night.

Once I make it to the edge of the bed, I shimmy off, landing on my feet with a grace and silence a cat would envy, then slowly tiptoe around the bottom of the bed and toward the bedroom door.

I look back at Peter, who is still sleeping soundly, his dark lashes fanned across his cheeks. A surge of affection for him pushes through my chest. But it isn't just *friend* affection. There's something else here. Something bigger.

I swallow against the sudden dryness in my throat.

I've been trying so hard to fight the idea. To resist. Because I have to resist. Because I really, *really* don't want to lose Peter.

I've been ignoring the signs. The little flutters of feeling. The new chemistry sparking between us. But I can't ignore them anymore. Not after last night. Not after lying in his arms and feeling every inch of my soul relax. I needed him last night, but I also craved his company in a way that was new and strange and exhilarating.

I like him.

Like like him.

My heart starts pounding.

What is happening to me?

And what am I supposed to do now?

Peter sleeps for another half-hour before he appears in the kitchen.

"Hey," he says, his voice scratchy from sleep.

I startle, my phone flying into the air before it crashes back onto the table. I grab it, checking the screen to make sure it's okay, then set it face down in front of me. "Hey. You're awake."

"You okay?" Peter asks, eyeing me with confusion.

"Yep. Just doing the crossword puzzle. You startled me."

He crosses through the kitchen and into the living room where he pulls a t-shirt out of a laundry basket he's currently using as a dresser. I gotta say, I'm sorry to see the view go.

"The Sunday puzzle?" he asks. "Any luck?"

I pick up my phone again and reopen the app. "I'm still working on Saturday," I say. "And I've made very little progress."

He drops into the chair across from me. "Want me to look?"

"Absolutely not," I say. "You'll know all the answers, and then I'll feel dumb."

He rolls his eyes. "You aren't dumb. Saturday is the hardest one. I can never do it without help."

"Right? Me neither. I'm solid on Mondays and Tuesdays, but after that, I can't do them without auto-check. Do you turn on auto-check?"

His lips twitch. "More like...I sometimes have to check one or two letters?"

"Peter!" I yell. "See? Now I do feel dumb."

He grins. "It just takes practice. We can work on it together if you want."

I slide my phone across to him. "Do you want coffee?"

"Yes, please," he says.

I make him a cup while he enters who knows how many answers into the puzzle. When I sit back down and put his mug in front of him, he slides the phone back, and the puzzle is close to a third done.

"Are you serious right now?"

He runs a hand across his face, and I notice the stubble dusting his cheeks. How have I never noticed how handsome he looks with stubble? How have I missed how deliciously sexy this man is first thing in the morning?

"I could be wrong," he says as he reaches for his coffee. "Just read them over and see what you think."

I try to read them over, but my focus is completely shot. With Peter sitting across from me, with his gravelly voice and his messy hair and his very sexy stubble, there's no way I'm answering any of these clues.

I need to have a conversation with Willa.

And possibly go for a very long walk. And then spend some time with my hands in the dirt so I can figure out what to do. I do my best thinking when I'm gardening.

Wait.

That's it.

The garden! I just need to get Peter onto the roof.

Every single time I've told Willa or Allison that dating Peter would be entirely too complicated, I've meant it. My relationship with Peter is one of the most important ones in my life. I don't want to lose him. I *can't* lose him. And if trying to love him meant losing him, I can't imagine it ever being worth it. Which is why I would never risk a relationship without some kind of guarantee.

But I *have* a guarantee. If the flower blooms for us, the risk is gone.

If it doesn't, then I'll know we aren't destined to be in love, and I've somehow gotten my feelings jumbled up. And we won't have to wreck anything trying to figure that out on our own.

"Hey, what are you doing today?" I ask. "Want to help me do some weeding up in the garden?"

Peter narrows his gaze at me, like he can't quite believe I asked, and I remember his allergies.

"So I can be miserable for the rest of the weekend?" he says. "I'm actually going to play racquetball with Archer today. Then he's taking me out for lunch. Don't worry, though. I'll absolutely be home in time to help with your date."

Ugh. My date. I forgot I had another one scheduled for tonight.

I have *several* scheduled for the upcoming week—probably because I've been working so hard to *not* like Peter. My dates have clearly become my defense mechanism.

The truth is, I've suddenly lost my enthusiasm for the whole project. Now, I just want to hogtie Peter and haul him upstairs to the garden so I can know one way or another and get on with my life.

But there is one happy part of what Peter just said, so at least for the moment, I shove my own problems aside and focus on the fact that I really, *really* love that Peter and Archer have become friends. And not just because of how much I love Willa. Even though Allison's worry is over the top, she isn't entirely off-base about Peter. He's always been a bit of a loner, outside of his friendship with me, and I get the same impression when it comes to Archer.

"I love that, Peter," I say. "That sounds so fun."

"Please don't turn this into a big deal," Peter says, like he can sense the glee simmering just under the surface of my words.

"But it *is* a big deal," I say. "You don't usually hang out with people who aren't me."

He runs a hand across his face, drawing my eyes back to the stubble lining his jaw. He really does look good with a little bit of scruff.

"Will you be okay weeding on your own?" he asks.

I wave a dismissive hand. "I'll be totally fine. It's no problem at all."

I yield the crossword to Peter and head into my room to get dressed for a little bit of gardening. I don't actually have a lot of weeding to do, but I did promise Mrs. Hathaway I'd repot a couple of her orchids that have outgrown their current homes, and the annuals I put in could use a little fertilizer.

I text Willa, hoping she'll be free if Archer is playing racquetball, and make plans to meet her on the roof as soon as the guys leave. When I finally come back out, Peter has changed into gym shorts and a t-shirt.

He turns to face me. "How do I look? Do I look like I could play racquetball with a billionaire?"

I press my lips together, fighting a smile. "You absolutely do," I say. "Have you ever actually played racquetball?"

"Not once. But I told Archer that, and he says it's an easy sport for beginners."

"I'm sure you'll do great," I say.

He frowns. "He's going to cream me, isn't he?"

I think of our very serious building owner. "Almost definitely," I say. "But I still bet you'll have fun."

As soon as he's out the door, I grab a book I've been meaning to loan Willa, swing by the Hathaways to pick up Jane's orchids, then head up to the roof.

Willa finds me a few minutes later standing at the potting bench pushed up against the backside of the stairwell wall.

"Can you get over this weather?" she says, tilting her face up. The sun is warm overhead, and the sky is a bright, vibrant blue.

"Amazing, right?" I say. "I love this time of year."

"Soooo," she says, turning and leaning against the table. "What's up? Anything big you need to tell me?"

I wrinkle my forehead as I look at her. She's asking like she already knows. But what does she think she knows? I grab the book from the side of the table. "Here," I say. "I just wanted to give you this. I finished it, and you're going to love it."

She flips through the book, then lifts it to her nose to

smell the pages. "Mm. Thank you for sharing. I'll read and report back."

I lift the first orchid out of its pot and shake off the loose moss. The roots are wrapped tightly around a plug of soil, and it's going to take some work to pry it free. "The first few chapters are a little slow," I say, "but if you hang on, it's totally worth it once you get to chapter five."

"Noted." She looks at the orchid. "So what are we doing here? Can I help?"

"We're giving Jane Hathaway's orchids a chance at life," I say. I break off a chunk of compacted soil and drop it onto the table.

"I gotta be honest, Soph," Willa says. "It looks like you're killing it."

"I promise I'm not," I say. "Orchids have air roots. They don't grow like regular plants, so the looser and less compacted their living conditions, the better." I free another chunk of the soil.

She picks up the second orchid. "Want me to do this one?"

"Sure. Just lift it out of the pot and pull away any dirt that's stuck to the roots." I point to the clod of dirt just like the one I'm currently trying to remove. "They sell them in potting soil so there's something to soak up and hold water while they're in stores and not getting proper care, but they'll be happier in a different substrate."

"You promise I'm not going to hurt it?"

"I promise. Just try not to damage the roots."

She nods and slowly starts working the soil loose. "So, when are you going to tell me about last night?"

I freeze. She knows about last night? Would Peter have told her? Maybe he told Archer on the way to racquetball, and Archer already texted Willa?

"It didn't mean anything," I say. "All we did was sleep. I

only asked him to stay because I had this weird experience when I was a teenager where I thought someone was breaking into my house, so when I heard Reggie, I just got really freaked—"

Willa holds up her hand. "Hold up," she says. "What are you talking about?"

I look at her, completely confused. What is *she* talking about, if not that? "About Peter sleeping in my bed last night."

Her eyes widen. "Wait, what?"

"What did you think I was talking about?"

"About Jake," she says, her voice getting higher and louder. "Peter said you guys went to get dinner last night, and he assumed that meant the flower bloomed."

That's right. Peter saw Willa last night. "He came to see you just to tell you that?"

"Of course he did! I was honestly surprised you didn't text to tell me."

"I didn't text because the flower didn't bloom," I say. "We *did* go out to dinner, but only because Jake said we could go as friends. I told him I didn't think we had any chemistry, which we really didn't, but he said he'd like to be friends. That's all that happened."

"So he's not your soulmate."

"Definitely not. Which is good because..." I hesitate, suddenly feeling nervous to admit this next part out loud.

"Because what?" Willa prompts.

"It's a bit of a plot twist, actually," I sheepishly say. "But I actually think I have a crush on Peter."

Willa freezes, her eyes going wide. "You what?"

I grimace. "Is that totally crazy? I know I've been all 'he's my best friend, blah, blah, blah,' but I don't know. This morning, I was looking at him while he was sleeping, and I just...I don't know. Something shifted."

"You looked at him while he was sleeping," she says.

"Should we pause and talk about how that makes you sound like a serial killer?"

"I promise it wasn't creepy," I say. "But he was in my bed, and he looked so peaceful, and he was so gentle and good to me last night, and—"

"Sophie," Willa says, cutting me off. "That's the second time you've mentioned him being in your bed. Please back up and give me some context here. Because so far, everything you're saying sounds creepy or naughty, and I need to know up front if we're dealing with either of those things."

I finally free the first orchid from all the soil compacted around its roots and grab my gardening shears to trim off the dead and damaged roots. I talk while I work, telling Willa about Peter comforting me last night when Reggie was scrounging around outside my window, then I back up even further, telling her about the handholding and the conversation when Peter told me I'm beautiful and all the other flutter-inducing things that have happened.

"Honestly, it's your fault," I say as I lower the orchid into a bucket of water so the roots can soak. "You're the one who suggested I try to look at him differently. Well, I did, and now I do, and I have no idea what to do about it."

"That feels pretty obvious, doesn't it?" Willa says. "You just go for it."

I roll my eyes. "I can't just *go for it*. I have no idea if he feels the same way. I also just started this whole big dating experiment," I say. "I have four more dates lined up this week."

"Why go on any of them?" Willa says. "Sophie, you and Peter are already so good together. Your relationship would barely change if you started dating. You know it would be great."

"It would absolutely change," I say. "Of course it would change."

"You would still have the same emotional connection," she says.

"True."

"And you'd still laugh and talk about all the same stuff."

"Also true," I concede.

"You'd just get to kiss while you're doing it."

My mind flashes back to this morning, when I woke up with my head resting on Peter's bare chest, and my face flushes hot. I lift my palms to my cheeks. "Oh my gosh," I say. "I can't think about kissing Peter."

Willa smirks. "Yeah, you can. You are right now." She reaches for my hands and tugs them down. "Also stop. You just got dirt all over your face."

I let my hands fall and take a deep, steadying breath. "So, I was thinking it would be really helpful if I could get Peter up on the roof with me," I say.

She furrows her brow, but then her expression shifts, like she's finally caught up with my reasoning. "Honey, why do you need the flower to bloom? This is Peter. You already know you love Peter."

"That's precisely why," I say. "You have to understand what's at stake here."

"Okay, tell me," she says propping her hands on her hips. There's a challenge to her tone that makes my defenses rise and fills me with unexpected emotion.

"He's all I have," I say, voice thick. "Every time my world falls apart, he's the one who makes me okay again. When my stepdad left, he was there. When I thought college wasn't going to happen, he did the research, helped me get my loans lined up. When my stupid prom date dumped me after graduation, it was Peter who made me laugh about it. Don't you see? If things don't work out with Peter, he won't be there to pick up the pieces of my life. He'll be gone, and I'll be on my own."

"He's your safety net," Willa says. "I get it. But you won't be on your own. You have me. And you're stronger than you think you are."

"Maybe. But I'm also a little more broken than I thought." I sniff and wipe at an unexpected tear with the back of my hand. "When I saw my mom last weekend, and then, when my dad came by to get his mom's journals, I realized something."

She steps closer and takes my hand in hers. "Okay. What was it?"

"All this time, I thought my relationships weren't working out because I'm a bad judge of character. Because I always pick the wrong guys. But I think it's really because I'm not very good at trusting people. I need the reassurance, Willa. And I don't think there's anything wrong with that."

She cocks her head to the side. "I'll be honest, Sophie. If you need the flower's reassurance, that sounds like the person you don't trust is yourself."

"Maybe I don't," I say. "But does it matter? I don't want to break his heart, Willa. And I don't want him to break mine either. The flower can make sure that won't happen."

She folds her arms across her chest. "Okay," she finally says, her tone soft. "I get it. I understand why you want the reassurance. But I really think you should just tell Peter how you feel. That man has shown you every single day how amazing it could be if you would let him love you. You already know everything the flower can tell you. You know he's good and kind and decent and worthy of your love."

"The flower will tell me he won't leave," I say, my tone sharp. "And I don't know that."

Willa's expression softens. "Sophie, yes you do. You know him."

I shake my head, but I don't look up, keeping my eyes on the second orchid. I lower it into another bucket of water and point across the table toward a bag of orchid bark sitting just past where Willa is standing.

"Can you hand me that bag, please?"

Willa wordlessly lifts it and slides it across the table.

"I'm going to tell him," I finally say. "I'm just going to get him on the roof first."

She sighs. "What about your other dates?"

"I'm not going to schedule any new ones," I say, "but I'm not sure how long the flower will be around, so I'm keeping the ones I already have planned. I don't want Peter to get suspicious. If I just stop dating cold turkey, he probably will."

Willa studies me for a long moment, then she puts her hands on my shoulders, giving them a tiny squeeze. "Sophie, I love you. And I fully believe in the magic of this building. But I think you're making this more complicated than it needs to be."

I bite my lip. I understand what she's saying, but she grew up in a house with parents who love each other, who modeled healthy, happy devotion. I grew up with an absentee father, a criminal stepfather, and a mom who deals with her losses through compulsive serial dating.

I wish I knew how to trust my own heart, but if I have a security blanket, I'm going to use it.

Chapter Eighteen
Peter

ARCHER TILTS his water bottle up and takes a long drink, sweat dripping down his forehead. We're sitting side by side against the wall in the back of the racquetball court at a nearby gym, and Archer just cleaned the floor with me three games in a row.

I'm at least getting better. We've played three mornings this week, and it's become my favorite way to work out, so I can't be mad at the guy for beating me so soundly.

"So let me get this straight," Archer says when he lowers his water bottle. "You've technically been offered *two* promotions."

"The second one was unofficial, but yeah."

"But you don't really want that one," he says, a statement more than a question. "The unofficial one."

"I do. It's the promotion I *thought* I was getting. I just want the one in Charlotte more."

"Because it pays more?"

"Yeah, but it's more than that. It's an incredible opportunity. It would give me access to the other side of data science. Right now, I do the research, but I'm not a part of interpreting it. In Charlotte, I would be. I would be presenting findings, making suggestions to the people who do the actual problem-solving. It would be much more challenging."

"So why are you hesitating? If it's a better job, and the pay is good and you want to do it, there are worse places to live than Charlotte. It's a great city."

"I like the city," I say. "I just—I don't know. Hard to leave a place that's always been home, you know?"

Archer nods. "But isn't your family moving to the South anyway? What will you still have in Serendipity Springs?"

"Sophie," I say without hesitation.

Archer lifts an eyebrow. "I thought she might be at the root of your hesitation."

"She matters," I say. "A lot."

"All right, let's say you turn down the job in Charlotte so you can stay in Serendipity Springs with Sophie. Then her dating scheme works, and she falls in love with someone else."

I shoot him a look. "This is some pep talk you're giving."

He lifts his hands. "What do you want me to say? You showed up on my doorstep a week ago and admitted you're in love with her. And she's taken how many guys up to the roof since then? Seems like you'd be anxious to let her know how you feel."

Archer isn't wrong.

I've had multiple opportunities to come clean, and I keep finding reasons to delay. To put off the conversation just a little bit longer. I might as well be right back in high school, planning and plotting a prom proposal until it's too late.

"I guess a part of me thinks if she felt the same way I did," I say, "she wouldn't need to go to all this trouble to meet other men. She wouldn't want to date anyone else."

"But how can she really make that call if she doesn't know you're an option?"

"I think it's the promotion that's making me hesitate," I say. "I don't want it to factor into her decision about me—*us*."

"How would it?" Archer asks.

"I don't know. Maybe it would make her feel pressured to date me because she knows I'll move if she doesn't? At the same time, I don't want her to think that if I do give the job up, that I'm doing it for her."

"But you would be," Archer says.

"But I don't want her to know that. That feels like a lot of pressure, too."

"Come on," Archer says. He stands up and offers me a hand. "Sophie deserves more credit than that. If she's factoring into your decision at all, she deserves to be a part of the conversation."

I take his hand and let him haul me to my feet.

He reaches for his racket. "One more game?"

"Are you serious right now? I can barely stand up."

He grins. "I'll go easy on you."

I sigh and reach for my own racket. "Don't do that. When I beat you, because I eventually will, I want to know it's because I earned it."

"Suit yourself," he says. "But when you can't walk tomorrow, it isn't my fault."

We play a bruising fourth game in which Archer decidedly trounces me, then he drives us back to The Serendipity. I'm hobbling my way across the lobby when Sophie comes rushing down the grand staircase.

"Peter!" Her eyes shift over my shoulder. "And Archer! Perfect. I need your help. Both of you."

"Right now?" Archer says.

"Can it wait? I really need a shower," I say.

Sophie's nose wrinkles. "You both do. But this will only take a second. Please?"

Archer looks at me and shrugs, so we follow Sophie back

outside to where a box delivery truck is sitting in the street. The back is open, and a delivery guy is standing with a clipboard in hand.

"Sophie Stewart?" he says as Sophie approaches.

"That's me," she says brightly.

"You got some muscle? This thing is really heavy." The delivery guy climbs into the back of the truck and shifts a wooden crate toward the edge of the bed.

She points over her shoulder at Archer and me. "That's what these guys are for."

"What is it?" Archer asks.

"A new ceramic planter for the garden," Sophie answers. "I just bought a gorgeous fiddle-leaf fig that needs a new home, and this planter is hand painted and so gorgeous and it's going to look amazing next to the rose trellis."

Archer is already stepping into place to lift the crate, but I'm scrambling.

Sophie wants us to carry this thing to the *roof*.

I can't go on the roof.

I definitely can't go on the roof with Sophie.

I won't say I haven't been curious. That I haven't thought about what it would mean if the flower bloomed for us. Sophie's been all-in, believing in the magic of the flower. If I want something to knock us out of the friendzone, that would do it faster than anything else.

But if it doesn't bloom, it would do the exact opposite.

It would kill my chances completely. And that's not a risk I'm willing to take. In Sophie's mind, no bloom for the two of us would close the door on a relationship between us with finality and certainty. And I desperately want that door to stay open. At least long enough for her to give me a fighting chance.

But it's getting harder and harder. This is the third time this week Sophie has needed me to do something on the roof.

The first two times, I managed to get out of helping. First, when she asked me to carry a new bag of fertilizer up the back stairwell, my mom called just as we were getting off the elevator on the fourth floor, and I was able to defer my pack mule responsibility to Matteo, who was, conveniently, getting on the elevator as we were getting off.

The second time, she wanted an opinion on how to string the new fairy lights she bought. Should they climb the trunk of the Japanese maple or line the rose trellis? She insisted showing pictures wouldn't be good enough, and could I please just come up and give her an opinion?

I claimed my work deadlines were far too pressing and annoyed her enough that she didn't talk to me for over an hour. But what else am I supposed to do?

I step up opposite Archer and lift the side of the crate, mind spinning the whole time. It's not actually all that heavy, though it probably would be if one person had to carry it all the way to the rooftop.

"You good walking backwards?" Archer says, and I nod before we make our way toward the front door.

Sophie stays behind, signing something on the delivery guy's clipboard, and for a fleeting moment, I wonder if we could get this upstairs and onto the roof before she catches up. But we're barely to the elevator before she comes trotting over, smile wide as she darts around us and pushes the button for us.

Once we reach the fourth floor, we'll have to walk down the hall to the back stairwell, the only one with rooftop access. I scour my brain for anyone between here and there who might intervene. But I come up with nothing.

I'm stuck.

And in less than five minutes, I'm going to be in the garden with Sophie.

"Hey, where's Willa?" I ask Archer as we step onto the elevator.

"I'm not sure," he says. "At this hour, probably about to start working."

"You should call her," I say. "Have her meet us up there. She'd probably love to see this, too."

"She's already seen it," Sophie says. "She was with me when I bought it. We met the artist and everything. Actually, that's not true. Willa saw a *smaller* planter, the one the artist had on display in her shop. I wanted one that was slightly larger, so the artist agreed to make it for me."

"See?" I say. "Then I'm sure Willa would want to see the bigger one. You should definitely call her."

Archer narrows his eyes at me, like he's trying to puzzle out why I'm so concerned about getting his girlfriend onto the rooftop. But she's my only hope at this point. That way, whatever the flower does or doesn't do, it'll be doing it for Archer and Willa no matter what's happening between me and Sophie.

"I'm sure she'll see it eventually," Sophie says. "I wouldn't want to disrupt her morning."

The elevator reaches the top floor, and we make our way down the hall, Sophie walking ahead. When she reaches the stairwell door for us, she holds it open, stepping to the side so we can pass by. I go up the stairs first, and I make eye contact with Archer.

"I can't go out there, man," I say, voice barely above a whisper.

He frowns. "Why?"

I glance around him at Sophie, who is coming up the stairs behind him.

"Because her flower is out there," I whisper.

It takes Archer a few seconds, but he finally seems to grasp what I'm saying. As soon as we reach the top of the stairs, he shifts his hands forward, pulling the crate into his chest. "I've got it," he says. "Go."

"Are you sure?"

When he nods, I let go of the crate, hovering long enough to make sure Archer really is in control of the cumbersome crate. When he nods one more time, I spin on my heel and head back down the stairs.

"What happened?" Sophie asks as I pass by her. "Are you okay?"

"Yeah, I just...sorry. I've got to..." I don't finish my sentence, I just wave a hand over my shoulder in what I hope indicates an urgent, unidentified need that I must attend to right this moment.

I take the stairs all the way down to the second floor, where I push through the access door, opting to head to my apartment instead of Sophie's. I haven't been there in a while, and I need to grab some clean clothes anyway. As soon as I step inside, the lights start flickering just like they were doing before I moved out.

I'm really, *really* getting tired of this apartment.

I rummage through my drawers, gathering the things I need, then head downstairs to Sophie's. It's only been a couple of minutes, so I'm banking on her still being on the roof unpacking her crate. I hope she is, because I don't want a confrontation right now, and I'm positive she's going to ask why I ran away.

Luckily, her apartment is empty, so nothing waylays me as I walk quickly to her bathroom. Once inside, I close and lock the door, leaning against it with a sigh.

I need a shower.

And something to eat.

And I really, *really* need to be honest with Sophie.

Tonight, I think. I'll tell her everything tonight. She has a stupid Operation Soulmate date, but as soon as she's back from that, I'm telling her everything. About the job offer. About my feelings. All of it.

I'm out of the shower, wrapping a towel around my waist when a knock sounds on the bathroom door.

"Hey," Sophie calls. "Just checking on you. Are you feeling okay?"

"Yeah. I'm good," I say. "Just got out of the shower."

"Okay," she says back. "I have Pepto Bismol if you need it. Or maybe some ginger ale?"

I frown. "Why would I need Pepto Bismol?" I ask, suddenly suspicious.

"Peter," she says, her tone almost chiding. "We've been friends for too long for you to be embarrassed. Archer told me about the gym. We don't have to talk about it. I'm just saying, if you need drugs, I'm happy to help."

"Okay," I say hesitantly. "I appreciate that."

"I've got to get to work," she says. "But I'll be in my office if you need me. Just text."

I listen as her footsteps recede toward her office, then I reach for my phone where it sits on the bathroom counter and send a text to Archer.

PETER

What, exactly, did you tell Sophie about the gym?

ARCHER

Not sure I follow your question.

PETER

Why did she just offer me Pepto Bismol?

ARCHER

Oh, that. I might have said something about explosive diarrhea. And implied that's why you had to run away.

PETER

Not funny, man.

ARCHER

Definitely a little funny.

Now tell her the truth, or I'm asking you
about your bowels every time we're
together in front of Sophie.

PETER

You will not.

ARCHER

It will be highly uncomfortable.

But I will.

For your own good.

Chapter Nineteen
Sophie

I DON'T SEE Peter until I emerge from my office to scrounge up some lunch.

He's working from the kitchen table, laptop open in front of him, but he's on a phone call, so I don't do more than wave. He waves back, offering me a small smile, then points to his phone with his free hand, mouthing the word *boss*. He looks like he's feeling better, at least. If he was even sick at all.

I'm beginning to wonder if Peter is avoiding my rooftop garden on purpose.

Archer is a lot of things. But he isn't a very good liar. At least, he wasn't this morning. But why would Peter be so determined to avoid the garden? His allergies aren't *that* bad, and if he's only in the garden long enough to drop off a shipping crate, that's hardly long enough for them to act up.

It *would* be long enough for the flower to bloom.

Which would be a welcome relief.

I've met up with three additional men this week. I invited Gary to meet me in the garden for coffee. Then Hendrix came over at lunch time, and a man named Richard insisted our first meeting be at a restaurant. I agreed, mostly because the idea of dinner sounded nice. But I didn't bother inviting him back to the garden because his ex-wife called in the middle of appetizers, a call he took before spending the rest of our time together telling me all the reasons why he hopes they can get back together.

It's all been very exhausting. And it's making me miss Peter. I miss our movie nights. I miss watching *Ted Lasso*. I miss feeling like we can talk about anything. And it hasn't felt that way since this whole Operation Soulmate thing started.

I finish making my lunch, not truly paying attention to Peter's conversation, but then he says, "I know, sir. I understand. I appreciate your patience. I'll definitely make my decision by the beginning of next week." His eyes flick up to me for the briefest second, then his cheeks turn a light shade of pink.

What decision is he making?

And why don't I know about it?

Does this have to do with the promotion he mentioned?

I take an extra-long time putting all the sandwich fixings back into the fridge. But as soon as Peter ends his call, he makes another, this time talking about numbers and code and a whole bunch of things that make zero sense to me.

If I didn't have my own deadline looming, I might linger a little longer, but I'd love to finish my current design before the end of the day, which means I only have a few hours left.

I take my sandwich back to my office, assuming we'll have time to talk before I leave for my date. But when I finally email my design to my supervisor and call it quits for the day, Peter is gone.

I pull out my phone to send him a text, but there's already one waiting for me.

I sigh, tapping my phone against my palm. My date tonight, Chad, is meeting me for dinner at Aria. I can't explain why, but when I made the plans, I didn't suggest he come to The Serendipity first. Something in his tone, I think. He came across as slightly entitled, like he already had expectations for how things would go.

I've been wrong frequently enough to know better than to trust my first impressions and instincts, so I still scheduled the date. But meeting at a restaurant instead of bringing him anywhere near my home felt like a safer bet. Aria was one of my favorite places to eat even before I discovered the head chef, Matteo, lives in my building, so I'm happy for the meal even if I'm less enthusiastic about the company.

And maybe Chad will surprise me?

Though honestly, I'm not sure I want him to.

The longer this week has dragged on, the more I've begun to sense that Willa was right. Maybe I am making things too complicated. My feelings for Peter have only intensified, and spending time away from him, especially when I'm with other men, is starting to feel silly.

As I move into the bathroom to do my hair and makeup, I bargain with myself. If Peter gets home before I'm finished with my face, I'll stay home.

When that doesn't work, I kick the deadline out a little. By the time my hair is done. By the time my shoes are on. By the time I'm walking out the door.

But all the deadlines come and go, and Peter still doesn't show.

Is he buying the entire freaking grocery store? How many things did he need to buy?

My stomach grumbles as I put on one last coat of lip gloss, and I breathe out a sigh.

"Fine," I say to my silent apartment. "I'll go have dinner at Aria. But I won't be happy about it."

Chad is waiting at our table when I arrive at the restaurant. He stands and smiles as I approach, then moves around the table to give me a hug.

He smells strongly of cologne, and I fight a wince as he envelops me. It's not a *bad* smell, but it's definitely about ten times too strong.

"Great to meet you, Sophie," Chad says. His grip tightens the slightest bit, and I shrink away, shrugging out from under his arms.

"Yeah, you too," I say as I step to my side of the table.

"Have you ever eaten here before?" he asks as I sit and open the menu.

"Many times," I say. "It's one of my favorites."

"Wow. Lots of times, huh? You'll have to tell me what's good. I don't frequently let myself indulge in Italian food." He pats his chest, which is admittedly chiseled under his dress shirt. "Too many carbs."

Oh, no. Is Chad one of those guys? The guys who count their macros and drink protein shakes all day? Don't get me wrong. I love a man who stays in shape. I just don't love it when it's his entire personality.

"Everything is good," I say. "Truly. The chicken marsala is probably my favorite, but all the pasta dishes are amazing."

He frowns. "Yeah, I can't eat pasta." His brow furrows as he studies the menu, then pulls out his phone, pulling up the calculator app and setting it down on the table in front of him.

I watch as he glances back and forth, looking at menu items, then typing numbers into his calculator.

I glance at my own menu, trying to figure out what information he could possibly be calculating. A steak on the menu has the number of ounces listed in the description, but otherwise, I can't imagine what he's gleaning.

Finally, I can't keep myself from asking, "Are you...adding something up?"

He looks up from his calculator app. "Hmm?"

I motion to his phone. "You just look busy over there."

"Oh. Right. Just adding up grams of protein."

"How can you do that when you don't know portion sizes?"

He shrugs his shoulders. "It's an approximation. Most restaurants of this caliber have a standard. Four ounces of meat. 6 ounces of pasta or another starch like potatoes or rice. Lower quality places serve larger portions, of course. So I make my best guess and order accordingly. I'm happy to calculate for you as well, if you like."

"No. That's okay. I don't really pay attention to stuff like that." I lean closer, not particularly impressed with Chad's calculating but also weirdly fascinated. "How do you know how much protein is in each menu item? Are you looking it up?"

"Oh, no." He taps the side of his head. "It's all up here." He gives me a confident smile. "I've done this a lot."

"You just know how much protein is in food? Like, *all food?*"

"Not everything," he concedes. "But most things." He glances down at the menu. "Everything they serve here. Want to quiz me?"

"Broccoli," I say, because I can tell by Chad's expression, he *really* wants me to quiz him.

"Three point two grams in four ounces," he says without hesitation.

"Pork," I say.

"Depending on the cut, anywhere from twenty-three to thirty-one grams."

"Wow," I say. "That's impressive." I close my menu and take a long sip of water. It is *not*, actually, impressive. At least not to me.

"You know," Chad says, "there are a lot of reasons why women should be counting macros too. It isn't just about building muscle."

Thankfully, our waiter arrives and takes our drink order. A glass of white wine for me and water for Chad, unsurprising because, as he so generously informs me, alcohol is full of empty calories.

Things don't get better as the meal continues. Halfway through our entrees, I'm itchy to escape. This date clearly isn't going anywhere, and I don't need my magic flower to prove it. If I hear one more thing about sugar content or ketosis or the glycemic index, I'm going to lose my mind.

I wonder what Chad's going to think when I admit my favorite beverage is a crème brûlée latte, and I like it best when paired with one of Willa's sugar cookies. I'm definitely going to tell him before the night is over. If only to make it as clear to him as it is to me that we are not, and never will be, a match.

"Would you excuse me for a second?" I say after taking my last bite of chicken marsala. I grab my purse and make a beeline for the bathroom. As soon as I'm locked in a stall, I pull out my phone and text Peter.

SOPHIE

HELP. My date won't stop calculating his macros.

PETER

That sounds like very important work.

SOPHIE

I swear, he hasn't asked me a single
question all night long. We have, however,
talked about the nutritional content of
everything on his plate and discussed how
my risk of cardiovascular disease is ten
times higher than it would be if I consumed
less sugar.

PETER

Sounds like a winner.

SOPHIE

Sigh. This date can't be over fast enough.

PETER

Did you drive yourself there?

SOPHIE

Yes—well, I walked.

PETER

Then leave.

SOPHIE

But we just finished eating. We haven't even
had dessert.

PETER

You really think that guy is going to eat
dessert?

SOPHIE

Ha. True. But I don't want to be rude.

PETER

He's been rude all night long. Cut your
losses. Skip dessert and come home. I'll
make you something sweet.

Warmth spreads through my chest at Peter's offer. I would much rather have dessert with him than dessert with Chad. Rather, dessert at Aria *while Chad watches*. And Peter is right. Chad *is* being rude. Not overtly. But he's been talking about himself for over an hour.

I don't have to stay for this.

I hurry back to the table, grabbing our waiter on my way. I hand him my credit card, letting him know I'll pay for the entire meal, then make my way back to Chad. I don't sit, instead sliding my chair all the way under the table and standing behind it.

Chad frowns. "What's wrong?"

"Actually, I just spoke with a friend, and I need to go."

"Oh," he says. "I hope everything is okay?"

"More than okay," I say. "I just have somewhere else I need to be."

The waiter returns and hands me my card and the receipt. I quickly add a tip and my signature, then smile at Chad one more time. "Thanks for the evening, Chad. Dinner was on me, but I don't think we should see each other again."

He leans back in his chair. "It was all the nutrition talk, wasn't it?"

The question makes me grimace, but I won't lie to the guy. "I'm sure you'll eventually meet someone who shares your passion, but that person will never be me."

His jaw tightens. "Yeah, well. You don't really have the muscle definition I'm looking for anyway."

And that's my cue to leave.

Fortunately, Aria is only a block or so away from The Serendipity. As soon as my feet hit the sidewalk, I feel an overwhelming urge to see Peter.

I don't even care that he keeps avoiding the rooftop garden. That I *still* don't know if he'll make my flower bloom.

But I don't want to fight this anymore. I just want to be with him.

I stop and loop my purse over my shoulder, then reach down and tug off my heels. Then I clutch them against my chest with one hand, lifting the hem of my dress with the other, and I run all the way home.

Chapter Twenty

Peter

I'M MIXING oatmeal into cookie batter when Sophie's apartment door opens, and she steps inside.

She's wearing an emerald green dress that ties at her waist and makes her eyes look especially bright, and her hair is up. A few curls have sprung loose, framing her flushed face in a way that makes me wonder if she ran all the way here.

My eyes drop down to her feet. She's barefoot, her heels dangling from one hand.

"Hey," I say, heart suddenly hammering inside my chest.

She's home, and she looks so incredibly beautiful, and tonight, right now, I'm supposed to tell her how I feel.

"You're home."

She drops her heels and walks into the kitchen, stopping a few feet away. "What are you doing?"

My cheeks heat the slightest bit. "Oh, um. Just making cookies."

Her eyebrows lift. "Have you ever made cookies before?"

I look down at my shirt and brush at a smudge of flour along my ribs. "No? But I said I'd make you something sweet, and I found a copycat recipe for the brown sugar oatmeal cookies we always get from Cookie's Coffee House, so I thought I'd give it a try."

Sophie bites her lip as she walks closer. I've never seen this look in her eyes before—a hunger that makes my throat go dry and my blood run hot in my veins. I drop the spatula into the bowl of cookie dough and turn just in time for her to wrap her arms around my waist. She presses herself against me, cheek against my chest, hands clasped at my back.

My arms drop around her shoulders, hesitantly at first because I have no idea what's happening right now. But then she breathes out a sigh, her body melting against mine.

I let out a little chuckle. "Everything okay?" I slide my hands up and down her back, the silk of her dress soft under my palms.

"Just glad to be home," she says. She leans back and looks up at me, but she keeps her hands clasped. We've never stood like this before, holding each other like we're in no rush to let go. This is more than just an embrace, more than a hug that has a beginning and an end. This is so much more intentional. Like we're here, and we're choosing to stay here, to stay *close*.

Sophie looks over at the counter where containers of sugar and flour and baking soda sit clustered around the bowl of cookie dough. "You did all this for me?" she asks.

"Of course I did," I say. "And I promise I'll clean up. I didn't mean to wreck your kitchen."

She shakes her head, smiling softly as she says, "I don't care about the kitchen." She looks into the bowl. "Is it any good?" She keeps one arm tucked around my waist as she uses the other to dip her hand into the cookie dough. She scoops up a generous chunk and plops it into her mouth.

I suck in a breath, suddenly nervous that it's terrible and she's going to start gagging any second, but then she closes her eyes and lets out a low noise of pleasure as she licks a bit of cookie dough off her pointer finger. "Oh my gosh, that's delicious," she says. "Did you actually brown the butter?"

"That's what the recipe said to do," I say. "Is it really good?"

She nods and helps herself to another bite. "Willa would be so proud. Here," she says, dipping her finger in the bowl one more time. "You try." She holds her finger up to my mouth.

Eyes locked on hers, I open my mouth and close my lips over her finger before she pulls her hand away.

The cookie dough really is delicious, but I'm too focused on the heat simmering in Sophie's eyes to notice.

Without breaking eye contact, she slides her hands up to my chest, her body fully tucked into the circle of my arms. "Peter, can I..." She closes her eyes for a moment, taking a shaky breath before she lifts her gaze back to meet mine. "Can I try something?"

I lick my lips. "Of course."

She bites her lip. "Don't freak out, okay?" she whispers. Then she lifts a hand to my cheek, pushes up on her toes and presses her lips to mine.

I feel the kiss—the softness of her lips, the featherlight touch of her hand sliding over my jawline. But shock keeps me from truly reacting, from kissing her back like I have dreamed of kissing her more times than I can count.

My feet are frozen, my hands gripping her back like she's the only thing anchoring me to this earth, but my lips aren't moving.

Why aren't my lips moving?

Sophie breaks the kiss and leans back. "Was that..." She lifts a hand to her face and covers her eyes. "Maybe I shouldn't have done that."

No. No! This isn't how this moment was supposed to go.

"Why would you say that?" I say, my voice breathy but

somehow still scratchy, cracking on the last word. I clear my throat, frustration with myself quickly growing.

"Because you didn't—" Her words cut off as she takes a step back, my arms falling away from her waist. "Oh, gosh," she says, hand still pressed to her eyes. "Did I ruin things? I was so afraid it would ruin our friendship. But I just thought —but if you didn't—" She winces. "You know what? Maybe I'm just tired? Exhausted from all the dating?" She lifts her free hand so now, both are pressed against her face, her shoulders hunched like she wants to hide not just from me, but from herself, too.

I have to fix this.

For years I've wanted to tell her how I feel, to *show her* how good this could be. I had the opportunity once before, and I blew it. I won't make the same mistake again.

Finally breaking out of my shock-fueled stupor, I step forward and gently wrap my hands around her wrists. "Sophie," I say gently. "Look at me."

She lets me tug her wrists down and slowly opens her eyes.

"It wasn't a mistake," I say.

She bites her lip. "Then why didn't you kiss me back?"

I slip my hand around her waist and tug her against me, then spin us around so her back is pressed against the refrigerator.

She lets out a little gasp at the impact, her eyes darkening as I lift my free hand and lean it against the fridge just beside her head. "When you've dreamed of kissing someone for such a long time, when it finally happens, it takes a moment for the shock to wear off."

Her eyes widen the slightest bit. "Wait. A long time? You've—"

I cut off her words with a kiss. "Can we please talk about this later?" I ask, mouth hovering just above hers.

"Mm," she says as her hands fist the fabric of my t-shirt. "Yes, please…"

I press my mouth to hers again, and this time, I kiss her with every ounce of feeling in my body. With every pent-up desire, every yearning I've kept dormant for years. I am a master at suppressing my feelings for Sophie, but I unleash all of them now, infusing every kiss, every touch, with just how much she matters, how much she means to me.

Her hands lift to my face, palms grazing over my unshaven jaw. I'm not sure why I didn't shave this morning—maybe because my routine was off with racquetball and hiding from Sophie—and I start to feel self-conscious about it, but then Sophie smiles against my lips.

"I like you with a little bit of scruff," she says, her voice low and sexy.

I let out a low groan as I deepen the kiss, pulling her closer, *closer*, until her air is my air, her body an extension of mine. We move together, touching, shifting this way and that, kissing again and again as we catalog each other in this new way.

I know so many things about Sophie. But I've never known this. The way her mouth tastes against mine. The way goosebumps erupt down her arms when I graze my fingers over the skin just behind her ear.

"Peter," Sophie says, her voice breathless as I press a line of kisses across her jawline.

"Hmm?"

"We're kissing."

I breathe out a chuckle. It's a very Sophie observation to make. "We are," I murmur against her skin. I lean back, palm shifting to Sophie's cheek. "How are you feeling about that?"

She leans into my touch, eyes falling closed as she smiles softly. "I'm feeling like it's a really good idea." She runs her hands up my arms, tucking them under the sleeves of my t-shirt. She curves her fingers around my biceps, making my muscles twitch. "When I left the restaurant tonight, all I wanted was to be with you. All week long, all these other dates, I just kept thinking things would be so much better if I were on a date with you instead. So when you told me to come home, I left. Right then. I paid for dinner, then I pulled off my heels and ran home barefoot."

She tugs me down, finding my mouth again, and kisses me with a tenderness that eclipses the intensity from moments before. Her touch is a brand on my skin, and I'm not sure I can ever go back to a day when I don't belong to her. I'm feeling too much, too fast, but we've been building to this for so long, I have no idea how to rein in my emotions. I know Sophie well enough to recognize that at some point, even if she isn't afraid in this precise moment, her fear will catch up with her, but I don't want her to freak out over this, and I can't stop worrying that she will.

"How long, Peter?" she asks. "How long have you wanted this?"

"It doesn't matter," I say. "It just matters that we're here now."

She tugs on my shirt. "Tell me."

I breathe out a sigh. "Years, Soph. Since high school."

She closes her eyes, lifting her hands up to cradle my face. She pulls me down for yet another kiss. "Why didn't you tell me?" she asks when she pulls back, but she doesn't move her hands away. She holds me close, looking directly into my eyes.

I shrug. "Because I was scared. Or you were seeing someone else. Or we were living apart in college. The timing never really worked out." I lift my hands and place them over hers, pulling her hand away so I can press a kiss to her palm. "I was going to tell you tonight. I couldn't bear the thought of watching you go on one more date without saying something."

She takes a slow, deep breath, then tucks herself against my chest, her head resting on my chest. "Are you still scared?" she asks, voice soft.

"Maybe a little," I say. "But I trust this. I want this."

She's quiet for a long time, but I can feel her body tensing, her body language shifting, like she's curling in on herself. I breathe steadily. I knew this would happen. That she would eventually panic.

I just have to convince her I'm not going anywhere. That she isn't going to lose me. That our relationship can still be what it was before. Now, it can just be *more* too.

"Peter, my relationships don't work," Sophie says. "We know this about me."

"They haven't worked in the past," I say gently. "But maybe that's because you were never with the right guy. I'm in this for life, Soph. We really only need *one* relationship to work, right? Why not this one?"

"Because I'll die if I hurt you. If it doesn't work out, and I —" Her words cut off as her eyes widen. "Wait. We just need to check." She leans back, stepping out of my embrace, and grabs my hand. "Come onto the roof with me."

My heart sinks.

I should have expected the question. Sophie doesn't want to trust herself. She wants proof we're meant to be together.

I squeeze her fingers. "Sophie," I say as gently as I can, "I'm not going onto the roof with you."

Her brow furrows. "Why not?"

I step away from her, moving back to the bowl of cookie dough. I shift the flour container to the right, then line the brown sugar up beside it, if only to have something to do with my hands. I just need a moment to calm my nerves, to say what I need to say in a way that isn't going to ruin what's happening between us.

Finally, when I feel a little more in control, I turn and lean against the counter behind me, arms folded across my chest. "Because I don't need a flower to tell me how I feel."

She scoffs. "That's not what it does."

"Isn't it?" I ask. "If we go up there and the flower doesn't bloom, what will you say about what just happened? That it was a mistake? Crazy hormones taking over?"

"I wouldn't..." she says, but her words trail off, and I know she's considering, asking herself if that *is* what she would do.

"But...Peter, what if that *is* what happened?" she finally asks. "What if we try this, and six months down the road, we realize we aren't going to make it? Relationships end all the time. People get hurt all the time. And I don't want to hurt you. More than anyone else in this world, I don't want to ever be the person who causes you pain." She moves toward me, reaching out like she's going to touch me, but then her arms drop, and she wraps them around her midsection. "If the flower doesn't bloom, we can acknowledge that this was one amazing make out, but we'll be better off going back to being friends."

My jaw tightens. "Please don't say that," I say. "Don't trivialize what just happened by suggesting we could ever go back to only being friends."

She sucks in a breath, and I realize too late it was the absolute wrong thing to say. In Sophie's experience, relationships *don't* work out. Men leave. She's seen it with her mom over and over again. And it's made her live on the defensive, protecting herself, shutting people out before they can ever get close enough to hurt her.

But I snuck in on the sly. Our friendship created an opportunity for us to get close without the threat of our relationship ending. She says she doesn't want to hurt me, and I believe her. I know she'd never do anything to cause me pain.

But more than that, Sophie doesn't want to get hurt

herself. She doesn't want to let herself fall, to *trust,* when she has no idea what it looks like when someone *stays.*

It's not a wonder she's scared.

"I'm sorry," I say. "I didn't mean to imply—we'll always be friends. Of course we'll always be friends."

"You say that, but it doesn't always work out that way," Sophie says. "This is why I've been trying so hard to get you on the roof. I just wanted to see, to know—" Her words cut off and she looks at me, eyes sharp. "That's why you've been avoiding the roof. You don't *want* to know if the flower blooms for us."

I take a slow, deliberate breath. "I didn't want *you* to know. I didn't want you to use it as a reason not to give me a chance."

"So no explosive diarrhea?" she asks, lifting one eyebrow.

I manage a grin. "Sorry to disappoint you."

"Honestly, it was worth seeing Archer so uncomfortable when he mentioned it." She gives her head a little shake. "Still. Aren't you a little bit curious? Don't you want to know if the flower thinks we'll turn into Mr. and Mrs. Hathaway?"

"You're giving it too much power, Soph," I say, my tone gentle. "Love is never a guarantee, but I'm not sure it's supposed to be. It's an action. If we want to be the Hathaways, still in love when we're old and gray, then we do the work. We make it happen."

"But that doesn't always work. Sometimes people do the work, and they still split up. They still lose each other."

I shrug. "Is that better or worse than never trying at all?"

"But it's different with us," she says, fire drained from her voice. "We've been friends for so long, and I don't want to mess it up." She looks up, eyes pleading. "Please? If we go up to the garden, we can know for sure. We'll know if it's worth the risk of ruining our friendship."

A part of me wants to say yes. To believe the flower *has to* bloom because there's no way we aren't meant for each other. That's how sure I am of my feelings.

But Sophie is hanging *all* her hopes on this.

I can't risk destroying my chances, and that's exactly what will happen if the flower doesn't bloom. She'll give up.

The trouble is, I might *also* be ruining my chances by saying no.

"That's just it, Soph. I already know it's worth it."

Chapter Twenty-One
Sophie

I STARE at my apartment door, a hollow emptiness creeping over me.

After pressing a very sweet kiss to my forehead, Peter told me he needed to take a walk, and then he left.

Walked right out the door like we hadn't just shared the most monumental kiss of our entire lives.

Or maybe *because* we'd just shared the most monumental kiss of our lives. That would be a very Peter-like thing to do. He always needs time to process how he's feeling.

I cross into the living room and drop onto my couch, settling into the cushions with an audible *oof.* I can't decide if I'm more upset that Peter left or more upset that he's so resistant to the idea of visiting the rooftop garden.

It doesn't make any sense. If he would just go up to the roof with me, we could know. We could save us both from the possibility of getting our hearts broken.

But *no.* Peter doesn't need a flower to tell him how *he* feels.

But that's not even how it works!

Okay, fine. That's exactly how it works. But doesn't he see the opportunity we have here? If we could just know, with absolute certainty, that there is the potential for *true love* between us, then we could know whether dating is even worth the risk.

And if it didn't bloom, well, then we would know that kissing *was* a mistake. We were caught up in the heat of the moment, but we could always go back to being friends.

But even as I think the thoughts, I know they aren't true. Nothing about that kiss was a mistake, and I'll never go back to looking at Peter like he's just a friend.

But where does that leave us?

Slowly, I stand and pad over to the front door, where I scoop up my heels, then head to my bedroom to change into pajamas. I can't remember if Peter took his keys when he left, but if he didn't, he'll probably be back any minute.

I find myself listening for him, stepping into the hallway while I'm brushing my teeth to see if he's coming down the hall. Peering into the kitchen in case he snuck in when the water was on and I missed it.

But he doesn't show.

Even when I'm completely ready for bed, bundled in my favorite flannel pajama pants and the MIT hoodie I stole from Peter the summer after he finished his bachelor's degree, he still hasn't come back.

I clean up the kitchen and, despite having already brushed my teeth, I bake a batch of Peter's cookies, then curl up on my couch with an entire plate of them, determined to stay up until he returns. The cookies are delicious, which only makes me long for Peter *more*. He didn't pick this recipe on a whim. He picked it because it's our favorite. Because these cookies are something we've always enjoyed together.

I gave Peter a spare key when he moved in, so technically, I could go to bed. But I feel a dull ache at the back of my heart, and I'm not sure it'll go away until I see him again.

I have no idea what I'll say.

What I even *want* to say.

I just know I'll feel better, more at peace, once he's here.

I won't watch *Ted Lasso* without Peter, so I pick a different show and make it through two full episodes. But Peter still doesn't show up.

I can't really be annoyed, but I *am* a little worried.

I stand and riffle through his stuff, trying to find his keys. I can't find them, so he must have grabbed them on his way out.

Which means he could be anywhere.

Back on the couch, I retrieve my phone from the coffee table and send him a quick text.

SOPHIE

Hey. Are you coming back tonight? Are you okay?

His response comes through almost immediately.

PETER

Staying at my place tonight. I had to water the plants.

I roll my eyes. Peter has *one* plant, a golden pothos on his desk, and I'm the only one who ever waters it. As fastidious as he is about everything else in his life, the man can't keep a plant alive to save himself.

SOPHIE

Plants plural?

PETER

Fine. Plant. I still watered it.

SOPHIE

Are you avoiding me?

PETER

Yes.

I have to at least chuckle at his honesty.

SOPHIE

Why?

PETER

Sophie. Don't ask a question when you already know the answer.

SOPHIE

But I don't know the answer! Are you mad?

PETER

I'm not mad.

SOPHIE

Are you sure?

PETER

I'm sure.

SOPHIE

So you just…need a minute?

PETER

Yes. And to spend a little time with my golden pothos.

SOPHIE

How are the lights?

PETER

Behaving, for now.

SOPHIE

You know you can come back if you need to.

PETER

I know.

SOPHIE

And you know how much I love you.

It takes Peter a very long time to answer this question, and I watch the dots appear and disappear several times before a message finally pops up. When it does, my heart squeezes painfully.

———

The next morning, I wake up to Saturday morning sun streaming through my curtains. It's just past nine, which is later than I usually sleep, but my rest was fitful last night, my brain flitting in and out of dreams that were a little too vivid. I dreamed of kissing Peter, but it was more than that, too. Snatches of a possible life together played out in my mind like scenes from a movie. Peter laughing at the kitchen table. Peter napping on the couch with a baby on his chest. Peter dancing with me in the rooftop garden.

I pull my pillow out from under my head and press it against my face, fighting the urge to squeal. Or maybe scream. Can I do both at one time? Is there a word for that? A screal, maybe? A squeam?

I want to be happy. I *am* happy. But I'm also terrified. The waffling back and forth between emotions already has me feeling exhausted, and I haven't even gotten out of bed yet.

"You can do it, Soph," I say to myself as I toss off my covers. "You can get up!"

I groan as the cool air hits my bare legs and I pull my blankets back over me.

Maybe just five more minutes.

I wonder how Peter slept last night. If his apartment *let* him sleep last night. Is he still in bed right now? Thinking about me like I'm thinking about him?

Even after the way things ended last night, a part of me still hopes he'll eventually come around to the idea of visiting the garden. But what if he doesn't?

Is that a dealbreaker for me?

Will I refuse to see him again? Date him? Unless he's willing to give me what I want?

I climb out of bed and head to the kitchen to make some coffee. I kicked off my pajama pants sometime in the middle of the night, but since Peter slept at home last night, I don't bother grabbing them. I only need a minute to make some coffee, then I'm going to jump in the shower anyway.

"I feel obligated to tell you I'm here, but I promise I'm not looking."

I startle at the sound of Peter's voice and spin around, nearly dropping the coffee mug I just pulled out of the cabinet.

Peter is sitting in the living room, hair mussed like he just woke up, his hand pressed over his eyes. I lift a hand to my chest and take several deep breaths, then look down at my lace-trimmed, pink and purple heart-covered underwear. They aren't my most scandalous pair, but they are a little cheeky, and the thought of Peter looking up and seeing me pantsless makes my face flush a deep red.

"Peter! You scared me!" I say.

"I know. I'm sorry. But that seemed like a better alternative than lurking while you're pantsless...and unaware."

"How gentlemanly of you," I say. "Hang on. I'll be right back."

I put down the coffee mug I've been clutching to my chest and hurry back to my room to grab a pair of leggings, hoping my blush will subside before I return to the living room.

The trouble is, I'm not blushing *just* because Peter saw me in my underwear. I'm blushing because he's *here*. He came back.

And now I have to talk to him. Look at that mouth, which I thoroughly kissed last night. Think about something besides the feel of his skin when I slipped my hands under the sleeves of his t-shirt and wrapped my fingers around his biceps. Focus on actual words instead of replaying the noise he made when I pressed a kiss to his neck just below his ear.

I take a slight detour before I go back to the living room and stop in the bathroom to look in the mirror.

My hair is *wild*. Frizzy, out-of-control curls stand up every which way, and mascara smudges make dark rings under both of my eyes.

I don't have time to tame the curls, so I force them into a bun, then tackle my face, cleaning up just enough that I won't look like a walking hangover but not so much that I look like I made an effort.

Even though I'm absolutely making an effort.

I finish by brushing my teeth and putting on a little bit of lip balm. I should probably go grab a bra, but I'm still wearing Peter's hoodie, and it's thick enough that I'll be okay without one.

And now I've *officially* thought about my appearance more than I ever have with Peter before.

He's up and making coffee when I get back to the kitchen. Glasses on. Hair tamed a little. He turns and glances at me over his shoulder, a new uncertainty to his expression.

It's comforting to see because it means he's probably feeling a little nervous, too.

These are completely uncharted waters for us.

"Sorry again," Peter says.

"Don't worry about it."

He hands me a mug of coffee made just the way I like it.

"So your lights started acting up again?" I ask.

"Around three a.m.," he says.

"Your apartment really isn't being nice to you right now," I say.

"Apparently not." He looks at the container of cookies sitting on the counter. "You made the cookies?"

I nod. "And they were delicious."

"I'm sorry I left a mess in your kitchen," he says.

"Don't worry about it. The cookies were worth it."

An awkward silence descends upon us, and I shift my weight from foot to foot, then take a long sip of coffee that's still too hot.

I wince the slightest bit, then set my mug on the counter.

Peter puts his mug down next to mine, then pushes his hands into the pockets of his pajama pants. He holds my gaze for a long moment. "I'm also sorry I left last night."

"No," I say, shaking my head. "I'm the one who should apologize. I'm sorry I made it seem like you had to go to the garden with me. I didn't mean to make it seem like—I mean, I do still wish you would go, but if you don't go, that doesn't mean I don't—that we can't—" I pause and frown. Am I completely incapable of saying a full sentence around Peter? Is this how it's going to be now? I shake my head and lift my gaze to meet his. "Sorry. Words aren't my friend this morning."

"Believe it or not, I think I understand what you're saying." He takes a step closer, his hands lifting to my arms. "I know you're scared, Soph. But what if we just take things one day at a time? We don't have to label anything or make any decisions about our friendship. We'll just take things slow. See how it feels to be together."

I lick my lips. "To be more than friends?"

His gaze drops to my mouth, and his expression heats. "Yeah. If that's okay with you."

I lean a little closer. "Will there be kissing in this new arrangement?"

He smirks. "I would like very much for there to be kissing." He reaches forward and slips his hands around my waist, tugging me toward him. "Nice sweatshirt," he says, and I smile.

"It's my favorite."

"Is it?"

"Yep. It always has been."

"Yeah? Why is that?" He leans down, brushing his nose against mine, his breath fanning across my cheek.

I close my eyes. "Cause the guy who gave it to me is my favorite."

Peter chuckles. "Pretty sure it was more a *taking* situation than a *giving* one."

I push up on my toes and press my lips to his. They're warm and soft and welcoming, and I think I could probably stay right here, kissing him, for the rest of the morning. "You know you wanted me to have it," I say in between kisses, and Peter grins against my mouth.

"You caught me," he says. His hands lift to my cheeks and cradle my face while he kisses me one more time. Minutes slip by as he explores my mouth, and I find myself thinking about all the years we've known each other, all the time we wasted, when we could have been doing this.

Maybe I don't need the flower to bloom for Peter. Maybe this really is good enough for me to lean in and trust it.

If there's anyone in this world I can trust to keep my heart safe, it's him.

But can he trust me with his?

Peter finally pulls his mouth from mine. His hands slide

down my arms until our hands are clasped, fingers entwined together. "So I was thinking," he says, a slight tremble to his voice. He sounds nervous, and he shakes his head, rolling his eyes like he's annoyed with himself. "I don't know why I'm nervous when I was *just* kissing you."

I bite the corner of my lip, suddenly struck by how endearingly perfect this man really is. "Don't be nervous," I say. "It's just me."

His expression softens. "That's precisely why I *am* nervous," he says. He takes a deep breath. "Sophie, will you have dinner with me tonight?" He squeezes my hands. "I'd like to take you on a real date."

"I'd love to," I say.

Because I would. Because even though I still have a million reasons to worry about what will happen if we try dating and it doesn't work out, now that Peter is here, all those worries seem so much smaller.

I just want to be around him. I want to be *with him*.

The realization washes over me, settling like a warm, comforting blanket around my shoulders. I've read a lot of romance novels, and they frequently describe feelings hitting like a lightning bolt, like some startling jolt of clarity.

This isn't that. It feels more like I'm accepting something I've always known. Finally seeing something that's always been right in front of me.

"I was thinking the cantina over by the library?" Peter says. "We could walk, probably. If the weather is nice. It's supposed to storm this afternoon, but the forecast says the rain should clear up by five or so."

"That sounds perfect," I say, and he nods.

"Good." Peter rocks on his heels, his cheeks turning the most adorable shade of pink. "Then it's a date."

A date. A real, actual date with my real, actual best friend.

I push up on my toes and kiss him one more time. "I'm really happy, Peter."

He smiles wide. "Yeah. Me too."

Chapter Twenty-Two
Sophie

PETER and I spend the rest of the morning cleaning my apartment. It's usually a task I hate, but with Peter helping, mopping my floors and scrubbing my toilet has never been so much fun.

While Peter is rearranging my pantry, I wipe down all the countertops and clean out the inside of my cabinets. I have no idea how I got crumbs inside the cup cabinet, but apparently, I managed it like a pro.

When I step off the stool I'm using to reach the top shelf, my hip bumps into the kitchen table, the motion waking up Peter's laptop.

It pretty much lives in the spot it currently occupies, and I've gotten used to ignoring it, but his email inbox is open on the screen, and the subject line of the message sitting at the top immediately catches my eye.

Charlotte Itinerary.

I glance into the pantry, heart hammering like I've already been caught snooping.

"Hey, you've got some expired oatmeal in here," Peter calls.

"Do I?" I ask. "We can toss it."

"I'll make a pile," he says. "I doubt it's the only thing."

"Sounds good," I say, but my eyes are glued to his laptop. I shouldn't look. But Peter's the one who doesn't have his laptop password-protected, which, that's the most surprising thing here. Seems like a data scientist for a cybersecurity company would have passwords and double encryption and a dozen other safeguards to protect himself and his personal information.

But what do I know?

I lean a little closer. I won't click on the email. That feels like a step too far. But the opening lines of the message are visible next to the subject line.

Looking forward to you meeting the team. You'll be a great add...

The rest of the word cuts off, but it's easy to guess what it says. You'll be a great addition. But addition to what? The Charlotte team?

A knot of dread forms in the pit of my stomach. Was Peter offered a promotion...in a different city? In *Charlotte*?

If he was, why hasn't he talked to me about it?

Bigger question: what would I do if Peter actually moved out of Serendipity Springs?

I just kissed the man like I want to spend the rest of my life with him. Not that long distance relationships can't work, but they are more complicated. And I really feel like I should have known this was on the table.

Before kissing him.

Before *falling for him*.

Peter pops his head out of the pantry, a box of cereal in his hand.

Acting on impulse, I reach forward and slam his laptop closed. His eyes follow my movement, and he frowns.

"Sorry," I quickly say. "I just didn't want to...break it. With all the cleaning."

"Okay," he says. "Do you want to keep these? I haven't seen you eating plain Cheerios, well, ever."

I wave a hand dismissively. "You can toss them. They're probably stale anyway."

"K. I'm just about done in here. What's next?"

I have no idea what to say. Do I confront him? Ask him? I have to, don't I? But I'm having a hard time with the hurt blooming in my chest.

I don't know why he didn't tell me. And I really hate that he didn't.

"Actually, I think I'm going to run up to the roof to cover the annuals," I say, suddenly desperate for a reason to escape. "I got an alert that says there might be hail with the thunderstorm coming through. I don't want to risk losing all the blooms off the petunias." The forecast really does call for hail, but I also need a minute to gather my thoughts and figure out how to talk to Peter about his move. *Possible* move? I wish I knew.

Peter frowns, and I immediately recognize his struggle. In any other circumstance, he would offer to help, but my petunias are in my garden, and so is the love flower.

"It's fine," I say, trying to reassure him. "It won't take me long. I don't need your help."

His jaw tightens like he doesn't quite believe me, but he nods. "Okay. I'll be here then."

It's windy when I reach the garden, the gathering clouds a deep, dark gray. I find a roll of plastic sheeting in the storage closet by the stairs and dig out a handful of small stakes from the bottom shelf.

It shouldn't take long, but I'm not sure I'll finish before the rain starts. Honestly, this actually would be easier with a second person, and I regret telling Peter to stay behind. With this kind of storm bearing down on us, we might not have even noticed the love flower.

A sharp gust of chilly spring wind ruffles my hair as I approach the flower beds that need covering. I'm not worried about the perennials and the heartier stuff that can handle a little bit of a beating. But the petunias and begonias and marigolds will get totally shredded in a hailstorm. A drop of rain falls onto my arm, and I glance up at the sky.

I *definitely* need some help.

"Hi. Are you Sophie?"

I look up to see a man standing a few feet away. He's tall and broad-shouldered, with sandy blond hair and deep brown eyes. He looks familiar, but I can't quite place him.

"Yes?" I say. "I'm sorry. Do I know you?"

He frowns. "I'm David. I think we have plans to have lunch together today?"

David.

Oh my gosh!

David!

My stomach sinks.

I have a date today.

A date with David the orthodontist, whom I met on Swipe Rite last week and then promptly forgot about. How on earth did I forget that we made plans?

Admittedly, I've been *slightly* distracted since I got home last night.

But still. To forget an entire *date*?

"Right. I'm so sorry. It's nice to meet you."

"You forgot about the date, didn't you?"

I look down at my overalls. I look like I'm dressed for house cleaning or gardening. Definitely not a lunch date. "I did, and I would love to give you a sincere apology, but do you think you could help me with something first?" I glance up at the sky. "I just need to cover the flower beds before the rain starts."

David's eyebrows lift. "Oh. Sure. Absolutely."

It takes less than five minutes to spread the plastic. With David holding it on one side, I stretch it tight and stake it down, then run around the bed to his side and repeat the same thing. Seconds after the final stake is in place, the clouds burst, and rain pours onto the rooftop.

I gather up the extra sheeting and the leftover stakes and make a run for the stairs, but then I stop short right in front of the Japanese maple.

Because my flower—my magical flower that has never opened for me—is in bloom.

Rain pelts my skin, running down my face and soaking through my clothes.

I look over at David, who is standing near the stairs, hand shielding his face as he stares my direction, likely wondering why on earth I'm just standing here.

It can't be true.

The flower can't be blooming for me and David.

But we're the only two people on the roof.

It's what I've wanted. What I've been hoping for all along. And now it's finally happened, and all I can think is that I really wish it hadn't.

"Sophie?" David calls. He takes a few steps toward me. "Are you all right?"

I look at the flower one more time. The maple tree above it is doing a decent job shielding it from the storm, but water is still collecting on its petals, making it droop just slightly.

But there's no question that it's in bloom. Big white petals. Deep pink center.

The rain falls faster, and I finally turn, spinning away from the flower and running toward the stairs. I open the storage closet door to throw my supplies inside, hoping I'll have time to make it into the stairwell, but when hail starts hammering the rooftop, I give up and step into the closet instead.

David steps in behind me, pulling the door closed enough

to protect us from the biting hail. "This is some storm!" he calls over the roaring weather.

I nod, but there isn't much point in talking. The storage closet is tucked into the side of the stairwell, and the rooftop of the small structure is metal, so the sound of the rain and hail beating against it is practically deafening.

David looks outside through the crack in the unlatched door. He's soaked through, his shirt clinging to his torso, his hair plastered to his head.

I take advantage of his momentary distractedness and try to take stock of my feelings. Physically, I'm cold and wet, practically shivering, but otherwise, I'm okay. But emotionally, I can't even begin to make sense of what just happened.

The flower *bloomed*. Opened up for David and me in the middle of a rainstorm. And so far, the flower hasn't been wrong.

That means David is my soulmate—my possibility for true love. But how can that be true? How can I belong with *this* man when my heart already feels so connected to someone else?

But then, my heart has *always* felt connected to Peter, from the very beginning of our friendship. Even before we kissed.

For a split second, I set aside my thoughts of Peter and try to study David objectively.

He has pleasing features, and he looks like he's in decent shape. And even though I've only just met him and we're currently standing in a closet together, I'm not getting any uncomfortable or predatory vibes. But I find myself utterly uninterested in making more than the most basic observations. I'm sure the man is nice, but my brain keeps shifting back to Peter, thrumming with a need to get out of here, to find him and assure him that I'm okay.

Even on the first floor, I'm sure he heard the hail, and he's probably worried about me.

Can David really be my soulmate if I can't stop thinking about someone else?

The rain finally eases up, and David looks at me over his shoulder. "Should we make a run for it?"

I nod and follow behind him as he leaves the closet and rounds the corner to the stairwell door. He holds it open for me, and I hurry inside, waiting as he comes in behind me.

He wipes the water from his face and looks over at me. "Wow," he says through a chuckle. "I haven't seen rain like that in a long time."

Footsteps sound on the stairs before I can respond, and I look down to see Peter quickly approaching, a worried look on his face.

"Hey," Peter says as he reaches the top of the steps. His hands fall on my shoulders, then shift down my arms, like he's cataloging my person, making sure I'm whole and well and safe. "I heard the storm and got worried. Are you okay?"

My eyes dart to David, who is watching our interaction closely, but Peter's attention stays wholly focused on me. "I'm okay," I say. "I managed to cover the flowers before the hail started, but I couldn't avoid the rain." My teeth chatter the slightest bit—the air-conditioned cool of the stairwell definitely lends a bite to my very damp skin—and Peter frowns. He yanks off his hoodie and wraps it around me, his hands chuffing up and down my arms to warm them before he finally looks over at David.

"Who are you?" he asks, his tone polite but cool.

"Um, this is David," I say. "He helped me cover the flowers." It's a stupid introduction, but what else can I possibly say? "David, this is my...friend, Peter." I hesitate on the word *friend* because Peter is definitely more than that now, but we're only a few hours into our new relationship dynamic.

Feels a little soon to be throwing around words like *boyfriend*, especially when we're supposed to be taking things slow.

David extends his hand to Peter. "Nice to meet you," he says as Peter shakes his hand. "Sophie and I were supposed to have a lunch date today, but apparently, the storm had other plans." David looks at me. "Listen, I'm sure you'd like to change into something warm and dry. I'm feeling the chill myself, so I'd like to do the same. Should we reschedule for another day? Maybe one with a sunnier forecast?"

I have to at least give the guy props for not reacting to Peter's presence with any hint of jealousy. Even though I'm technically supposed to be his date, and I'm standing here wearing Peter's hoodie, David still seems perfectly cool and confident.

I nod. "Sorry about forgetting. And thank you for your help with the flowers."

David steps toward the stairs. "No problem," he says with a wink. "It'll make a great story if we're ever asked how we met." He looks at Peter. "Nice to meet you, Peter. Sophie, I'll call you."

Peter and I are silent as David makes his way down the stairs. One flight, then two, three four before we hear the echoing click of a door opening, then falling shut.

Peter takes a deep breath, then holds out his hand. "Let's get you downstairs and into some warm clothes."

I slip my hand into his and let him tug me down the steps, but I can't do this. I can't walk with him, talk to him, let him take care of me without telling him the truth.

"Peter?" I say, giving his hand a quick squeeze.

"Don't worry about it," he says without pausing his steps. "You had a lot of dates scheduled. And this just happened between us. I get it. You don't need to explain anything."

"That isn't it," I say.

Peter is walking faster now, and I'm struggling to keep up,

my wet sneakers squelching on every step. He grips my hand a little tighter.

"Peter, wait. Can we stop a second? I don't want to fall."

This, finally, snaps him out of whatever blind emotion was driving him down the stairs, and he turns, stopping two steps below me so we're almost eye to eye.

His eyes are full of something I can't quite read. He almost looks frustrated, but it isn't that. It's more like he's *tormented*.

"I'm sorry," he says, his voice soft. "I'm being an idiot."

"You aren't," I say. "That was a really weird situation up there."

He licks his lips, his hand tightening around mine. "You forgot you had a date scheduled?"

I nod. "I made the plans a few days ago. I'm not sure how he got into the building. I told him we'd meet in the garden, and I planned to have you let him inside. But then, after we—after last night, I completely forgot until he showed up right before the rain started."

Peter takes a deep breath, his eyes turning glassy for a second, like he's remembering something.

I need to tell him.

I *have* to tell him. I can't keep standing here, holding his hand, with this giant thing hovering in the air between us. If I don't tell him, I won't stop thinking about it. And if I can't stop thinking about it, I'll never be able to let it go.

I open my mouth to speak, but Peter beats me to it.

"Did you know I was going to ask you to senior prom?"

I close my mouth. "Really?"

He nods. "I bought a cake," he says. "The icing on the top said *Will you go to prom with me?*" He lets out a disbelieving chuckle. "I bought a cake, and I had this whole plan where I was going to invite you over to watch a movie and then get up to make popcorn and come back with a cake instead."

My heart hammers painfully in my chest. I don't have to guess what happened next.

"But then you texted and asked if you could come by," Peter says. "Said you had some exciting news." He meets my gaze.

"Jack Larson had asked me to prom," I say, and he nods.

"I waited too long," Peter says. "I planned and I practiced, and I put it off day after day because I was so scared to tell you the truth. To admit that I—" He gives his head a little shake. "Anyway. When I saw you standing at the top of the stairs with David, I thought of Jack Larson. That's why I was acting so weird. I was thinking about him swooping in because I was too chicken to tell you how I felt." He drops my hand and runs his fingers through his hair. "It's stupid that I'm telling you this now, when you're standing here shivering, but I just didn't want you to think I was jealous or angry or anything else. I was just caught up in my head because a part of me still thinks this is too good to be true. And now I'm rambling and you're still freezing, so we should—"

"Peter, the flower bloomed," I blurt out, cutting off his words.

He stares, his frown making his forehead wrinkle and his eyes turn down. "What?"

"It bloomed," I repeat, voice trembling. "When I was on the roof with David. The flower bloomed."

Chapter Twenty-Three
Peter

I HAVE no idea how I made it back to Sophie's apartment.

How I kept it together while I started a bath for her and made her some tea and promised we would talk as soon as she was warm and dressed.

Now, I'm pacing around her living room while she's in the bathroom, and I want to scream at the entire world.

The freaking flower *bloomed*.

It bloomed for a *stranger* while I was down here organizing the seventy-five million kinds of tea Sophie has in her pantry.

A part of me wonders if, had I not been so stubborn, the flower would have bloomed for *me* and Sophie. Had I just gone up on the roof with her, we could have avoided all this drama. But it's too late for that. Too late to know what might have happened, because now, the flower has bloomed for someone else.

I drop onto the ottoman in Sophie's living room and reach for a basket of my laundry. I fold it wordlessly, thoughts spiraling the entire time.

In a perfect world, the flower blooming for David wouldn't matter. Sophie would feel confident enough in what we have together that she wouldn't hesitate to ignore the bloom, opt not to see David again, and continue what we started.

But is it selfish to wish for that? To assume that, despite magic or fate—or whatever the flower is—saying otherwise, I'm truly the best option for Sophie?

What if I'm wrong and David whoever-he-is actually *is* better equipped to love her like she deserves?

What if I'm not—and never have been—destined to be her *one true love*?

After I finish my laundry, I set it aside and reach for my phone. I got an email late yesterday afternoon suggesting I take a trip down to Charlotte this coming week to meet the team I'll be supervising should I take the offered promotion.

My travel, of course, will be on the company, and they'll put me up in a nice hotel downtown, right next door to the corporate office. I think they're beginning to worry I won't say yes, and this is their attempt to wine, dine, and woo me to Charlotte.

I was planning to tell Sophie about the job offer tonight, but now it feels like it will only complicate things. Whether I want to admit it or not, she has a choice to make. She believes in the flower—in the magic it holds—and she's been chasing the assurance of its bloom for weeks now.

That's an assurance I can't give her—especially not now, when the flower has already bloomed for someone else. It's not that I want to walk away. But if she chooses to be with me, I want it to be without any hesitation, without any doubts or questions lingering in her mind.

When the newness of our relationship wears off, and she's tired of my idiosyncrasies or my exacting ways, I don't want her wondering if she could have had a better relationship with someone else.

With David.

The bathroom door squeaks open, and I quickly stand, shoving my phone into my pocket.

Sophie emerges, her body wrapped in a fluffy white bathrobe. Her hair is damp, brushed back from her face, and her cheeks are flushed from the heat of her bath. She looks beautiful, but the weariness in her expression makes my gut tighten.

"Feel better?" I ask as she moves into the living room, and she nods.

"Yeah. I can feel my toes again." She sits down on the far side of the couch, so I sit on the opposite side, body turned sideways so I can face her. She keeps her eyes down, but I know she's thinking because she keeps tugging on her bottom lip with her teeth, like she's afraid to look up, afraid to talk to me.

"Peter," she finally says, "can we pretend for a minute that you're just my best friend again?" She lifts her gaze to mine. "Because you give really good advice, and I could use some good advice right now."

"Give me just one sec." I reach up and tap my fingers against the side of my head, like I'm adjusting my programming. Then, in the most robotic voice I can muster, I say, "Recalibrating, recalibrating, recalibrating...best friend mode activated."

Sophie breathes out a chuckle. "Are you serious right now?"

I grin and drop my hand. "Sorry. Just wanted to do something dorky enough to wipe all memories of sexy Peter from your mind."

"Oh, got it," she says. "He's like your alter ego, then. There's Best Friend Peter, then Sexy Peter?"

"Indeed," I say, "and right now, I'm fully Best Friend Peter. Hit me. Let's talk this out."

Sophie's expression softens, her shoulders relaxing, and I

know I've made the right call. We've been friends a lot longer than we've been anything else, so I can do this. I can be objective.

Mostly.

Hopefully?

"So there's this guy," Sophie says. "And I really like him."

"Tell me about him," I say, and Sophie shoots me an amused expression. "Average height, lean build. Good muscles though. Built like a swimmer, which is exactly what I like."

"Sounds handsome," I say.

"Oh, he definitely is," Sophie says. "Big brown eyes, and these glasses that add just the right amount of sexy professor energy."

This entire conversation is absolutely ridiculous, but it's doing an excellent job of lightening the mood, and that's something I think we both need.

"He owns a few too many hoodies, but I'm willing to overlook it because on the rare occasions when he wears a suit, he *really* knows how to wear it." Sophie smirks, shooting me a teasing look. "But more importantly, he's kind and considerate and he works hard, and he's really good at taking care of me."

Warmth spreads through my chest at her words. I enjoy nothing more than taking care of Sophie, so it feels good to hear the compliment.

"So what's the problem, then?" I say. "This guy sounds really great, and you sound like you really like him."

She bites her lip. "Yeah. I do. But I think he might be keeping something from me. Something with his work? And that's not anything he's ever done before." She swallows and looks at me, expression searching. "Kept secrets."

I take a deep breath. This isn't at all how I expected our conversation to go. How does Sophie know about the promotion?

"What makes you think he's keeping secrets?"

She shrugs. "I saw an email on his laptop, which was weirdly not password protected."

I frown. My laptop usually *is* password protected, but I just reconfigured my security settings and had to turn off the facial recognition component to do it. I must have forgotten to turn it back on.

"I didn't read it," she says. "Or even click on it. But the subject line made me think there's something he's not telling me. Which only matters because our relationship has recently shifted, and I feel like I deserve to know if something is going on. Do you think that's fair?" she asks. "If you were me, would you want to know?"

"It's definitely fair," I say, kicking myself for keeping the secret for this long. "I'm guessing he probably has reasons for keeping you in the dark, even if those reasons aren't justified."

"Yeah?" she asks. "What do you think they might be?"

"Fear, probably," I say. "If your relationship *has* recently shifted, I'm guessing he doesn't want to lose you or screw anything up. Maybe he didn't tell you about his work promotion because he was scared it would be a reason you wouldn't give him a chance."

Sophie nods, holding my gaze for a long moment before she says, "They offered you a job in Charlotte?"

I nod.

"And it's a good job?"

"A really good job. Exactly what I want."

She takes a steadying breath. "Are you going to take it?"

I lean forward, propping my elbows on my knees. "Honestly, Soph, if staying in Serendipity Springs means being with you, I'll give up the job in a second. That's how much I want this."

She shakes her head. "But I wouldn't want you to give it up for me. Not if it's something you want."

"*You're* something I want," I say. "That matters too."

"Were you ever going to tell me?" she asks, her voice small.

"Of course I was. I wanted to tell you tonight. Up until last night, I was trying to figure out how to tell you how I feel, and I felt things shifting between us, shifting in a good way, and I didn't want to screw that up. I didn't want a potential move to get in the way."

"But it *will* get in the way, won't it? You can't give up the job for me, Peter. I won't let you."

I sink back into the couch. "I have to be honest," I say, pressing a hand to my forehead. "When you came out here, this isn't what I thought we'd be discussing."

"I'm not worried about David," she says, but her words come a little too quickly.

I look at her, lifting an eyebrow, and she winces.

"I'm *mostly* not worried about David," she says.

"You don't have to apologize if you are," I say. "I know the flower's magic is important to you."

We sit in silence for several moments. I carefully weigh my next words. I don't want to regret them, but I also don't see any other path forward.

"Sophie, I don't want you to have this question hovering over you. If you and I are together, I want you to be sure that a year down the road, or five years down the road, you aren't wondering if you missed out on the man you were supposed to be with."

She shakes her head, like she doesn't like my words any more than I do. "So what do we do?"

"I think...I go to Charlotte this week—I'm supposed to go anyway—and maybe you spend some time with David. Get to know him. See if you feel anything that makes you think the flower might be right."

She presses her lips together, tears brimming in her eyes. "Why does the thought of that make me so sad?"

"Because we care about each other," I say. "Because I don't think either one of us wants to see the other get hurt."

She lifts her hands and wipes at her tears, then tucks her arms around her middle. "What happens after this week?"

I shrug. "I don't know. Maybe we'll both have a little bit of clarity about what we want."

She nods. "Maybe David is terrible, and I'll hate him right from the start."

"And maybe I'll hate Charlotte," I say. "It could be a terrible city."

She shakes her head. "It's not a terrible city," she says.

"I know," I say. "But it might be a terrible city for me."

It will be, I think to myself. As long as she isn't in it.

I stand and offer Sophie a hand. When she slips her fingers into mine, I tug her to her feet and pull her into an embrace.

She melts into my chest, her cheek pressed against me, and I lean down and press a lingering kiss to the top of her head. "It'll be okay," I say. "Whatever happens."

"Peter, I'm scared," she says, her voice barely above a whisper.

"Yeah," I say. "Me too."

Me freaking too.

Chapter Twenty-Four
Sophie

DESPITE MY INSISTENCE that he stay, Peter decides to go back to his own apartment after our conversation.

We also decide to delay our date tonight.

I get it.

We're definitely at some sort of crossroads, and living together, dating like everything is normal, will only make it more difficult for us to be objective, to think clearly.

But I miss Peter when he's gone. I miss his belongings stacked in the corner of the living room. His laundry basket beside the couch. I miss his laptop and his work things on the corner of the kitchen table. I just miss *him*. The way he makes me feel anchored, happy no matter what's going on at work or with my family or anywhere else. It feels good to be around him, and it only takes a few minutes for his absence to feel more like a gaping hole in my life than a smart decision.

As soon as he's moved out the last of his things, I finally get dressed and head back up to the roof to uncover the flowers. It's nearly dinner time now, and my stomach grumbles on my way up the last flight of stairs, reminding me that with everything that's happened today, I haven't had anything to eat. Not since the coffee Peter made for me this morning.

Was that really only this morning? When I stood in my kitchen and kissed Peter's coffee-warm lips? It seems so long ago.

On the rooftop, the early evening sky is clear, the air crisp and clean after the afternoon's storm. Most of the plants look okay, despite the hail that fell earlier. Some leaves are damaged, but nothing severe enough to keep any of the plants from recovering.

Removing the plastic is much easier to do on my own, and it only takes a couple of minutes to pull up the stakes and roll up the sheeting. The flowers underneath look perfectly happy, blooms intact, leaves lifting toward the sky.

Once everything in the garden is tended for the night, I put away my supplies, then head back downstairs. When I reach my apartment, I find a brown paper to-go bag sitting on the floor in front of my door with a note stuck to the outside.

I reach down and pick up the note.

Pretty sure no situation exists that isn't improved with tacos. Enjoy.
—Peter

I carry the food inside, setting it on the table before pulling out my phone to send Peter a text.

SOPHIE

Really? NO situation? Are showers better with tacos? Or pap smears? What about a prostate exam?

PETER

Honestly, if I had to endure a prostate exam, I might enjoy the distraction of a good taco.

SOPHIE

Okay, fine. Same with the pap smear. But a
shower? You can't argue that one.

PETER

I could. For the right taco. You'd just have to
eat fast. Have you eaten yet?

SOPHIE

Not yet. I was up on the roof uncovering the
flowers.

PETER

Eat! Before they get cold. And be sure to
use lime. You always forget and then
complain when you remember after your
taco is already gone.

I grin at my phone. He really does know me so well.

SOPHIE

Thank you for feeding me.

You should come back and get your
groceries. You left a lot here.

PETER

If I take my groceries, you'll have nothing to
eat. Plus, I'm leaving on Monday morning.

My heart pinches painfully at the thought of Peter leaving, flying to Charlotte to try on a new job. A new life. A life that wouldn't have me in it. At least not like his life now.

SOPHIE

I guess that's true.

How are your lights?

213

The text exchange goes a long way to easing the discomfort and uncertainty that's been dogging me all afternoon. So I do eat my tacos. And they're the best ones I've eaten in a very long time.

On Monday morning, my boss sends over a proposal request for a new commercial complex on the other side of town. It's normally the kind of thing that would make me grumble and groan. Boring parking lots. Minimal green space. But this week, I'm happy to have anything to focus on that isn't my very confusing love life, so I pour myself into the project and finish it in record time. My boss gave me until Friday, but he's got a fully workable proposal on his desk by Tuesday afternoon.

I am in desperate need of a shower, I haven't seen actual sunshine in thirty-six hours, and five of my last six meals have all been takeout, but I'm still calling it a win.

The only problem: with my work done so far ahead of schedule, I have nothing else to do to occupy my time.

Which is why, when David texts and invites me to have dinner with him Tuesday night, I agree.

That was the plan, after all. While Peter is checking out a new city, a new job, I'm supposed to be checking out *David*.

The idea of two people destined to love each other was exciting when I was thinking about other couples, but it's a different story now that it's me. It's disconcerting to know that I'm supposed to fall in love with someone who, so far, hasn't triggered any kind of emotional or physical response.

Maybe we just need to spend more time together? We didn't touch the entire time we were together last Saturday, even in the tiny storage closet on the roof. It didn't seem to matter with Jake, but could that be the missing piece with David?

Or is Peter the reason I can't look at David with any sense of clarity? Maybe my heart is already so full, there isn't room for me to consider anyone else.

But after everything I've been through, if I'm turning my back on the flower that promises a true-love guarantee, I have to do it with my eyes open.

So I'm going on this date.

Whether I want to or not.

And I'm going to be as objective and honest with myself as possible.

I arrive at the Thai place David recommended a few minutes early, so I sit in my car and pull up the thread of text messages with Peter.

We've chatted a few times over the last couple of days.

I asked him to let me know when he arrived safe in Charlotte. He did.

He asked me to check his mail for him and make sure his golden pothos is watered in his absence. I promised I would.

But other than that, we haven't said much. I have a million questions, but I haven't asked any of them because I don't want to seem like I'm inserting myself into the middle of his decision. I don't want to *need* him so much that he decides not to take the job because of me.

I wish I could text him right now. He always knows the exact thing to text when I need a boost of confidence or reassurance, but that feels even worse than asking about his trip. I'm supposed to be thinking about David right now. Not Peter. I definitely can't text Peter and ask him for encouragement so I can successfully *date David*.

I groan and drop my head onto the steering wheel.

My life is ridiculous.

Utterly and completely ridiculous.

When my phone buzzes in my hand, I lift my head to see a call coming in from my mom. I still have ten minutes before I'm supposed to meet David, so I go ahead and answer. We're supposed to have lunch tomorrow, and we still haven't firmed up our plans, so that's probably why she's calling.

"Hey, Mom. How are you?"

"Oh, my gosh, Sophie," she starts, "you aren't going to believe what I'm doing right now."

"No? What's up? What are you doing?"

"I'm packing!" she practically singsongs. "For a trip to Paris!"

"Wow. Really?"

"I hate to do it, honey, but I need to cancel our lunch plans for tomorrow. Michael just got this amazing invitation to join a few friends in Paris for the week, and he's asked me to go along!"

I can't even believe I'm asking the question when I say, "Mom, who's Michael?"

"Oh. Haven't I mentioned him? You'll love him. He's handsome, rich. A total silver fox."

"Do you really think it's a good idea to go to Paris with someone you just met?" I ask, though I don't know why I bother. My reservations have never influenced Mom's behavior before.

"We didn't *just* meet," she says. "I've known Michael for years. We've just never dated. He just got a divorce, poor thing. So this trip to Paris is exactly what he needs."

"Then...I guess I hope you have a good time," I say, despite my hesitations. Honestly, at this point, what do I know? Mom seems happy. Who am I to say that flitting from one man to the next isn't the perfect way to live? But I can't keep myself from asking something I've never asked her before. Maybe it's because my emotions are all so raw, but I just can't pretend anymore. I can't pretend like what we went through is normal. "Mom, why did you and Dad split up?"

She's quiet for a long moment, so I know my question surprises her. "Well, where did that question come from?"

"I've been thinking about our conversation, when you said I was the one who's hiding." I pause and take a deep breath. "The thing is, I have a really big thing happening in my life right now. A person I think I might be in love with, but I'm so crippled with fear and anxiety about what might happen, and I just—I worry it screwed me up to see you dating so much." The words surprise me, not because I don't think they're true, but because I've never said anything like them to my mother before.

"Oh, Sophie," she says gently. "It's impossible that it didn't. That's the hard part about being a parent. You do your best to handle your problems, to shield your kids, but there's always fallout."

"You did a good job, Mom. I was happy, healthy, safe. I just don't have a lot of confidence in love. I mean, Dad left. Charles left. And every other man you've dated—they've all left, too."

"Honey, your father didn't leave. We got a divorce, but he didn't *leave me*. We both wanted to end the marriage."

A weight drops into the pit of my stomach.

"What?"

Mom breathes out a sigh. "We weren't happy, Sophie. We were never happy."

"Then why did you get married?"

"Because I was pregnant with you." She chuckles lightly. "And believe it or not, because a fortune teller at the county fair told me your father was my soulmate."

"Wait, what? How have I never heard this story?" I lean back in my seat, glancing around the parking lot in search of David. I'm happy when I don't spy him anywhere, because I really want to know what my mother is talking about. I always knew I was conceived before my parents' wedding. Mom is visibly pregnant in all the wedding photos. But I've never heard anything about a fortune teller.

"It wasn't really about the fortune teller," Mom says. "It was more about you. But your father and I—we didn't get along all that well. We had great physical chemistry, but we fought all the time. We never saw the world the same way, but I'd just found out I was pregnant, and I wanted to believe we could turn ourselves into a family. When the fortune teller claimed she'd had a drink of the famed Serendipity Springs water and could see love, I latched onto the claim with my whole soul. And we did try. Both of us did. But six years is a long time to live a lie. We finally decided to call it, figuring the younger you were, the easier it would be for us all."

"So you *weren't* heartbroken when he left," I say.

"I mean, it was a change, sure. But no. Your father did not break my heart."

"Then why do you date so much?" I ask, still struggling to believe Mom's version of her life. "I thought you were trying to protect yourself. To avoid another heartbreak by never letting a relationship get serious. That's textbook behavior, Mom. You of all people should know that."

She chuckles. "True. But that isn't the case for me. I know it's hard for you to believe, Soph, because your heart is so different from mine. But I really am happy. Maybe I will settle down one day, if I ever meet a man who makes me want to. But I've always been a free spirit. I like being my own person. I like spontaneous trips to Paris and eighty-day world cruises, but I also like knowing that at the end of the day, I don't need anyone else to be happy. I have myself, I have a gorgeous daughter I'm proud of, and that's enough for me."

I sit in silence and let my mother's words sink in.

"Sophie," Mom says gently. She's using her therapist voice now. "I probably *was* hiding a little at first. Protecting myself from the possibility of heartbreak. And I won't pretend that every choice I make is perfect or that I don't have things to work through on my own. But I want you to listen to me very closely, okay?"

I sniff against the threat of tears. I really don't want to cry seconds before I go on a date. Though something tells me this date might not actually happen after all. "Okay," I say, voice shaky.

"You're different than I am," she says. "Your heart is so big and so pure. You've always been made for loving people, for giving people your whole heart."

"Then why have I never been in love?" I ask. "I've tried, Mom. I've dated and dated. But I've never had a relationship last longer than a few months. And I've been so scared that it's because I'm just like you. That I'm subconsciously pushing everyone away."

It's the reason I latched onto the idea of using the flower to find my *own* happily ever after. It was a guarantee in a world that usually doesn't offer one.

"You have, though, haven't you?" Mom says. "Your relationship with Peter has lasted years."

"Yeah, but we were just friends. That's different."

"I would argue you've always been a lot more than *just friends*," Mom says. "But even if I'm wrong and your relationship is purely platonic, friendships are still relationships. They require vulnerability and honesty and commitment. There's nothing wrong with your heart. You're still so young. You have plenty of time to fall in love. And if you want it, you'll absolutely find it."

"Wait," I say. "You always thought Peter and me were more than friends?"

"Honey, *everyone* thought you were. That boy looked at you like you were the sun, moon and stars all at once."

The tears are definitely falling now, and I don't stop them. "He was pretty great, wasn't he?" I say. "He's still pretty great."

"I ran into Evelyn the other day," Mom says. "She said something about Peter moving to Charlotte. How are you feeling about that?"

A familiar knot tightens in my chest. "He's there right now," I say. "Checking things out. It's supposed to be a really good job. Perfect for him."

"Hmm," Mom says. "Well, Charlotte is a lovely city. I'd love to have a reason to visit."

I scoff. "What do you mean? He's the one who would be moving, Mom. Not me."

"Ah, well, either way," Mom says. "Listen, I really have to go. But let's have lunch as soon as I'm back in town, all right?"

I wipe at my eyes and sniff one more time. "Okay. I'd like that."

"You're not me, Soph," Mom says. "You're so much better than me, and you deserve the biggest, brightest, best kind of love."

I end the call and drop my phone into my lap. Numb. A little shell shocked. But the longer I sit, the more certain I become.

I *do* deserve the biggest, brightest, best kind of love. And I know exactly where to find it.

Chapter Twenty-Five
Sophie

IT'S JUST past seven when I pound on Willa's apartment door. My knock is admittedly more forceful than it needs to be, but there are *big* things happening inside my brain, and I really need to talk to someone about it.

She swings the door open, and I barrel into her apartment. "Hi. Are you busy? Am I interrupting? Is Archer here?"

She closes her door and turns. "Not busy. Just making dinner. Archer isn't here, but he'll probably show up any minute."

I follow her into the kitchen. Whatever she's making smells really good, and it makes my stomach rumble with hunger. I did *not* end up eating Thai food with David, and now I suddenly wish I'd at least picked up something to go.

"What's up?" Willa continues. "Why are you so keyed up?"

I grab a tangerine out of her fruit bowl and start to peel it. "Do you realize we haven't had a conversation in six entire days?"

Willa looks over her shoulder and shoots me an apologetic smile. "I know. I've been so busy with work. I had this huge order come through for a party on Sunday night, and I literally feel like I've done nothing but ice cookies. What have I missed? How's everything with Peter?"

I pop a few segments of tangerine in my mouth and settle myself on one of Willa's barstools. "Let's see. Do you want to hear about the amazing kissing first? Or the fact that Peter's possibly moving to another state? Or should I tell you about the flower blooming for me and another guy?"

Willa slowly turns. "Oh, wow. We have a lot of ground to cover."

We do, and *we do*. I talk until dinner is ready. Until Archer comes in, kisses her hello, takes one look at me, then takes his plate and heads right back out again. I talk right up until Willa sets a plate of teriyaki chicken and rice in front of me and hands me a fork, and I don't leave anything out.

"How did David take it when you bailed on dinner?" Willa asks. She sits down on the barstool next to mine with her own plate. "Eat," she says, motioning toward my food. "It's getting cold."

I scoop up a forkful of rice. "He seemed disappointed, but he was nice about it," I say. "I mean, we hardly know each other. It's not like he really had time to hope for an actual relationship."

"Yeah, I guess not," Willa says. "And you feel really good about your decision, yeah?"

"What do you mean?"

"Like, you aren't worried about regretting your decision not to date David."

I put down my fork. "What are you really asking here?"

"Just let me be pushy for a second, okay? Answer the question. When you think about never seeing David again, about having a relationship with Peter instead, are there any lingering doubts or fears still troubling you?" She scoops up a bite of her food. "Take a minute to think about it. I want a real, honest answer."

My brow furrows as I take another bite and really consider her question. As much as I worried and questioned before, now, my mind feels calm and clear. Something happened when I talked to my mom. When she used Peter as an example of a positive relationship in my life. Something clicked and shifted, and my perspective completely changed.

"No doubts," I say. "I don't want to date anyone else. I don't want to get to know David. I *do* want to be with Peter."

"And the flower?" Willa asks.

I frown. "I don't understand why the flower bloomed for the wrong man. I really wanted it to work for me, and I believed that it would. But I'm a grown woman, with a heart and mind of my own. I know what I want. *Who* I want. I don't have any doubts about that."

Willa smiles. "You're absolutely sure?"

"I'm absolutely sure."

"Good," she says. "That means I can tell you the flower didn't actually bloom for you and David."

I freeze. "What?"

Willa bites her lip. "Don't be mad, all right? I had no idea until you just now told me what happened, or I would have cleared this up the minute it did."

"Willa," I say, suddenly desperate to understand. "What are you saying right now?"

"Saturday afternoon, when the big hailstorm hit? Archer and I were on the roof."

"No you weren't," I say. "I was the only one up there until David showed up. I would have seen you."

Willa rolls her eyes. "We were, and you didn't see us because we were hiding behind the rose trellis."

"Doing what?" I ask, still struggling to wrap my head around what she's telling me.

"Nothing! Just—"

"Willa," I say, my voice firmer this time.

"Fine! We were making out. Is that what you want me to admit? We saw you coming, and we didn't feel like stopping, so we snuck behind the trellis and then David showed up, and it felt totally silly to just emerge from the bushes in front of a complete stranger, so we stayed hidden until the storm started."

"But I would have seen you leave," I say. "I stood in the rain and stared at the flower long enough to get totally soaked."

Willa's cheeks heat the slightest bit. "We kissed in the rain long enough to *also* get thoroughly soaked," she says. "We only ran once the hail started."

"When I was already in the storage closet," I say. I drop my head into my hands. "All this time!" I groan. "All this time, I've been absolutely miserable because I thought I was supposed to be with some rando, and it's your fault! Why didn't you tell me this earlier?"

"I didn't know there was anything to tell!"

"No, I mean, why didn't you tell me earlier *tonight*? When I first told the story?"

Her expression clears. "Ohhh, I see what you're asking." She shifts on her stool to face me. "I just wanted to make sure you had your feelings sorted out. You've never been particularly good at trusting yourself, Sophie. You doubt your judgement, your ability to maintain relationships, your worthiness of friendship. It's big that you decided to love Peter even without the flower's approval. I wanted you to hear yourself say it out loud."

"Because I don't need a flower to tell me how to feel," I say, remembering Peter's words the first night we kissed.

Willa nods. "I mean, it's pretty fun when the flower agrees with you. But it's even more fun that you get to choose."

Emotion wells up in my chest. "I *do* get to choose."

"Yeah. You do." She reaches over and grips my arm. "Honey, does this mean you're moving to Charlotte?"

I choke out a laugh with a sob caught somewhere in the middle, and suddenly I'm crying into what's left of my dinner.

Willa stands and retrieves a paper towel, handing it to me to wipe my nose. "It's too soon to actually think that, right? I mean, we're not even together. And it might not even come to that. He might not like the job. He might decide to stay here instead."

"He might. But if he doesn't—would you move to be with him?"

I think about my job. About my boring bosses and the life they strip out of every single one of my designs. I love Serendipity Springs. It's been my home for a decade. But I'm not sure how much it would still feel like home if Peter wasn't in it. "Yeah, I think I would. Is that totally bonkers?"

"Maybe a little. But it's not like you just met the guy. He's been in love with you for a long time. Your history matters here."

I look at her and frown. "He's been in love with me? Is that something you know for a fact?"

Willa grimaces.

"Wait, are you serious? You *do* actually know it as a fact?

"I mean, it's pretty obvious just from the way he looks at you. But yes. The night you had dinner with Jake, Peter came here, drank with Archer, and basically told us everything."

"And you didn't say anything to me about it?"

"It wasn't my information to tell," she says. "And Peter wasn't ready for you to know. Not when you were in the middle of Operation Soulmate."

"But then I came to you and told you I liked him, and you still didn't say anything!" I say. "What kind of a best friend are you?"

"The kind who knew you needed the journey more than

you needed the information. You needed this, Soph. You needed to believe in yourself more than you believed in the flower. I have zero regrets for keeping Peter's secret." She rubs her hands together. "Now. What's the rest of your week look like? Because I think you need to fly to Charlotte to surprise your man."

Chapter Twenty-Six
Peter

A PART of me hoped I wouldn't like Charlotte. That I would come down here and feel like the city is too big or the office is too corporate.

But I've found the exact opposite. The thriving city nestled into the foothills of North Carolina is bustling and busy and beautiful, and it only takes a couple of days for me to imagine myself living here.

The team at IronKey is smart and interesting and fully engaged in their work—work that impresses and inspires me. The work environment is relaxed and comfortable, and Valeria, who will, should I accept the position, be my direct supervisor, is warm and kind but also exacting in a way that works for my brain. I can already tell I would enjoy working for her —with her—and leading a team of scientists I've already grown to respect would be incredible.

By the time I'm back at the hotel on Thursday evening, it's hard to imagine *not* taking the job.

The only trouble is, it's equally difficult to imagine living without Sophie in my life. It's taken all my willpower not to call her the last few days. We've texted a few times, but we haven't spoken. And the distance feels unnatural. I've been keeping a list of all the things I'd like to tell her when we speak again, everything from the serious and important—Valeria told me point blank that I'm the brightest talent in data science she's seen since she started with the company ten years ago—to the completely random—they sell this soda in North Carolina called Cheerwine that Sophie would definitely love, even though it's too sweet for me.

The past few nights, right before falling asleep, I've let myself indulge in the idea that maybe I could have the best of both worlds. I could take this job, build a life in Charlotte, and Sophie could live here with me.

I would never ask her to make such a sacrifice. Serendipity Springs is her home, and she's always loved it there. She has her mom, her friendship with Willa, her job, the rooftop garden. But all those logical thoughts aren't doing a very good job of convincing my heart to stop wishing for it anyway. To stop wishing for her.

But then, all the wishing in the world won't matter if she decides to be with David.

I tug at my tie, loosening the knot before pulling it free and tossing it onto the bed. *Those* thoughts have also been dogging me all week, doing their best to squelch my optimism and hope and replace it with a sort of melancholy acceptance.

The flower hasn't lied to Sophie so far.

Why would it be wrong this time?

One more day in the office, then I'll fly back to Serendipity Springs on Saturday morning, and I'll have to face Sophie and find out the truth. I just don't know what *my* half of the truth will be.

Will I take the job? Or will I stay in Serendipity Springs for her? For us?

Maybe I won't be able to make a choice until she makes hers.

I toe off my shoes, then unbutton my dress shirt, but then the hotel room phone lets out a jolting ring, and I pause—I didn't even realize hotels still have room phones—leaving the shirt on as I cross to the desk to answer it.

"Hello?" I say into the receiver.

"Good evening. This is Joni from the front desk. You have a visitor here to see you. Are you expecting anyone this evening?"

"Uh, no, not that I know of."

"Very good, sir," Joni says in a very professional tone. "Your privacy is our utmost concern, so I'll let the visitor know."

"Wait," I say. "Can you tell me who it is?"

Joni sniffs. "One moment." A brief pause passes before Joni returns and says, "She says her name is Sophie Stewart."

My heart starts hammering in my chest. Sophie is here? In Charlotte?

"Please send her up," I say. "Right away."

"All right," Joni says. "Room five forty-two," she says, presumably to Sophie, then back to me, she adds, "She's on her way."

I make fast work of stripping off my dress shirt and pulling a t-shirt over my head. I think about changing out of my dress pants, but I'm too anxious to see Sophie, so I forget about my mismatched outfit and grab my room key before heading into the hallway and hurrying toward the elevators.

It takes about ten seconds for the elevator to stop on my floor with a ding that makes my heart climb into my throat. I don't know why Sophie is here, but right now, in this moment, there's nothing that I want more than to see her.

When the elevator doors slide open and Sophie sees me, her expression brightens before she offers me a sheepish smile. "Hi, Peter."

I shake my head, blinking once, twice, because I have to

be dreaming. Sophie looks beautiful enough to make my chest ache just from looking at her. She's more dressed up than I usually see her, wearing black pants and heels and a white blazer over a shimmery green top. She looks polished and professional and not like she just got off an airplane. Her hair is down, curls framing her face, and I know, with sudden clarity, that if I have the opportunity to spend the rest of my life with this woman, I'll take it no matter where I have to live to do it.

I stand there staring, unmoving, long enough that the elevator doors start to close, pausing my racing thoughts and jolting me back into the moment. I lunge forward, sticking my arm into the doors to keep them from closing and gesture her off the elevator.

"You're here," I say, once we're both on the same side of the doors. "How are you here?"

She shrugs. "I needed to see you."

It's all I can do not to pull her into a hug, but the look on her face keeps me from doing it. She looks nervous, a little trepidatious, like she has to say something really important and she doesn't know where to start.

"Can we hug?" she asks, like she's reading my thoughts. "I really want to hug."

I let out a little chuckle, opening my arms as she steps into my embrace, her arms wrapping around my waist. She sighs as she presses her cheek to my chest.

I lean down, nose to her hair, and breathe in a lungful of Sophie-scented air.

"I missed you," she says, her voice soft.

"Yeah, I missed you too." It feels so good to hold her like this, and I soak it in, trying not to stress too much about why she's here or what she's going to tell me. Because there must be something if she came all this way. "How did you find me?"

"An educated guess," she says. "IronKey is right next door.

I figured they'd put you up somewhere close. Though I wasn't sure Joni was going to cave," she says, arms tightening around my waist. "She did *not* want to tell me your room number."

"Come on," I say, reaching for her suitcase. "It's not far to my room."

She follows behind me as we cover the short distance down the hall. I pull the key out of my pocket and unlock the door, then hold it open for her as she makes her way inside.

I leave her suitcase by the wall, and she shrugs out of the bag she's wearing on her back, setting it down on top of the dresser. Then we just stare at each other, the silence heavy between us.

I want to ask so many questions—and she probably has questions too, but it's hard to know where to start.

"Do you want to sit?" I finally ask, motioning toward the king-sized bed.

"Sure," she says. She sits on one corner of the bed, while I sit on the other. I spend too long wondering if I should have taken the chair by the window, avoided the awkwardness of us both sitting on the bed.

It's a stupid thought though because it wasn't that long ago that we *slept* in the same bed, the night Reggie scared Sophie into needing my company.

Finally, Sophie closes her eyes, face scrunched. "Peter, why does this feel so awkward?" she asks, squinting one eye open and looking at me.

"Should I have taken the chair?" I say, quickly standing. "I can—"

She grabs my arm as I move past her, stopping my progress. "You don't need to sit in the chair," she says with a chuckle. "It's just me." She tugs me down on the bed so I'm sitting directly beside her. "I think I'm just nervous," she says. She threads her fingers through mine, giving my hands a squeeze. "I spent the entire flight rehearsing what I was going to say and how I was going to say it, and now everything is gone. All my words." She lifts her free hand and makes an exploding gesture with her fist, opening it and spreading her fingers wide. "Poof," she says. "Just like that."

"Take your time," I say. "I don't have anywhere I need to be."

She finally looks over and smiles at me, her eyes so full of warmth, of *love,* I feel a sudden, driving need to kiss her. I won't though. Not until I know why she's here. Until I know she wants me to.

"How has it been this week?" she asks.

I almost deflect the question. I don't want to talk about work. I want to talk about us. But I only want honesty between us, so I swallow and tell her the truth. "It's been amazing. I really like the team."

She squeezes my hand. "That's good. Really good. I had a feeling you would. And you like the city?"

"I do. The NASCAR Hall of Fame is nearby. That sounds exciting."

She wrinkles her brow. "You do not want to go to the NASCAR Hall of Fame."

"No," I say, smiling. "I don't. But I did get a pretty thorough tour of the city on Tuesday afternoon. It's nice. A lot of great parks. Nice museums. Oh! And a Chinese place I think you'd love. Best kung pao chicken I've ever eaten."

"I can't wait to try it," Sophie says. She drops my hand while she shifts on the bed, kicking off her shoes before pulling her legs up so they're crossed under her and she's facing me. She reaches forward and takes both of my hands in hers. "So, I have a small confession."

I swallow against the nerves clawing at my throat. "Okay."

"I actually arrived in Charlotte early this morning," she says.

"I wondered," I admit. "You're pretty dressed up just for a flight."

"I had a business meeting," she says, holding my gaze, but that doesn't make any sense.

"In Charlotte?" I ask, and she nods.

"It's a pretty crazy story, actually," she says. "Yesterday, I called my grad school mentor, Dr. Finley, over at UMass. It's always nice to check in and say hello, but this time, I had a very specific question." She licks her lips, and I notice a slight tremble in her exhale.

I give her hands an encouraging squeeze, and she smiles softly before continuing.

"Dr. Finley is really well-connected all up and down the East Coast. From guest lecturing to publishing to all the students she's mentored, I thought it might be worth asking her if she knows anyone in the Charlotte area."

I furrow my brow, still not fully grasping what she's trying to tell me.

"Unsurprisingly, she has a former colleague who recently left academia and is opening his own firm here in Charlotte. It feels incredibly hard to believe, because everything happened so quickly, but she made a phone call to him, he suggested we meet, I mentioned I was going to be in the city the following day, then I booked a flight for the literal crack of dawn the next morning, jumped on a plane eight hours later, and met with him today. He's still a few months out from hiring, but we had a great lunch today—we really vibed and hit it off—and then he took me over to his new office building, which is still under construction, and I met his wife and his twin daughters, and I just like him so much, and he says if I'm interested, he'd love to bring me on as a junior designer."

My breath catches in my throat. "Sophie, what are you— are you saying you would work *here*? In Charlotte?"

She bites her lip and nods. "Probably not until late summer. August or September, maybe. Which isn't ideal. But I'm really excited about the way Gregory talked about design. It's so much more in line with my own principles. So much *more* than what I've been doing with Trowbridge. I really think it will be a great fit for me."

"In Charlotte," I repeat, almost afraid to let myself get excited. Does this mean what I think it means? That she would move here—for me?

"Peter, I'm in love with you," she says. "And I feel like that's a really important distinction because I've *loved* you for years. But this is more than that. Which, I realize it's a little wild to say that because it happened so fast, but when we kissed, something shifted and suddenly all that love I already had for you just—it morphed into something else." She lifts her shoulders in a shrug. "Meeting with Gregory today was just a bonus. What I really flew down here to do was tell you that I want us to be together. And I'm ready to move to Charlotte to make it happen."

Heat floods my chest, and I lean forward, taking her face in my hands as I press a kiss to her lips. "Are you serious right now?" I kiss her again. "Is this for real? Are you for real?"

She laughs in between kisses. "I'm absolutely for real, and I'm absolutely serious."

I pause, another question popping into my brain. "But what about your flower? What about David?"

She shrugs her shoulders dismissively. "Someone really smart once told me he doesn't need a flower to tell him how he feels, so I decided I don't either."

I can't stop the grin that spreads over my face at her words. "I don't even know what to say."

She presses a kiss to the tip of my nose. "You could start with I love you too," she says playfully.

"I do," I say, hating that I needed her prompting to say it

when it's been pulsing in my mind and heart for weeks, months—even years. "I love you so much." I pull her against me, breathing her in, hoping she senses how much she means to me. "I've loved you for so long, Soph."

This time, when we yield our words to kisses, we don't stop for a long time. There are so many things I still want to know. Questions I want to ask. Logistical things my brain is already sorting through. But all those things can wait.

Right now, I just want her to know how much I love her. I love the softness of her lips, the wildness of her curly hair, the shape of her body. I love her exuberance and her cheerful nature and the joy she brings to everyone she meets. I love her eye for color and design. I love that she's so good at growing things and making spaces beautiful. I love that she's never given up on me. Even when I'm anti-social. When I'm too boring or too logical or too scientific. She still sees the good in me. And she reminds me of that good like it's second nature. Like my worth is so obvious, she shouldn't even need to say it out loud. But she says it out loud anyway because that's Sophie's way. To lift and encourage and make people feel good.

Eventually, as our kisses slow, I whisper all of this to her, as we touch and taste and explore this new aspect of our relationship, I tell her all the things I've held back, that I've been too afraid to say for fear of scaring her away. And she whispers right back. Promises of love, but also admissions of the fear she wrestled to get here.

"You know what's funny?" she eventually says. We're sitting against the headboard, side by side, Sophie's head resting on my shoulder. "It was a conversation with my mom that finally nudged me into accepting how I feel."

"Your mom? Really?"

She yawns and snuggles a little closer. "Yeah. I was in the parking lot at this Thai place where I was supposed to have dinner with David, and she called. We talked about my dad a little, and I just—I don't know. I think I had some things wrong in how I viewed their relationship—ways that impacted both how I view my mom and how I view myself. Also, she told me she always thought we were secretly in love with each other when we were in high school. So, there's that."

"I was in love with you in high school," I say.

"I was so clueless, wasn't I?" She tilts her head up and looks at me. "It makes me a little sad to think about all the time we lost."

I lean down and press a kiss to her forehead. "Don't think about it like that. We were still friends. Maybe we both had some growing up we needed to do."

"But the kissing, Peter," Sophie says. She lifts a hand to my cheek and guides my lips to hers. "We could have been doing so much kissing."

I chuckle against her mouth. "Okay, true. We definitely missed out in that regard."

"I'm hungry," Sophie says when she finally breaks the kiss. "Think it's too late for kung pao chicken?"

I glance at my watch. It's just past eight, and I've already had dinner once, but I'll eat again if it means eating with Sophie. "It's never too late for kung pao chicken. You want to order in or go out? We could walk to the place from here, so either way, it's pretty easy."

She scoots to the edge of the bed and stands. "Order in, please. I'm exhausted and really want to put on pajamas and crash."

I make quick work of ordering takeout while Sophie wheels her suitcase into the bathroom, presumably to change clothes, then I do my own lightning-fast change, swapping my dress pants for a pair of soft gray joggers.

Sophie emerges a few minutes later with her hair up and

her face washed, dressed in leggings and the MIT hoodie I love to see her wearing.

"Sooo, I realize I didn't exactly ask," she says, "but if I promise to behave, are you okay with me staying with you tonight? Because I gotta tell you, this hotel is *very* expensive, and if I'm moving in a few months, I need to save every penny I possibly can."

"What does behaving look like?" I ask as I reach a hand toward her. I'm sitting on the edge of the bed now, and she steps into the space between my knees, letting me wrap my arms around her.

"You know. Basic roommate stuff," she says. "Keeping my clothes in one place. Not getting toothpaste on the bathroom counter. Pretending not to notice if you fart in your sleep." She looks around the suite. "I'm happy to sleep on the couch."

"I wasn't sure until that last one," I say. "But now I'm okay with it. You can absolutely stay." She lifts her hands to my hair, fingers scratching gently against my scalp as I marvel for the millionth time that she's actually here. That this woman is willing to move *for me*.

"Hey, Soph?"

"Hmm?" Her hands still, and I tilt my face up to look at her.

"It's important to me that you understand something."

"Okay," she says expectantly.

"If you want to stay in Serendipity Springs, I'll stay with you. I've got a good job there. We could be happy there. I don't want you to feel like the only way for us to be together is for you to give up your home."

She holds my gaze for a long moment, her hands sliding down to my shoulders. "Here's the thing, though. *You're* my home. I'll love living in Charlotte because we'll be together. Besides, your job here is better—it's your dream job. If we stay in Massachusetts, you're giving up a lot more than I'm losing by moving. You've met Leonard Trowbridge, Peter. I do *not* have my dream job, but I think working with Gregory might become just that. This move is a win for us both."

"You're sure?"

She leans down and kisses me. "Absolutely sure."

Over the next hour, we eat our kung pao chicken and talk our way through the basics of what the next few months might look like. A long-distance relationship won't be fun, but it's easier to wrap our heads around it knowing it will be temporary. Plus, so much of Sophie's work is remote, she'll be able to spend a good bit of time in Charlotte until her lease is up at The Serendipity and a job has fully materialized down here. And Valeria already mentioned the possibility of limited remote work for me, at least at first, so I'm sure she'll be flexible as long as I'm in the office more than I'm not.

Together, we google the cheapest direct flights between Serendipity Springs and Charlotte. We search neighborhoods and price apartments and start lists of restaurants we're excited to try together. When Sophie adds a Thai place to the list, I remember a comment from earlier that I meant to ask her about but didn't.

"Hey, did you end up having dinner with David? At the Thai place?" I ask.

She quickly shakes her head. "Nah. I cancelled on him last minute. Which, I hated to do it, but I'd finally admitted to myself I was in love with you. I would have been a terrible date. Which is what I told him, actually. That I'd finally acknowledged my feelings and needed to go home and pack so I could come to see you and tell you as much."

"You told him all that, huh? How did he take it?"

"He said he appreciated the honesty, but he wasn't surprised. Not after he saw us together after the storm."

I think back to that afternoon, to how worried I was

when I found Sophie at the top of the stairs, shivering and soaked to the skin. "I maybe came on a little too strong that day," I say.

"You didn't," Sophie says. "It was sweet, the way you were worried about me." She stabs her chopsticks into the half-eaten kung pao chicken and sets the container to the side. "Okay, I'm going to tell you something, but I don't want you to think it's the reason I'm here."

"Keep talking," I say, reaching for her discarded food. I can't quite reach, so she grabs it and hands it over.

"The flower never bloomed for me and David," she says, and I freeze, mouth open, the bite of chicken I just picked up falling back into the container with a plop.

"It didn't?"

She shakes her head no. "But it's important to me that you know I decided to come here *before* I learned the truth about what happened. You aren't my backup plan, Peter. You're my *main plan*. My *only* plan."

"But you *did* see the flower bloom, right? So...I don't understand. If not for you and David, then...?"

"For Willa and Archer," she says. "They were on the roof at the same time. I didn't see them because they were making out behind the rose trellis, but they were definitely there. Willa remembered specifically because of the storm."

I breathe out a chuckle. "And to think how much trouble they caused," I say.

"That's what I said!" Sophie says. "But also, it was the nudge I needed, so maybe I'm not so mad about it."

I'm not sure I'll ever be mad at anything again as long as Sophie is beside me. Not even when, right before I drift off to sleep, she whispers into the darkness, "Just for the record, we definitely *are* going to the NASCAR Hall of Fame before we fly home on Saturday. Whether you like it or not."

Chapter Twenty-Seven
Sophie

PETER and I try to get on the same flight on the way home on Saturday, but it proves to be more logistical trouble than it's worth, so I arrive home to The Serendipity before he does. I'm restless waiting for him. Pacing my apartment. Too preoccupied to do much of anything until he's home.

Even though Peter has been a part of my life for a very long time, I am currently obsessed with him in new and miraculous ways. I cannot get enough of him. Of his kisses. Of the little smirk he gives me when he's trying to be flirty. Of his open admiration. The man gives me compliments like he's making up for lost time, and I am here for it.

When he finally texts that he's arrived and invites me up to his apartment, I practically run the whole way there, sprinting up the grand staircase to the second floor and flying down the hall to Peter's door. I'm raising my fist to knock when the door swings open and Peter is standing there, wearing the NASCAR t-shirt I bought him in the hall of fame gift shop after our tour yesterday afternoon.

I smile when I see it, then I launch myself into his arms.

He laughs and stumbles back with an oof. "Sophie, you

saw me this morning. It's been what, nine hours since we were last together?"

"I don't care," I say before pressing a kiss to his neck. "It was the longest nine hours of my life."

"So this is how it's going to be now."

"Mm-hmm," I say. "You started it. Now I'm hooked." I press another kiss to his skin, moving toward the curve of his jaw. "Besotted," I whisper. Another kiss. "Obsessed." My lips move to the corner of his mouth. "Madly in love."

He lets out a low groan, his hands sliding to my face. He kisses me soundly, thoroughly, until I'm breathless and weak in the knees. But then he pulls back and grins. "This isn't what I called you up here for."

"But it's so fun," I say, my hands skating up his chest. He catches my hands with his and takes a step back. "Come on. I want to give you something." He leads me into the kitchen and has me sit at his table, then he disappears into his bedroom.

I glance around, noting how clean and ordered his apartment looks, despite the construction zone it's been over the past few weeks. I'm still laughing about Steve's final advice to Peter about how to handle his flickering lights, but I'm guessing now that we're together, they won't be giving him any more trouble. I'm as sure of that as I am that if Peter and I ever do make it onto the roof together, the flower will definitely bloom.

Not that I need it to.

I don't. Not anymore.

The happiness and assurance in my own heart is all the sign I need that Peter is my happily-ever-after.

Peter reappears in the kitchen, and I gasp when I see what he's holding in his hands. He sets the LEGO greenhouse down on the table, fully constructed and perfect.

"Peter! It's beautiful."

"I added something to the inside," he says, his tone a little sheepish. The greenhouse is lined with glass—or plastic that's supposed to look like glass—and the interior walls are covered in tiny LEGO plants with colorful plastic blooms. But there's only one flower sitting in the center. A white one with a deep pink center.

"This way, the flower is always in bloom for us," Peter says. "No matter what happens in your rooftop garden."

I sniff, emotion making my chest tight. "I love this so much, Peter."

"It's yours," he says. "It was always supposed to be yours. This, too." He tosses an envelope down beside the greenhouse, then lowers himself into the chair perpendicular to mine.

I open the envelope, heart squeezing when I pull out a single sheet of paper containing Peter's familiar handwriting, one of his number codes filling the center of the page.

"Oh, my gosh. I haven't seen one of these in years." Peter used to make cyphers for me whenever we were bored in AP Chemistry. The messages hidden inside them were always totally ridiculous. *Mr. Finnigan looks like a penguin. I'm really in the mood for Doritos.* Totally inconsequential stuff. But something tells me this one isn't so inconsequential. Not if Peter still has it after all these years.

"I found it when I was packing up my old bedroom," he says. "I was planning to give it to you after the prom, assuming you would actually say yes and we would go to the dance together. Since we didn't..."

"You never gave it to me," I say.

He nods. "You dated Jack until we graduated. Then we were going to different colleges, and...I guess the moment passed."

I hold the paper in my hands, staring at the numbers like I'll be able to puzzle out the code just by staring at it. "It's been a long time, Peter. I don't know if I can still figure one of these out."

"I promise you can," he says. "This one isn't that complicated." He stretches behind him and opens a kitchen drawer, retrieving a pen and a pad of paper, which he hands me. Then he stands and leans down, pressing a quick kiss to my lips. "I'm gonna get us some food while you work."

"For real? You're giving me homework? On a scale of one to ten, how hard should I expect this to be?"

He pauses at his apartment door and grins at me over his shoulder. "It's Monday-crossword-puzzle hard. Maybe Tuesday. I promise you're qualified."

"Barely qualified," I mutter as he leaves me alone in his kitchen. But it only takes a few minutes for me to puzzle out the pattern. It's a familiar one—one he used frequently in AP Chem. Each number corresponds to a letter but in reverse, except for vowels, which are assigned numbers one through five starting with A. So A is one, E is two, and so on. Then the rest of the alphabet counts down from six, starting with z, all the way back to the beginning, skipping the already numbered vowels so that b is twenty-six.

Once I sketch out the alphabet and determine what's what, I have Peter's message in front of me in a matter of minutes.

Dear Sophie, I know I made you work really hard to be my friend. It was only because I was so in awe of you, I kept waiting for the punchline because it had to be a joke. You couldn't actually want to be my friend. But you didn't give up. You tried and you tried, and eventually, you wore me down. I'm so glad you did, because now, I've fallen in love with you. It's the best thing that's ever happened to me, Soph. Even if you never love me back, I feel so lucky to know you. To be your best friend. I hope you will love me back though. If you're reading this, it means I felt confident enough to give it to you, so fingers crossed. I love you. Peter.

I read it again and again.

It's hard to believe he felt this way all those years ago, that he's been carrying these feelings around with him for so long.

It makes me want to go back to give high school Peter a hug and kick high school Sophie right in the shins. How did she not see him for how incredible he was? How did she miss it?

Peter would tell me to be gentle with my younger self. And I probably should be. We have our whole lives ahead of us. Lives *together*. And maybe Peter is right, and we really did need some distance apart. Maybe things wouldn't have worked out had we started dating in high school.

But I'm determined to *see* Peter from now on. To recognize and honor the privilege it is to be loved by him.

Half an hour later, Peter returns with cheeseburgers from my favorite burger place, mine made just the way I like it, and a Greek salad without olives. It's something he would have done a month ago, order food based on what he knows I like, but it feels different now that we're together. Like I'm so incredibly lucky that I get to have my very best friend be my boyfriend, too. I'll never take that for granted.

"Did you figure it out?" Peter asks as he swaps half of my sweet potato fries for half of his regular fries.

"Yes, I did," I say. "You were quite the wordsmith in high school."

He reaches for the paper and picks it up. "I don't even remember what it said." The color in his cheeks deepens as he reads, then he groans. "Oh, man. I really wish I'd just thrown that away."

I snatch it out of his hands. "Don't say such a thing! It's perfect."

"It's cheesy."

"Perfectly cheesy," I say. "I'm never throwing this away. My first love note from my first love."

His eyes meet mine. "First, huh?"

I shrug. "It's only ever been you."

He leans forward and kisses me. "You stole my line," he whispers against my lips.

Later when we're snuggled on his couch watching *Ted Lasso*, I look up at Peter and press a kiss to his jaw. "Hey," I say. "We've been in your apartment for hours, and your lights haven't flickered one single time."

"I guess Steve was right," Peter says. "It really wasn't a wiring problem. It was a relationship problem."

I breathe out a chuckle. "And here I thought my flower would lead me to true love. But your apartment did all the heavy lifting."

"I feel kinda bad for how much money Archer spent rewiring the place."

"If anyone can afford it, Archer can," I say through a yawn. "I should call Willa. She'll be happy to know we finally figured ourselves out."

"Yeah. Archer will be too," Peter says. "Have you told Willa about the move?"

"*Ish?*" I say. "She knows it was on the table, but I haven't told her we've decided anything for sure. I should though. *We* should."

"We will," he says, brushing a kiss across my temple. "But only if you're sure it's what you want."

"At some point, you're going to have to stop asking me that. I'm sure. Please trust me."

"I do," he says. "Of course I do. It just seems too good to be true. I've been wishing for this on every birthday cake since the tenth grade."

I tilt my face up and press a long kiss to his lips, my hand lifting to brush along his jaw line. "Was it really every single birthday wish?"

"Every single one," he says.

"Peter, that's a lot of wishes."

"It is a lot of wishes," he says, love and warmth in his gaze. "Thanks for making them all come true."

I smile, then I kiss him again. Because making his wishes come true is exactly what a main character would do.

Epilogue
Sophie

Six months later

THE LATE OCTOBER air in Serendipity Springs is crisp and cool, but not so uncomfortable that it's unpleasant to be outside. My rooftop garden still looks beautiful, despite my absence the past few months, which eases the slight ache that squeezes my heart over being here, over recognizing that The Serendipity isn't my home anymore.

Reggie, of all people, the college coed who lived next door and scared me into forcing Peter to sleep in my bed, apparently has a green thumb and happily took over care of the garden when I moved. He's done an amazing job. He even convinced Archer to install a gas fire pit in one corner, surrounded by several comfortable outdoor chairs and couches.

Peter steps up beside me, two large pizza boxes in hand. "Where are we sitting?" he says, looking around the garden.

"Over by the fire pit," I say, gesturing to where Willa and Archer are already waiting for us.

It's the only reason we're on the roof together. If Willa

and Archer are on the rooftop too, we'll know the flower—which seems completely impervious to the cooling temperatures—is blooming for them no matter what it would or wouldn't do for us.

It's good to be back with Willa and Archer again, though it hasn't been all that long since we actually moved. It took us a long time to both get to Charlotte permanently. Time for leases to run out and jobs to become available. Our relationship was partially long-distance at first, but we got really good at traveling back and forth, taking advantage of long weekends and working remotely as much as our jobs allowed. But now, we're both in Charlotte full-time. I'm working with Gregory and loving every minute of it, and Peter is thriving in his new job.

We're only back in Massachusetts to celebrate my mom's birthday, who is, believe it or not, in a relationship that has lasted longer than all the others. His name is John, he is *not* wealthy, and I think he just might be perfect for her.

I follow Peter over to the fire pit where Willa stands and gives me an enormous hug. I hug Archer next, then we all dig into the pizza.

"Hey, Archer," Peter says, in between bites. "Why don't you tell us who won our racquetball game this morning."

Archer frowns. "One game, Peter. You won *one game*. How many times have I won?"

"Doesn't matter," Peter says. "You can't ruin this victory for me. It tastes too sweet."

We all laugh, then fall into easy conversation about life in Serendipity Springs and our new life in Charlotte. I tell them how much I love working for Gregory, and they give me updates on all our mutual friends from The Serendipity.

Then Willa surprises me when she suggests that maybe sometime soon, she and Archer could come to Charlotte for a visit.

Willa has always struggled with travel, with leaving Serendipity Springs, so it's big that she's suggesting it.

Archer drops a hand on Willa's shoulder, his expression gentle and full of warmth.

"You know I would love to have you visit," I say, and she grins.

"Oh! I almost forgot. I made a batch of cookies just for you! Let me go grab them."

She jumps out of her seat and heads across the garden, but she must not make it far, because only seconds go by before she calls my name.

"Sophie?" she calls. "Can you come here a sec?"

I put down my pizza slice and go in search of her, only to find her standing just past the rose trellis next to the Japanese maple.

"What's up?" I ask as I approach.

I follow her gaze to my magical flower and let out a little gasp.

The flower is blooming just like expected, just like always, except this time, I see two blooms instead of one.

Two blooms.

"Have you ever seen it do that before?" Willa whispers.

"Never," I say. "Do you think it means..." I meet her gaze, and Willa gives me a hopeful smile.

"Two blooms for two couples?" she says.

I close my eyes. I don't need the flower to bloom for me and Peter. I am completely, even *desperately*, in love with him. So in love with him that even six months in, I still think about pinching myself because our relationship doesn't seem real.

But if the flower *is* blooming for us, well. I can't say the confirmation wouldn't feel good. Like a true full circle moment. Is it wrong that I kind of want it now that I know it's a possibility?

"Should we test it?" Willa asks.

I open my eyes. "How would we do that?"

She shrugs. "I don't know. Maybe Archer and I could leave for a second? Then you could watch and see what happens?"

"Okay, yeah, let's do that," I say before I can lose my nerve. "But do it in a way that doesn't alert Peter."

"Alert Peter to what?" Peter says as he comes up behind us.

I spin to face him, and I see the exact moment his gaze lands on the flower. His eyes widen, his mouth falling slightly open.

"That's it?" he asks, and I nod, suddenly wondering why we didn't stop and look at it on our way in. His hands were full of food, and I was so excited to see Willa, I didn't even think about stopping to see it.

Peter leans down to study the flower, his finger gently brushing across the petal.

While he's distracted, I nod to Willa who runs over and gestures to Archer. Together, they sneak around the opposite side of the garden and head downstairs.

I hold my breath as one of the blooms slowly closes, leaving only one bloom on the plant.

Peter stands and looks over his shoulder, surprise on his face. "What just happened?"

I smile, warmth spreading behind my ribs. "Archer and Willa went downstairs."

He looks at the flower, then back at me again. "So that means..." His words trail off, and I step forward, wrapping my arms around his waist.

"It bloomed for us, too," I say.

He lifts his hands to my face, cradling my cheeks as he presses a kiss to my lips, long and slow. "Now that we know," he says, "it feels kinda stupid that I avoided coming up here for so long."

"It's not stupid," I say. "It's sweet. We took our destiny into our own hands. Love isn't magic, it's an action. And we're doing the work of loving each other."

He kisses me one more time. "Loving you isn't work, Sophie. It's like breathing." He looks over at the flower. "What would you have done had the flower bloomed for us before you'd actually fallen in love with me? Do you think you would have been surprised?"

I cock my head, like I'm considering. "In this hypothetical situation, does the flower bloom before or after I see you in your tiny running shorts? Because that was a pretty significant turning point for me."

Peter rolls his eyes. "What is it with you and those running shorts?"

"It's your fault," I say. "You're the one with the distracting—"

Peter swallows the word *thighs* with his kiss, but he knows well enough what I was going to say. I comment about his running shorts every time I see him wear them, and it still makes him blush when I do.

"Should we tell Willa and Archer they can come back now?" I ask. "I'm ready for my cookies."

He holds my gaze, his palms running up and down my arms. "Not yet, actually," he says, a new trepidation in his voice. "I think...I want to ask you to marry me first."

I suck in a breath, heart suddenly pounding against my rib cage. "Are you serious right now?"

"I wasn't planning on doing it now, here, but..." He reaches into his jacket pocket and pulls out a tiny velvet bag. "I do have this ring, and the flower bloomed, and honestly, I just don't want to wait anymore." He drops to one knee and pulls the ring out of the bag. "I've been in love with you for years, Sophie. Will you marry me? Give me what I've wished for on every birthday cake since the tenth grade?"

Tears spring to my eyes as I take in the beautiful ring. We've never even talked about engagement rings, but this one is perfect—a single diamond surrounded by clusters of gemstones in pink and green and blue and purple. The smaller stones are arranged to look like flowers, and it's the most beautiful thing I've ever seen. "Peter, it's perfect," I say.

"The second I saw it, I knew it was the one I had to buy. It looked just like you."

I let him slip the ring on my finger, then I tug him to his feet and jump into his arms. "I would love to marry you," I say. "My answer is yes."

He kisses me with reverence and tenderness, and my heart aches with a joy that's almost painful for how good it is—for how right this feels.

Six months ago, Peter told me our relationship was too good to be true.

It feels that way now, but it won't be the last time I think so.

I think it when my mom walks me down the aisle on our wedding day.

When Peter holds our baby girl for the first time, tears streaming down his face.

When we buy our first house.

But I also think it whenever Peter wears his NASCAR t-shirt to bed. A significant point because he only pulls out the t-shirt when he knows he's made me mad and he wants us to be friends again.

Maybe it's the adorably sheepish look on his face whenever he puts it on. Maybe it's the genuine love in his eyes. Maybe it's because Peter is *really* good at apologizing—with his words *and* his kisses.

Or maybe it's just because that t-shirt reminds me of how long he waited for me to love him back. Steady, patient, unyielding Peter.

Kind, good, generous Peter.

I can't help it. That stupid t-shirt works every time.

The End

For bonus content, including a bonus epilogue for Petals and Plot Twists, visit jennyproctor.com and click on Bonus Content.

Only Magic in the Building
a whimsical romance series

The Serendipity
Emma St. Clair

The Cupid Chronicles
Courtney Walsh

Petals and Plot Twists
Jenny Proctor

Misfortune and Mr. Right
Savannah Scott

Clean Out of Luck
Carina Taylor

Off the Wall
Julie Christianson

Signed, Sealed, and Smitten
Melanie Jacobson

The Escape Plan
Katie Bailey

Acknowledgments

Throughout my career, I've had some wonderful collaborative experiences working with other authors, and Only Magic in the Building is no different. I loved getting to know the whimsical world that exists inside The Serendipity, and I loved writing a love story for Sophie and Peter that included a little extra dose of magic and fun.

Courtney and Kiki, thank you for your dedicated leadership and for holding us together through all the ups and downs of collaborating. Christina, Patty, Julie, Carina, Melanie, it's a privilege and honor to write and release along side you. Thank you for being such lovely friends.

I wrote this book in a ridiculously short amount of time. I didn't start drafting until the last week of January, and the book released on March 19th. It was an almost impossible deadline, and I couldn't have done it without the patience and and support of my family. Josh, as always, thanks for hanging with me. Henry, Ivy, Jack, I do it for you. Thanks for loving me even when my brain was stuck in Serendipity Springs!

Emily, your edits are brilliant and I couldn't finish a book without you. Thanks in particular for all your efforts to help me get the motivations right. And of course, thank you for adapting to my impossible deadline by meeting the equally impossible deadline that I gave you.

Sandi, Abigail, Megan, Tiffany, Caitlin, Abigail, Keri, Alicia, Mary, Tera, Janell, and Sabrina, thank you for reading and providing the last bit of polish the book needed!

And finally, to my Facebook reader group, you guys keep me going! Thank you for your enthusiasm and your continued excitement for every new book. You mean the world to me! It means so much that when I post and beg for a handful of advance readers, it only takes minutes to have willing volunteers, even when I tell you I need you to read in less than twenty-four hours. I will argue with every breath that I have the very best readers. THANK YOU!

Also by Jenny Proctor

The Some Kind of Love Series

Love Redesigned

Love Unexpected

Love Off-Limits

Love in Bloom

How to Kiss a Hawthorne Brother Series

How to Kiss Your Best Friend

How to Kiss Your Grumpy Boss

How to Kiss Your Enemy

How to Kiss a Movie Star

The Oakley Island Romcom Series

Eloise and the Grump Next Door

Merritt and Her Childhood Crush

Sadie and the Badboy Billionaire

The Appies Hockey Romance Series

Absolutely Not in Love

Romancing the Grump

Other Novels

The Christmas Letters

Her Last First Date

Just One Chance

Love at First Note

Wrong For You

Mountains Between Us

The House at Rose Creek

About the Author

Jenny Proctor is an award-winning author of more than fourteen romantic comedies and an Amazon bestseller.

She began her career in publishing in 2013; her writing has been a constant since then and is now her full-time focus, but in the past, she spent several years as the owner and managing editor of Midnight Owl Editors and as the chair of the Storymakers Conference.

Wired for relationships, Jenny loves public speaking, teaching, and building lasting connections.

Jenny was born in the mountains of Western North Carolina, a place she considers one of the loveliest on earth. She loves to hike with her family and spend time outdoors, but she also adores lounging around her home, reading great books or watching great movies and, when she's lucky, eating delicious food she did not have to prepare herself.

Jenny currently resides with her husband and children in the Charleston, South Carolina area. To learn more, find Jenny online at www.jennyproctor.com.